HIGHLAND GAMES

EVIE ALEXANDER

EMLIN
PRESS

First Published in Great Britain 2021 by Emlin Press

ISBN (eBook) 978-1-914473-00-5

ISBN (Print) 978-1-914473-01-2

A CIP catalogue record for this book is available from the British Library.

www.emlinpress.com

EMLIN
PRESS

For Pash Baker

PRAISE FOR HIGHLAND GAMES

'A hilariously funny and sizzlingly sexy romp in the Scottish Highlands. This book had me crying with laughter and begging for more...'
Margaret Amatt, author of *The Scottish Island Escapes* series

'Is there a reason you're just discovering Evie Alexander? Where have you been?! Evie's writing crackles and pops with the most delightful characters and wit. And don't get me started on the steam! I can NOT wait until the next book.'
Kelly Kay, author of *The Five Families Vineyard* series

'A fantastic, funny and oh so sexy story, full of Highland mischief and romance!'
Julia Jarrett, author of the *Dogwood Cove* series

'This book is bloody brilliant. It's snortingly funny, honest, page turning and downright fabulous. As soon as the book starts you know you are in a safe pair of hands. The writing is tender and intelligent and moves quickly to engaging and provoking. I was hooked.

Zoe, Rory and all the characters are one hundred percent believable. The plot itself is a hoot and at no point is Zoe the helpless victim waiting to be rescued, no matter how many screw-ups she gets herself into. Even when she does have to be rescued she turns it to her own advantage.

Now, let's talk about sex. Highland Games has smoking sex scenes, and I mean the pages were on fire, but they are also fun. Evie Alexander writes sex like it's fun and joyous and bouncy. Imagine two otters having the time of their lives in a bowl of trifle. If this isn't the best rom com of the year then I don't know what is.'

Liz Hurley, author of *The Hiverton Sisters* series

ALSO BY EVIE ALEXANDER

THE KINLOCH SERIES

Highland Games

Zoe's given up everything for a ramshackle cabin in Scotland. She wants a new life, but her scorching hot neighbour wants her out. As their worlds collide, will Rory succeed in destroying her dream? Or has he finally met his match? Let the games begin...

Hollywood Games

The only way for Rory to save Kinloch castle is to throw open the doors to a Hollywood megastar. However, Brad's plans for Braveheart 2 involve Rory's girlfriend as well as his home. By saving his estate, is Rory about to lose the love of his life?

Kissing Games - September 22nd 2022

Valentina's worked without a break to craft her acting career. But she's never truly lived, and everything's built on a lie. Bodyguard Charlie's done too much living, and is on the run from his demons. Can they let go of the past, or will their love remain a Highland fling?

Musical Games - Early 2023

After lying to a Hollywood megastar, Sam needs Jamie to write an album with her in one week. He's got the voice of an angel and the body of a god, but fame is the last thing on his mind. Will he help make her dreams come true?

By Evie Alexander and Kelly Kay

EVIE & KELLY'S HOLIDAY DISASTERS SERIES

Evie and Kelly's Holiday Disasters are a series of hot and hilarious romantic comedies with interconnected characters, focusing on one holiday and one trope at a time.

Cupid Calamity

Featuring Animal Attraction & Stupid Cupid

Patrick and Sabina have ditched their blind dates for each other. Ben's fighting a crazed chimp for Laurie's love. Insta-love meets insta-disaster in these laugh-out-loud Valentine's day novellas.

Cookout Carnage - June 2022

Featuring Off With a Bang & Up in Smoke

Cute farm boy Jonathan clings to a love ideal, blissfully ignoring what the universe has planned, while keeping track of his pet pig. Posh Brit follows his heart into the American Midwest in search of Sherilyn, his digital dream love.

Christmas Chaos - November 2022

Featuring No way in a Manger, & No Crib and No Bed

In Scotland, Zoe and Rory attempt to have a civilised and respectable rite of passage, but straightforward is not their style. In Sonoma, Bax and Tabi attempt to throw a meaningful Christmas celebration. But there are too many people involved and it's nothing like they expect.

PROLOGUE

Zoe sat by the side of the bed, holding her great-uncle's hand as he slept. She stared at the framed pictures on the wall: watercolour prints of countryside scenes, taking the viewer somewhere peaceful and calming, whilst the roar of London traffic outside reminded them they were anywhere but. Great-uncle Willie had spent almost his entire life alone in a remote corner of Scotland. Living off the land, in a one-room cabin, doing odd jobs for the Kinloch estate. It was a life of open space and freedom, but now his last breaths would be the acrid tang of exhaust fumes and disinfectant.

The sound of his breathing changed and she turned to him, running her thumb across the back of his hands, the hills and valleys of veins, bones and sinews, the landscape of a lifetime. His hair used to be a mirror of her own, a crazy cloud of red curls. But now the colour had left, leaving wisps of white behind. He opened his eyes and she moved closer.

'Uncle Willie, it's me. It's Zoe.'

He moved his head and she stood up and perched on the

edge of the bed. He spent so much time asleep now, and she was never really sure if he recognised her when he was awake. A spark flickered in his eyes.

'Princess Zoe?'

Her eyes stung. 'That's me,' she replied, jaw tight with emotion. She tried to smile.

'Dinnae cry for me, lassie,' he whispered. 'I've had a good life.'

Zoe swallowed. 'I...'

Willie looked past her. 'Your mum?'

Zoe shook her head. Tears dropped onto their clasped hands. 'She's having a cup of tea with Dad. They'll be back in a bit.'

Willie looked back at her, raising up an inch off the pillow. 'I've left you something. Ye have to take it,' he whispered, urgently.

What? Great-uncle Willie didn't own anything.

'The cabin. It's yours. Go have an adventure. You don't have to always do what your mum and dad want. Do something for you, love.'

He sagged back into the pillow, his eyes closing and a sigh rushing out between his dry lips.

'Follow your heart,' he whispered, before falling back to sleep.

❧ I ❧

THREE MONTHS LATER

This was it. She was going to die.

Die being mauled and eaten by a bear. Why had she left her flat, her job, her friends, her life, for this wild fantasy only to die on the first night?

And she wasn't even wearing her best underwear.

Adrenaline shot up Zoe's body, turbocharged by alcohol, straight to her frantic heart. *Think! Can I barricade the door?* She tore her gaze from the grimy window, fighting the darkness inside the deserted cabin. The chairs looked rotten and the table too heavy to move without making a noise. *What happened to the rest of Willie's furniture? And why did I neck half a bottle of Prosecco the minute I arrived? On an empty stomach?*

She peered back at the large shape shuffling in the blackness outside. It was huge; bigger and broader than a man. But hang on, were there even bears in Scotland? She ran through her memories – a scrambled montage of wildlife documentaries – trying to pick the right country from ice caps, rain-

3

forests, and savannah. There had been a film, years ago, about bringing native species back to the Highlands. Had they reintroduced bears? Or was it beavers? She went to Google it, then remembered there was no phone signal.

God, this place really is the ends of the earth.

She tiptoed to the cabin door. It didn't lock or even close properly, hopeless against a creature that big. She peered through the crack. It was by the outhouse. Maybe it was searching for food. Could she throw it something to eat? She locked her eyes on the figure and bent her knees, her fingers fluttering into the shopping bags on the floor. They knocked against a can and it tipped, tumbling with a crash.

The figure's head snapped up. Zoe heard a low growl: the sound of a creature preparing to kill.

Shit, shit, shit!

Her hand closed around a loaf of bread. She yanked it out, pushed the door open and catapulted the loaf into the air. It arced overhead and landed with a soft thud at the bear's feet. The growl changed to a frenzied bark, and a wolf stalked out from behind the outhouse.

Oh god, wolves and bears!

She was doomed. The bear put a paw out, silencing the wolf, bent down and picked up her weapon.

Zoe was white with fear but Prosecco made her bold. 'Shoo! Shoo! Be off with you!'

The bear raised itself to its full height.

'A loaf of bread? You threw a loaf of bread at me?'

Oh god, it was a man. A man-bear. Out of the frying pan into the fire. 'I've got a gun! Get off my land! Or... I'll shoot you!'

The man-bear slouched back against the outhouse, tossing the loaf from paw to paw. 'No, you don't, and this isn't your land.'

'Yes, it bloody well is!'

Zoe was furious. She was thirty per cent cold, sixty per cent drunk and one hundred per cent scared so stupid she'd thought bears roamed wild in Scotland. To top it off, some intruder was now saying this wasn't her land? She reached back into the bag, grabbed a can and threw it with pinpoint accuracy, hitting him on the shoulder.

It bounced off. *He must be made of steel.*

'Let me guess,' he drawled. 'Baked beans?'

She pulled out another and threw it at him. 'Get! Off! My! Land!' she yelled; each word punctuated by another grocery item sailing through the air. When the bag was empty, she balled it up and threw it after her food. It unravelled and fell to the floor by her feet.

'Have you finished?'

Zoe was silent, thinking of what else she had left. Her boots? The man-bear walked towards her, holding the loaf at arm's length. The wolf – okay, dog – at his heels, wagging its tail. They climbed the steps to the porch where she was standing.

'Yours?' If words were an eyebrow, this one was arched.

Zoe snatched it, squinting up at him. His face was obscured by the darkness. 'I told you,' she hissed, 'get off my fucking land.'

He leaned in and she leaned back. 'It's not your fucking land,' he whispered.

'Yes, it bloody well is! My great-uncle gave it to me.'

He stepped back, surprised. 'Mad Willie?'

'It's great-uncle Willie to you!'

He crossed his arms in front of him. 'So then, niece of *great-uncle* Willie, is the land freehold or leasehold?'

Zoe paused. How did he know? 'I own the leasehold for the next thirty years.'

5

'Ahh, so it's not really yours then. It belongs to the Kinloch estate.'

Zoe was beyond anger, beyond fear. This massive oaf had nearly given her a heart attack and now he was telling her it wasn't her land? She took a big breath, intending to let him have it, when he interrupted.

'So, may I ask why you threw a loaf of bread at me?'

Zoe stopped, set off course. 'I thought you were a bear,' she replied without thinking.

Silence.

Then the man-bear started laughing.

The sound was even bigger than him, splitting the darkness with unrepressed joy and echoing across the loch to the other side of the valley. Zoe's toes tingled as the deck reverberated under her feet. He laughed as if he couldn't stop, his huge frame doubled over as he gasped for breath. He was wheezing now, each howl punctuated by 'A bear! A *bear*!'

'I don't see what's so funny.'

The man tried to control himself. 'It's Scotland, not bloody Yellowstone! Have you come here looking for pixies? Maybe a little Nessie spotting?' He started laughing again at his own joke, guffawing at her.

'I'm here to live, you buffoon! And it's not funny. You scared the shit out of me. And anyway, who the hell are you? And what are you doing sniffing around my house in the dead of night?'

The man-bear stopped laughing, and straightened up. 'Okay. First, it's not the dead of night, it gets darker quicker up here than in the home counties. Second, I work on this land and saw a piddly little sports car abandoned on the track. I came to see what was going on and got attacked by a lunatic armed with a loaf of bread. And third, you can't live here; it's not fit for human habitation. I'll show you the way to the village. There's a pub with rooms you can stay in, and tomorrow you can go home.'

Zoe clenched her jaw and spat out her words like bullets. 'Listen here, Mr Know-it-all, let me get one thing straight. This is *my* land and *my* home and I intend to live here. I don't need an enormous, overgrown yeti trespassing on my property and frightening the crap out of me. Now bugger off.' She held up the loaf of bread. 'I'm going to make myself some beans on toa—' she remembered there was no electricity, 'bread, and have a quiet night in.'

'Maybe watch some telly?' he replied. 'Surf the web? Have a nice hot bubble bath? Good luck with that.'

He stepped off the porch and strode away, whistling for the dog to follow him. Zoe stalked into the cabin and slammed the door as hard as she could. It rewarded her by falling off its hinges and landing with an almighty crash on the front deck.

The man didn't look back.

She gulped in a breath, catching it in her throat. Tension spiralled inside her, pushing up tears she wasn't ready to shed. *What have I done?* It was all going wrong before it had even started. She'd arrived too late, there was no phone signal, and her new home had no door, let alone the bed she remembered from her childhood. She shook her head. She would not cry here. She wouldn't give the man-bear, or anyone else, the satisfaction of being right. She was going to have something to eat, get a good night's sleep, and know that, as her mum always promised, everything would be better in the morning.

She counted to sixty, then went to find the jar of jam she'd pitched at the yeti. It was stuck in a patch of mud. She tugged it out and took it to the stream that ran down the hill, cleaning off as much as she could in the glacial water. Back at the cabin, she sat on the front deck, dipping slices of bread into the jam.

Swigging Prosecco from the bottle, she watched the dark hills in the distance and the faint shimmer of starlight on the loch.

It was like another world or stepping back in time. Early yesterday morning she'd set off from the small suburban flat in London that was no longer her home. The people, traffic, lights, pollution, and background hum of the city had never been that noticeable, but now their absence was deafening.

It was so dark. So quiet. So *empty*.

She felt a thrill of nervous excitement and a giggle hiccupped out. God, no wonder her parents and friends thought she'd lost her mind. Giving up a good career to go and live in a cabin left to her by her dead great-uncle. In another country. At least she spoke the language. Sort of.

Her stomach was filling and the alcohol was helping lift her spirits, but there was no easy solution for bed. Could she drive into the village now and look up Morag? No. It was late and she couldn't give up an hour into her new life. She sighed. Nothing was going according to plan and the oaf-bear was right: she couldn't stay here. Despite the Prosecco, she was shivering and desperately needed the loo.

The outhouse wasn't an option. Had she arrived earlier she could have cleaned out the cobwebs. But now there was no way she was going to step into that box of spiders, sit over a black hole and pee. She crouched next to the side of the cabin instead, then cleaned her teeth, swilling her mouth out from a bottle of water. The basics done, she scooped up her bag and walked back to her abandoned car.

Siena was a beautiful little MG; perfect for city life. However, she wasn't entirely at home in the Highlands. Mud was spattered across her sky-blue body, and she was far too delicate to have handled the rough track down to the cabin. Zoe was relieved she'd left her near the main road, so she could easily reverse out in the morning. She threw her bag in the back, reclined the front seat, and attempted to manoeuvre herself into a sleeping bag like a clumsy caterpillar. Caught in her old London patterns, she inserted earplugs and pulled on an eye mask, not that it made any difference to her comfort.

She'd never slept in a car before and now she knew why. All five foot ten of her was never going to be able to stretch out in comfort. Her feet kept hitting the pedals, the headrest was hard, and her arms were too cold outside the sleeping bag and too constricted inside.

She considered going to Morag's again but dismissed it. She wouldn't admit defeat and wanted to face her in the softer light of day, not showing up in the middle of the night, a ghost from the past.

It was going to be a long and miserable night.

2

Zoe's eye mask had dislodged in the night and she woke with the sunrise hitting her face like a golden mallet. She'd been lost in a looping dream of racing great-uncle Willie from the cabin to the loch. Twin flames; one tall, one small. Wild red hair, overflowing with life, whooping and screaming as they tumbled into the cold water. It was Zoe's stuck record of happiness. The dream that had brought her back to Scotland after so many years.

She tentatively moved her limbs. She felt as if her body had been taken apart, then put back together again by someone who had thrown the instruction manual out with the box. Her feet were backwards, her knees sideways, her left shoulder swapped with the right, her bottom so numb it had disappeared. Her mouth had been stuffed with cotton wool dipped in sour milk and her head had been used as a pincushion. Everything just hurt.

Slowly, she pulled out her earplugs and unzipped the sleeping bag, extricating herself and pushing open the car door. She gingerly swivelled her legs around and, like a newborn foal, stood up, swaying slightly. She stretched her arms as if to touch the morning sky, then lowered them and looked around.

In the half light of yesterday and after the exhaustion of the drive up, she hadn't had a chance to take in her surroundings. The track was only wide enough for one car and was dwarfed by the tall trees either side of it. The air was still and the branches were almost completely bare. It was November now and autumn was at its end. A solitary beech leaf floated down and she instinctively caught it, rubbing its softness between her fingers and thumb. She reached into her pocket and brought out her phone to photograph the leaf. Close up, with the sun turning the browns into gold, held up to the sky with the sunlight behind it, in her palm, and with the dark backdrop of the trees beyond. Her professional-style SLR camera nestled in the boot, but her phone was more than adequate this morning. Two weeks ago she'd opened an Instagram account, ostensibly for the friends she was leaving behind to share her journey, but also as a place to explore a different side of her. A side not associated with spreadsheets, cities and work. A side locked in this landscape and her memories.

She walked around the car, holding her phone in the air to find a signal. Nothing. She grabbed her bag and walked back down the track to see the cabin in the daytime.

Rounding the corner and seeing it in the amber morning light brought memories flooding back. For a few precious months of her childhood, this house and this land had been her home, almost her entire world. A new wave of emotion coursed through her. She swallowed it back down. This wasn't the time. She needed to make an objective assessment of the cabin and work out how to make it habitable once more.

It was situated at the top of a couple of acres of open grassy ground, which gently sloped to the edge of the loch. The cabin was one room, rectangular, made from thick pine logs. No kitchen, no bathroom, no bedroom, but four single-paned windows, dirty and cracked, and a porch running along the front. The roof was tiled in wooden shingles and had grown a head of mossy hair. Zoe shuddered. It was most likely a breeding ground for all sorts of creepy crawlies, and she'd need a ladder and a lot of courage before she could take a proper look.

Walking up the steps onto the front porch, she heaved the solid door to one side so it was no longer blocking the entrance, and walked in. Last night, lit only by her phone, the interior had been a place of shadows and unknowns. But now, with the sunrise sending streaks of gold across the wooden floor, she could see everything. And it was worse than she could have possibly imagined.

Willie had lived a simple life but she remembered a bed, a chest of drawers, cupboards, and a large dresser. Where had they gone? The only things left were a solid oak table that had seen everything from Coco Pops to animal butchery, and a couple of chairs, probably only good for firewood now. Against the right-hand wall was a wood-fired Rayburn stove that looked like it was out of the Ark. Her parents had come for Willie three years ago, when he became unable to take care of himself. Had they cleared everything else out?

The cabin didn't have running water or a sink. Whenever her great-uncle chose to wash, which was pretty infrequently, he used the loch or the small stream that ran down the hillside next to the cabin. When Zoe had come to stay as a child, he'd rigged up a gutter and drainpipe which he used to fill an old cattle drinking trough outside for her to wash in. He also constructed the outhouse for her; no more than a tiny hut with a wooden box and toilet seat inside set over a big pit. To make it more appealing to a ten year old, he'd painted it gold and daubed 'Princess Zoe's Throne' in purple over the door.

She hadn't wanted to ask where he'd gone to the toilet before...

As a girl, the cabin had seemed like a mansion, but now it felt shrunk in the wash. She was used to living in small spaces, her London flat had been tiny, but at least it had separate rooms and a bathroom. She sat on a wobbly chair at the oak table, and dropped her head into her hands. What had she done?

Willie had left her the lease for the cabin in his will less than a month ago and now she was here; using her holiday allowance to leave her job early, not even staying in her flat until the lease ran out. She hadn't told anyone her plans, not even her parents until the day she left. She didn't want them, or anyone else, to talk her out of it. Her best friend, Sam, told her she was having a midlife crisis because she was nearly thirty, and Zoe could see how it looked. She should have done a recce before moving up; made plans based on what the cabin was like in reality, not in her childhood memories from decades ago. At least waited until spring before she changed her life. She sighed, and brought out the remains of the loaf of bread to eat with the last of the jam. She knew she'd made a rash decision, but she'd wanted an out for a long time, and the cabin was it. Willie told her to follow her heart and she had. Now the decision had been made, nothing was going to sway her from it. She just needed a plan.

The Rayburn stove was her first priority. She needed to get it going for warmth and cooking. Water she could drink from bottles or take from the stream. She'd paid a removal company to take her furniture and belongings to a storage unit an hour and a half's drive away. She'd keep everything there until she was sure the cabin was watertight. The cabin walls may have been sturdy but it was missing a front door, the windows needed replacing and the roof was alive. There was also the sad but inevitable task of trading in Siena for a more appropriate vehicle.

There was so much to do but she was up to the challenge. She took her laptop out of her bag, flipped it open and made a list.

ZOE'S FIRST PORT OF CALL WAS TO BE INVERNESS, ABOUT forty minutes south of Kinloch by car. But before she could get there, she needed to phone home. With no signal at the cabin, she hadn't been able to ring her parents last night when she arrived and knew her mother would be having kittens. She crept along the narrow winding roads until her phone beeped with notifications. She pulled over into a lay-by and called home.

It picked up after the first ring.

'Hello!'

'Hi, Mum, it's me.'

'Oh, darling, we've been worried sick! ARNOLD! IT'S ZOE! SHE'S ALIVE! Your dad said there wasn't much signal, but I couldn't remember, so of course have been imagining the worst.'

'Mum, I'm fine! It's all good!'

'Is it? Hang on, love, your dad's here, let me put the phone on loudspeaker so he can listen in. Just a minute. Arnold love, I can't see which button to press. Why do they make them so small? Have you got your glasses? Here, you take a look.'

Zoe grinned as she heard her dad take the receiver.

'Which button is it, Mary? There's one that looks a bit like a rainbow, shall I try it?'

Zoe could hear the beep of a button being pressed, then her mother was back, speaking slowly and loudly.

'Zoe, it's Mum! Can you hear me?'

'And I'm here too! It's your dad! Can you hear me?' said her father, as if reading the shipping forecast.

Zoe was so full of love for her parents, her eyes began to sting. She couldn't cry or she'd never stop, then her mum would be set off and her father would feel torn apart, with the two most special people in his life upset and in different countries.

'I can hear you both loud and clear!'

'Wonderful, darling, now tell us all about it. How is the cabin holding up? Your father told me, when we left, the front door was hanging off by its hinges.'

'How's the roof, love? Any leaks? Got the Rayburn going yet?' interjected her father.

'The front door is great,' Zoe lied. 'And the Rayburn is running perfectly. The roof only has one small leak from a couple of detached shingles, but I'm getting them replaced later today.'

'Well, if you're sure, love?' replied her mum. 'You know we can come up, we just need to book the time off work.'

'No bother, love, no bother at all. Just say the word,' agreed her father.

She felt so loved, so safe and protected by their unconditional kindness, but the last thing she wanted was for them to come up and discover their darling girl was heading into a Scottish winter, camping in a wooden colander with no front door. They were freaked out enough already by her decision, plus the fact she'd kept them in the dark about it.

Her parents had always wanted her to have a career, something that would never go obsolete, or be outsourced to another country. They had learned this lesson the hard way when her father had been made redundant from his manufacturing job on the wrong side of forty. They had lost their house, then Zoe's mother had been diagnosed with cancer. It had been the worst time of their lives. When it was over, and they had a new roof over their heads, they wanted to know Zoe would be able to provide for herself. Music, history, languages, all had to take a back seat to maths and science.

They were helicopter parents; hovering, helping, pushing Zoe down paths she may have never chosen for herself, never quite trusting her to chart her own course through life. Zoe loved them, understood their motives, wanted to please them, but now she needed to make her own decisions, no matter how crazy they seemed. The pressure had been building for the last few years, to the point where life was feeling unbearable. Willie's death and legacy was her release.

She reassured them whilst gently putting them off, got off the phone, took a few more photos for Instagram and set off for Inverness, for possibly the last drive she would have in Siena.

After the wilds of the cabin, it seemed as busy as London. Within a few hours she had traded in her beloved sports car for a fairly shabby navy Toyota pickup truck, with bull bars and an extended three-year warranty for reassurance. It felt enormous and she crept along the roads convinced she was about to take out anything that came near her. After trips to a hardware store, builders' merchants, camping shop and a large supermarket, she managed to park it and treated herself to a roast dinner in a pub she remembered coming to decades before with her parents. At least that hadn't changed. The pictures on the wall, depicting hunting scenes, were still the same, as were the faded burgundy velour chairs. She sat at a table by the window, filling her belly, and watched the world go by.

In some ways, it wasn't much different from what she had left behind. The same shops on the high street, the same grey sky, but just in an unfamiliar setting. She got out her phone and flicked through the photos she'd taken that morning by the cabin. The brightness, the colour, the openness of the landscape. She uploaded them to Instagram with the ironic hashtag #braveheart2 then opened her messages.

She smiled as she read through them. They were from Sam, the best friend she'd met in university halls and who she'd spent three years sharing a house with. Sam had studied theatre studies and was an actress, finally getting her big break with a small part on Elm Tree Lane, a popular soap.

Sam: Yo! Babe! You alive? Wearing a kilt yet? xxx

Sam: Do they really eat deep-fried Mars Bars? Lol

Sam: Have you had any salty porridge?

Sam: What's the hovel like? Met Rumpelstiltskin?!

Sam: Any hot Scots? XXXXXXX

Sam: When are you coming home?!!

Zoe messaged back.

Zoe: Had Sam Heughan round for shortbread and whisky last night, and deep-fried Mars Bars count as one of your five a day – everyone knows that lol. Not coming home till I've found you a Scottie hottie xxx

It was only three days since they'd had goodbye drinks but it could have been a lifetime ago.

Only one other friendship had come close to the one she shared with Sam, the one with Fiona and Jamie, the children of her mother's childhood friend, Morag, who ran the post office in Kinloch. Fiona was the same age as her, Jamie two years younger, and during the summer she had spent with Willie, the three of them had slotted together perfectly like pieces of a puzzle.

It had been nearly twenty years since she had seen them but the memories were as fresh as yesterday. Would they remember her? Even though her mum still kept in touch with her old friend, it was very sporadic, and Zoe hadn't wanted

Morag to know her plans to move to the cabin. The last thing she wanted was her checking it out before Zoe's arrival and informing her mum it was uninhabitable. She put her phone back in her bag, paid for her food and drove back to Kinloch to find her.

Kinloch was what Willie called 'a one-horse town'. A village built around the castle with one main street running through it. Small shops lined each side for less than a hundred yards, including a butcher, an ironmonger, uninspiring takeaways, generic charity shops, a bookies and the post office. Zoe parked 'The Beast', as she'd named it, and stood at one end of the high street; memories swirling around her like snowflakes before settling on the tarmac to melt away.

Everything was so small, so changed. She paused at the post office door, suddenly shy and nervous. Morag had always been so warm and loving, easing the pain of being far from home. But what if she didn't recognise her? What if she wasn't as pleased to see her as Zoe had hoped? She hadn't been back since that summer, hadn't written. She was only a child but should she have done more than a signature on the bottom of an occasional Christmas card from her parents?

The little bell above the door tinkled as she opened it, setting off sparklers in her tummy. She stood awkwardly as she heard a familiar voice from the back room calling out.

'Coming!'

There she was: greyer hair, smaller than Zoe remembered, but still, unmistakably Morag. A lump formed in her throat and she opened her mouth but no words came out.

'As I live and breathe!' Morag crossed the distance between them and crushed Zoe to her. 'Zoe, my love! My dear wee girl!' she cried as Zoe felt the weight of the last weeks and months tumble out in tears.

Morag smelled exactly the same, a combination of cornsilk powder, home cooking and love. She was just as soft and warm; a walking, talking comfort blanket.

'Fi! Get out here, love, it's our Zoe!' Morag yelled over her shoulder.

A woman with dark wavy hair ran out holding a baby, and the three of them held each other tightly; as if they dared to let go, the spell would be broken and Zoe would vanish in a puff of smoke.

A confused wail from the baby broke them apart.

'Oh, Zoe, you haven't changed a bit! How long are you here for? Where are you staying? Can you stay here?' Fiona rattled out, bouncing the baby, whilst Morag herded Zoe to the back of the shop.

'Come out the back, love, I've got a date, apple and walnut cake cooling, I must have known you were coming!'

Morag steered Zoe into the comfiest chair by the fire, grabbed a couple of tissues and gave the box to her. 'What are we like? Now all we need is Jamie. Let me ring him.'

Morag blew her nose loudly, lifted up a cordless phone and speed-dialled whilst Fiona continued her barrage of questions and statements. 'Look at you! Do you do Pilates? There's a class on in the hall but I haven't been yet, or Zumba? Oh, and this is Liam, say hello Liam! He's seven months old now. His dad is Duncan, did you ever meet him? I was sweet on him for forever.'

Fiona smiled at private memories, then Zoe was back between two conversations.

'Jamie! Jamie! Come home, love, you'll never guess who's just walked through the door!'

'So, he works out on the rigs,' said Fiona. 'Two weeks on, two weeks off and it's awful, and I worry and think about what happened to Dad, but the money's good and so for the two weeks he's away I come back and stay at Mum's.'

'No, not the Queen, you big lump, better! Guess again!' encouraged Morag in the background.

'So, what are you doing back? I'm so sorry about Willie,' said Fiona, her forehead creasing. 'Are your mum and dad okay? Are they here with you?'

'No, no and no! It's our Zoe!' Morag proclaimed. 'Yes! Zoe! Come back now and see her!'

'You're so gorgeous, and I'm a frump, covered in food and baby sick,' Fiona moaned. 'Oh, we have to go out! How long are you here for, please stay a few days, it's been so long. Wasn't that the best summer ever?'

'What do you mean you can't come now? It's Zoe!' Morag shouted into the phone. 'She might be gone again this afternoon. Yes, of course I'll make her stay. All right, son, love you, bye, bye.'

Morag put down the phone with a flourish and pulled up another chair in front of Zoe. 'So, my darling, tell us everything!'

There was a sudden silence as even baby Liam looked at her, awaiting a response. Zoe felt like a scrawny girl again. 'I, I don't know where to start. Mum and Dad are fine. I've been living in London and working mainly as an accountant, but then Willie got sick...'

Morag squeezed Zoe's knee. 'I'm so sorry, pet, that must have been very sad for you and your mum.'

Zoe nodded. 'He didn't even remember Mum at the very end. And he had changed so much. But then he left me the lease on the cabin, and I decided to make some changes in my life. So... I've left my job and come up here to live.'

After a short, stunned silence, Fiona and Morag whooped with delight. 'Oh, Zoe love, that's wonderful news! Businesses always need accountants, and of course you can stay here, you can bunk in with Fi and Liam, unless you fancy sharing with our Jamie?' Morag said, giving her a sly glance.

'Mum! Stop! Zoe might have a boyfriend,' said Fiona to her mum before focusing her laser eyes on Zoe. 'Do you have a boyfriend?'

Zoe blushed. 'No. But—'

'That settles it then!' exclaimed Morag, getting up as Liam began to wail. 'I need to tell everyone the good news. Oh, and the cake. Let me get the cake.'

'But, but...'

Morag stopped. 'Yes, love?'

'I appreciate the offer to stay, I do, but—'

On cue, her potential roomie Liam screamed the kind of high-pitched baby cry that would wake even Sleeping Beauty.

'I'm going to be living in the cabin.'

3

Two hours later, Zoe left the post office in a daze. Part cake coma, part emotional overload. Her life at a desk in an office seemed to belong to a completely different person. Morag and Fiona had been dismayed and worried that Zoe intended to live in what they could only describe as 'a great big heap of firewood' and tried their best to dissuade her. And with every new customer brought out the back to see Zoe, the same questions and statements were issued. Sadness for her great-uncle. How was her mum? Did she have a boyfriend? She couldn't possibly stay at the cabin, wasn't she beautiful, oh, and did she have a boyfriend?

Zoe felt a twinge of guilt she had lied so shamelessly to everyone about the state of the cabin. She was banking on the fact that none of them had been up there in years. According to Zoe's telling, the cabin just needed a rag rug and some pewter plates and she'd be the Laura Ingalls-Wilder of Kinloch. Morag, keen to find any way that Jamie could be involved, had volunteered him for the job of chimney sweep and had press-ganged him into going around later that afternoon.

Now she needed wood for the Rayburn. Getting it going meant she could cook and keep herself warm. Morag had said there was a labourer chopping wood in the back courtyard of the castle, and suggested Zoe see if he might be able to sort her out.

THE CASTLE LOOMED OVER THE SMALL VILLAGE, ITS GRANITE walls touching the sky and casting a domineering shadow over the nearby buildings. She brought out her phone to take some snaps for Instagram and made her way to the back of the castle, the 'tradesman's entrance' as Morag described it. It was the more human back door, where for hundreds of years servants came to and fro, along with the animals, delivery carts, wood, and everything else needed to maintain the front of the house in opulent splendour.

As she walked down the narrow street next to the high wall, she could see the opening up ahead. The gates had long gone but the cobbles of the courtyard remained, gently spilling out to meet tarmac and double yellow lines. The sound of wood splitting echoed towards her and she rounded the corner with a spring and a smile before stopping dead.

The courtyard was old and utilitarian. Part car park, part workshop. A muddy truck, bearing a coat of arms, was parked haphazardly next to a pile of logs. The courtyard looked like a place for dumping things for dealing with later or never. But it was also a place where the heavens had opened and flung out a god. To the side of the courtyard, facing away from her was Thor's better proportioned brother. Thor got the hammer, but this guy got an axe. He was splitting wood with ease and precision, his movements effortless and exact, a fusion of man, metal and wood.

He was shirtless, wearing faded trousers and brown leather work boots that looked so used he must sleep in them. His body appeared chiselled from golden marble, with not an ounce of fat to hide his perfection. Zoe watched, mesmerised, as he casually swung the axe down, his muscles moving in exquisite harmony. She stared at the expanse of his back and arms, a body created by work outdoors, not pumped up in a city gym. His hair, wavy and wild, skeins of dark honey and gold, almost grazing his shoulders. She felt dizzy, discombobulated, a ringing sounded in her ears as her unconscious mind and hormones roared into life. She shook her head, confused by her reaction to the sight in front of her.

He bent over to pick up another log and Zoe's eyes slid down to the peachy perfection of his backside. She breathed faster, her jaw slack, her mouth dry and heart pounding. He might have had a face like a dog's dinner but she didn't care. She would just worship his back, and arms, and bum, and – oh no. It was happening again. *Not now!*

In stressful social situations, Zoe's default reaction was to laugh. The more inappropriate the situation, the more hysterical she became. Zoe was the child who cackled like a hyena at funerals, who wet herself when her elderly neighbour was carted off in an ambulance with a broken arm. It was embarrassing, uncontrollable and socially unacceptable. The sight of the most incredible man (back half) she had ever seen started out as hyperventilation, then careered out of control into a screeching car crash of a laugh.

The god turned around, still holding the axe. Zoe had a glimpse of a ten pack of abs before she doubled over, one hand clapped to her mouth trying to disguise the hysteria as a coughing fit.

He put down the axe and pulled on a faded plaid shirt, slowly and deliberately doing up the buttons from the top to the bottom. It was a striptease in reverse but Zoe had never seen anything so erotic before. She had to get control of herself. She needed this guy's wood.

I need this guy's wood... she thought, compressing her lips together so tightly her hysteria had no other exit than her nose. She snorted so hard her eyes watered from the pain, then the fake cough to cover it up made her throat raw.

Still, Thor's brother patiently waited.

'I'm so sorry!' she gasped. 'Something caught in my throat!'

Get it together! she inwardly screamed as she straightened up, brought herself back under some semblance of control, and looked at the stranger.

As her eyes met his, a jolt of electricity shot through her. He had the eyes of a wolf, the ice blue of a glacier, rimmed with grey, striations of silver shooting out from bottomless black irises. They held her as the rest of the world dropped away. She took in the pure maleness of him; his features strong and powerful, a slight bump on his nose from being broken, full lips, high cheekbones, all set in the bronzed face of someone who lived his life under the open skies. His hair was a golden shaggy mess and had clearly not seen a brush for years, yet Zoe wanted to reach up, run her hands through it and bring his mouth crushing down on hers. *What is happening to me? Speak to him!*

'Er, hi, erm... Morag who runs the post office said you might be able to sort me out? I mean, I need some wo—fuel for my Rayburn. I'm Zoe by the way,' she trilled manically, thrusting forward her hand as if to shake his.

He didn't move. She faltered and dropped her arm, chewing nervously at her bottom lip. God, she had done it this time. Or was he a deaf-mute?

'I know who you are,' said the man-bear. 'You're the wildlife expert.'

Zoe shut her eyes. Oh god, oh god, oh god, oh god, GROUND OPEN NOW! She sighed, opened her eyes and faced him down.

'Look, I think we got off on the wrong foot last night. I was scared and you were, er, something. Now, as you can see, I'm here to stay for at least the next thirty years before I give my home back to your boss, so please can I just buy some wood, then I can get out of your hair.'

Zoe could have sworn a glint of humour flashed across his face as she spoke, but then the lights went out.

'No.'

'Er, what?'

'No, you cannot buy any of the estate's wood.'

'What? Why not?'

'Because I say so.'

'What if someone in the village wants some?'

'They can buy as much as they like.'

'Then I'd like to buy some for Morag.'

He smirked. 'Nice try, but still no. And don't come back in ten minutes wearing a wig and a moustache, you're unforgettable.'

Obviously not in a good way, she inwardly groaned. 'But why won't you let me buy any?'

He paused. 'Because I'm not enabling your insanity any further. Have you ever spent a winter in the Highlands? Have you even considered what you need to do to the place? The first time you set a fire, whatever is currently nesting in the chimney will go up in flames taking you and the cabin with it. I'm not going to be the one who sold you the wood that killed you.' He raised his massive, calloused hands, ticking off each point. 'One, it doesn't have electricity; two, plumbing; three, water; four, a phone line; five, mobile signal; or six, sewerage. Christ, it doesn't even have a frigging door! You need to get back in that lovely little car of yours and go back home. You don't belong here.'

You don't belong here. Zoe's throat constricted. This was the only place she had ever felt she truly belonged. Tears pricked at her eyes before anger replaced them.

'How dare you! And who are you to decide what I do or don't do? Lord of the bloody manor? I'm not taking orders about my life and my land from someone who looks like they sleep in a hedge. And you're a fine one to talk about belonging. You don't even sound Scottish!'

Thor's brother shrugged, turned his back, picked up the axe and started chopping again.

Unbelievable! As he moved to pick up a new log from the pile, Zoe leapt forwards, grabbed the pieces he had just split and legged it out of the courtyard with a victorious yell. She was going to have his wood whether he liked it or not...

❧

RORY WATCHED HER RUN OUT OF THE COURTYARD. HE THEN buried the axe in the tree trunk he was splitting the logs on, walked over to a long, low building on the side of the courtyard and through the door. This was his workshop. He'd made it his kingdom and his world.

An old German Shepherd, asleep in a dog bed to one side, woke as he entered, getting up, tail wagging happily, to greet him. Rory walked to the large workbench in the centre of the room, scratching behind the dog's ears. Lying on the bench was a large wooden door, almost finished. It was a door he was making for the cabin, the cabin he wanted for himself.

When Mad Willie left, Rory presumed it would revert back

to the estate. No one in their right mind would want to live there. No one except him. He was used to hardship, to solitude, and now he craved it. He wanted isolation, he wanted freedom. But now this city girl had arrived and put a spanner in his works.

He knelt down. 'Bandit, my friend, how about a W-A-L-K?'

Bandit nuzzled his head against Rory's neck, then trotted to the door. Rory followed him out, striding to the estate's 4x4 and opening the cab door for Bandit to bound in. The truck was powerful; built for the territory and capable of taking on any weather the Highlands could throw at it. The loathsome coat of arms of the MacGinleys was emblazoned on the bonnet and doors but nicely covered with a veneer of mud. Rory preferred it that way.

He negotiated the narrow streets around the castle with ease, driving out of Kinloch and along the road towards Inverness. A few miles out he cut left up a muddy track, to unload several bales of hay and feed for a tenant farmer's Highland cattle and check the stream had not frozen over. It would soon be time to move them from the higher ground so they could be fed more easily and find better shelter. Once the cattle had been checked, Rory and Bandit left the truck and headed out onto the glen.

The landscape opened up before them; the undulating hills shrouded in mist, seamlessly merging into the slate grey sky. It was still and quiet, as if the world was holding its breath, poised on a knife edge of change, waiting to see which way to fall.

As his feet picked up the pace, he breathed in deeply through his nose; smelling the cold, damp peaty air, inhaling the wide-open space. He'd adopted the trick of nostril breathing from his army days. On exercise in Africa, he'd woken early one morning to find long distance runners passing by their camp. They were there, then they were gone. Light and lithe, a whisper through the landscape. The next morning, he got up earlier, and ran beside them for a few miles, puffing and panting as they hooted with laughter at the man who outweighed them all combined. Rory knew he was fit, but they were effortless. On day three he studied them. They only ever breathed through their noses, matching their respiration to their stride. By day four he had mastered it, and the runners rewarded his observation skills with high fives. He could see this had been the beginning of a lifelong interest in mastering his body and his mind; skills that helped in the darkest times of his life.

He stopped, and turned to see how far they had walked, winding his fingers into Bandit's fur.

'What should I do, Bandit?'

Bandit's warm body pushed against his leg. Old memories clung to his skin. They tightened and itched.

His childhood had been nasty, brutish and short. The only moment of colour had come one summer, when his parents brought him to Kinloch and left him to his own devices. He'd set off the first morning to explore, armed with sandwiches and his grandfather's walking stick. Coming from Edinburgh, the mountains of his homeland were always set behind the grey stone of the city. Now he was immersed in nature. When the sun was high in the sky, he found the cabin and Willie. It was the first time in his life he'd ever felt like he belonged. In those two short months, Willie had been more of a father to him than his own, and each day had been full of discovery and fascination. Willie taught him how to set a fire, stalk a deer, and run naked into the loch roaring like a lion.

And now, after over twenty years, he was back. Some responsibilities couldn't be put off forever. Joining the military had been the ultimate escape from a domineering father. But when his father died, he had to come home; first to Edinburgh, and now here. He owed it to his mother to take care of her, but couldn't live with her in the small flat forever. He wanted to be like Willie. To live in the cabin, free of materialism, complications, stress, and other people. Three months ago when they returned to Kinloch, he'd gone straight to the cabin, finding it derelict and abandoned. He'd cleared out the rotting furniture, leaving only the table and a couple of chairs, and had started making a new door and new window frames. By Christmas he had wanted to be in.

But first, he had to get this Zoe person out.

Last night it had been a surprise to see a car by the edge of the road by the track, and a shock to see the cabin occupied by someone other than him. Someone drunk, but still sober enough to be a dead shot with a can of baked beans. In daylight she was even more chaotic. Tall, with gangly limbs, an unruly mass of bright red curls, and freckles thrown haphazardly across her face. She looked like a firework mid-explosion, every part of her shooting out, defying gravity and coherence. Despite not having any wood, she was full of fire, he'd give her that. But the fire would go out. She'd be just like all the other city people with bagpipes for brains. The fantasy of life in the Scottish Highlands wouldn't last when they realised Starbucks wasn't at the end of the road, and they couldn't get quinoa at the corner shop. He needed to hasten her inevitable departure but didn't know how.

Rory looked at the pale grey sky, then at his watch.

'Time to go, buddy. Any ideas of how to get shot of crazy lady?'

Bandit tilted his head to one side, then set off, tail wagging, down the side of the glen. 'Race you!' yelled Rory.

They thundered down the mountain, whooping and barking. It was always a foregone conclusion who would win, even though Bandit was getting older, but he waited patiently for Rory to catch up every few hundred yards. They were soon back at the truck, and Rory recovered, leaning on the gate to the field with the Highland cattle. He practically knew them by name. They were such placid animals. They were clustered around the new bale of hay inside the gate, tearing mouthfuls off, their hot breath condensing in the cold air.

Had she really thought bears lived in the Highlands? He shook his head. She'd probably think these cattle were woolly mammoths. He looked down the track towards the main road. The cabin wasn't far from here. Maybe the cattle needed a change of scene?

❧

THE LACK OF MOBILE SIGNAL AND ELECTRICITY AT THE CABIN meant Zoe needed to stay in town. Fortunately there was a small library attached to the community centre off the high street. It had three computer terminals, a printer, and signs in VERY large letters informing the older generation that help was always on hand. Zoe sank gratefully into a plastic chair and opened up her portal to all the knowledge she would ever need. Within five minutes, her phone and extra battery packs were on charge, she knew where to buy wood locally, how to fix and use a Rayburn, and had a plan for the lack of a front door.

Accountancy may not have been her dream career but she was the queen of spreadsheets, the empress of organisation, and within an hour had drawn up a battle plan for the cabin. She placed bids on a back boiler to fit her Rayburn that would provide the cabin with a supply of hot water. There was only one available that was the right model, and it looked even older than the castle. She only hoped if she won it, it worked.

She would show that smug arse – the one with the *incredible* arse – she had no intention of leaving. She would succeed as much for herself as to spite him. It was easier to hate him than to dwell on the turbulence he'd created within her. That was a weird, one-off reaction to someone who was clearly the village idiot with ideas above their station and it wasn't going to happen again. No. Definitely not. Not ever.

It was three o'clock by the time she left the library, and even though her stomach was calling, the sun was already starting its descent to bed and she needed light. She drove back to the cabin and unloaded her supplies.

The outhouse got a glittery toilet seat, chrome toilet roll holder, and a powerful battery-powered camping light. The cabin got solar and battery-powered lights, cleaning tools and products, plastic boxes for her clothes, and the pièce de résistance, a tent, which she put up in the far corner of the cabin. The cabin may not have had a front door, but it did now have a bedroom.

She then filled her empty plastic bottles from the stream. This was where Willie had got his water supply, but she needed to fix the gutters and drainpipes he had put up when she stayed so she could collect rainfall and have it closer to the cabin. Drinking water was a different problem. She didn't want to keep buying bottles; it wasn't so much the cost as the plastic. As she mentally added a filtration system to the long list of things the cabin needed, she heard a car pull up. She walked out to see a familiar, yet unfamiliar, man getting out. He gave her a friendly wave. 'Hey, Zoe.'

'Jamie!' Without a second thought, she barrelled herself towards him with her arms outstretched.

He stood, an embarrassed smile on his face, his cheeks pink, as she gave him the same treatment she had received from his mum and sister.

'Look at you! You're all grown up. You're taller than me now. It's so amazing to see you again. Thank you so much for coming. Your mum tells me you're an electrician? Come see the cabin!'

Zoe dragged him by the hand, exactly as she'd always done, but this time with a strapping man, whilst he also reverted to the past and followed without a word like the little boy he had been, always following his elder sister and her best friend around.

'Ta-da!' Zoe dropped his hand and used hers to present the interior of the cabin. 'As we enter the majestic building, with its unique entrance, we move onto the kitchen – perfectly formed if yet not functional.' She sashayed around as if presenting a property show on TV. Jamie was grinning at her but a knot of anxiety was tying tighter in her stomach. He was the first person, apart from the man-bear, to have seen the true state of the cabin and she was dreading him having the same reaction. 'We move onto the open-plan living area. Here we have a brand-new invention – not a walk-in closet, but a pick-up-and-walk-off closet.' She lifted the plastic boxes containing her clothes and ceremoniously placed them down again, a few inches away. 'And finally, the master bedroom! Bathroom currently non-en suite, but definitely on property.' She presented the tent with arms spread and jazz hands as if showing off the latest toaster on a home shopping channel.

There was a pause and Jamie cleared his throat.

'Well, Zoe, I think you've got a palace on your hands. Nothing a bit of graft and a door can't fix.'

Zoe leapt forward and grabbed his upper arms as if clinging onto the life raft of his optimism for dear life. 'You think so? Oh, Jamie, everyone thinks I'm mad, but I have to make it work.'

His smile was warm. 'You'll be fine, Zo, but we won't have

light for long, so let's see about the stove, then if there's time, we can look at the door.'

Zoe followed him back to the car like an obedient puppy and gamely held onto sticks and brushes as they walked back into the cabin.

'Now, this could get a little messy, so just clear as much room as you can,' he said, laying newspaper over the top of the Rayburn. Zoe moved everything to the far side of the cabin and Jamie opened the cleaning door to the flue pipe.

'Pass me the first brush, would you?'

Zoe complied, feeling like she was a surgical assistant at an operation. Jamie had brought ash shovels of various sizes and was soon scooping out black soot into a bag.

'Can you take a look outside and let me know when I'm out?' he asked as he screwed more extensions to the brush.

Zoe ran outside, taking pictures with her phone, and yelled with delight as she saw the brush triumphantly exit the chimney, sending a bird's nest catapulting up into the air, then rolling down the roof to the ground. She snatched it up and ran back inside.

'We've made a family homeless!'

Jamie grinned, his face starting to blacken from the soot. 'They're long gone, it's nearly winter now. But it'll make good kindling.'

Zoe held the nest protectively to her body. 'No! It's my first piece of art for the cabin.' She laid it down carefully on top of one of her plastic boxes and Jamie closed the flue.

'That wasn't bad you know, but let's clean the rest out and get it lit.'

She helped him manhandle the heavy iron plate off the top and they set to work with brushes, cleaning out the vents and firebox whilst Jamie talked her through the complexities of a wood-fired Rayburn. Zoe listened to his deep Scottish voice talking about damping down, sliders and spin wheels. *This* was what someone who lived in Scotland should sound like. His voice was a melodious lullaby and she let herself wander off into a daydream, walking through purple heather under a bright blue sky, her great-uncle at her side. She turned to look up at him and recoiled from herself as her mind conjured up the man-bear, shirtless in a kilt.

'Zo? Zoe?'

She started as she realised Jamie was talking to her.

'Er? What?'

'A fireside companion. Do you have one?'

'What? Like a cat?'

Jamie laughed. 'No, a poker, tongs, shovel and the like. I'll leave these here tonight and run you up one in the morning.'

Zoe flushed with embarrassment and gratitude. 'Thank you, Jamie, thank you so much.'

The Rayburn was ready, so they made a little pile of paper and kindling in the firebox and Jamie gave the job of lighting it to Zoe. She felt a thrill seeing it catch. They grinned at each other and high fived.

'Now for the door!' Zoe cried.

They went outside to look at whether or not they could fix it. The frame had started to rot so the hinges had finally given out and the door itself was also warping.

Jamie shook his head. 'This isn't going to be a quick fix.'

'Don't worry,' said Zoe, 'I've had an idea.'

She showed him a pile of plastic sheeting and wood.

'My plan is to make a frame and staple sheeting to either side. What do you think?'

Jamie smiled and squinted out toward the mountains on the other side of the loch. 'Well, I reckon we've got about an hour of light left so let's see what we can do.'

They worked quickly to assemble the frame, then Jamie

took the hinges off the old door and they hung the new one in its place. The fit was far from perfect but it would have to do for now.

'Tomorrow I'll run up a few old fleeces from Alan's farm,' Jamie said as he helped Zoe tidy up. 'We can fix them between the plastic for insulation and you can use them as a draft excluder along the bottom. I'm afraid my skills don't stretch much further than this, so you'll have to find someone else to fix the door properly, but I can give you some names.'

'Thank you so much, Jamie, you've been a lifesaver today.'

ZOE STOOD ON THE PORCH WAVING HIM GOODBYE, SMILING ruefully at Morag's hopes they would be more than just friends. He was as wonderful as she remembered, but a brother, not a lover. And anyway, the last thing on her mind was finding a boyfriend. She hadn't been in a relationship for years. Not since Joe, who had lasted through uni and a couple of years beyond. Things had always been plain sailing with Joe, apart from where his parents were concerned.

They were steadfastly upper-middle class, and after investing their money in the right education and social circle for their son, were supremely dissatisfied by his choice of lower-middle-class girlfriend. The fact Zoe's father was a cashier in a bank, not a hedge fund manager from the city, and her mother worked in a charity shop rather than being on the board, was further proof Joe was wasting his time with the lower orders.

During the five years they were together, Zoe could never get them to accept her, and always experienced a gnawing sense of inferiority and anxiety around them. Joe was nice, but their relationship was no grand passion, and it was a relief for them both when his parents engineered a job for him in

America and they could let it all come to an end. Since then, she'd tried internet dating but had been left disillusioned by the whole process. One liar after another. It didn't matter what the lie was, it was always going to come to the surface sooner or later, like a boil.

Most men lied about their age and appearance. Using profile pictures from decades ago, or photos of their friends. Then they lied about their jobs, their families, their kids. They lied about smoking, they lied about how they felt. They were just incapable of telling the truth.

Zoe had been so optimistic, taking every man at his word, pouring her expectations, heart and soul into each date. She had even slept with one, who turned out to be married with three children and another on the way. Within six months of dating she was soiled by the whole experience. A boyfriend was at the bottom of her priority list. Top of the list was a good night's sleep. An enormous yawn unfolded out of her, so big she couldn't stifle it. She brushed her teeth, crawled into the sleeping bag, and listened.

It was so quiet. Back home there had been hundreds of people within a few feet of her at all times. Even in her flat, she could hear people moving about on the other side of a wall. Now it was just her, and an endless expanse of emptiness outside. She oscillated between a sense of loneliness and excitement, before excitement won out.

She popped in her earplugs, put her eye mask on, and groped to turn off the light. Lying on her back, she thought about Jamie, Fiona and Morag. Thank god for that family. With them on her side, life in Kinloch would be so much easier.

4

After the previous night in the car, sleeping on the floor in a tent was the height of luxury, and Zoe woke with a lazy smile, pushing up her eye mask and checking her watch to see she had slept for nearly twelve hours. Her heart was full with excitement for a new day, however her bladder was fuller, and she remembered with a groan that a sleepy morning stagger to the bathroom meant boots, a coat and a walk outside.

She pulled out her ear plugs, shuffled out of the sleeping bag, and walked to the Rayburn which was still warm to the touch. Jamie had shown her how to fill the firebox with wood last thing before she went to bed; 'banking' it, so it was ready to get going the next morning. She refilled it and brought out a stove-top kettle to fill with water for the essential morning cup of tea. Her brow furrowed in concentration as she attempted to get water from the five-litre bottle into the kettle, without transferring most of it to the floor.

A bellow came from outside, and she dropped the bottle in fright, straight onto her foot. It tipped over, and water glugged out. She yelled, grabbing at the bottle to right it, then sat on the floor in a giant puddle, rubbing her foot.

'Owwww!'

'Moooo!' came an answering call from outside.

What in god's name was that? She dragged herself up to stand, and limped to the front door. Everything was blurry through the plastic, so she tugged it open a crack and peeked out.

A shaggy head framed by enormous horns peered back at her, its eyes obscured by long auburn hair. Condensed air puffed thickly out of its dark wet nostrils, its front hooves were on the first step leading up to the deck, and its jaw was moving in circles as it chewed.

'Mooooo!' it called again in greeting; the sound waves vibrating the plastic sheeting of her makeshift door.

Answering moos came from the rest of her land, as more horned heads raised up from the eternal task of eating, to see that a human had been spotted. Humans equalled food, and *en masse* they ambled up to the porch to jostle with each other for front row seats.

Zoe closed the door, petrified with fear. Where the hell had they come from? And even more importantly, how on earth was she going to reach the outhouse? Cycling through her options in rapid succession, she squatted over the washing up bowl to pee, mortified she'd sunk so low on only her second full day. Maybe if she ignored them, they would go away? It was the only option she could even consider, so she got dressed and made herself a bowl of porridge, putting her ear plugs back in to help her ignore the sounds from outside.

Fifteen minutes later, she took out her ear plugs and checked through the dirty windows to see they had dispersed again. Now she just needed to make it to the truck and she'd be away. As she looked from cabin, to cows, to truck, planning her escape, she noticed stalks of hay lying on the darker grass.

39

There weren't many left, but they were concentrated at the top of her property, leading away down the track towards the road. Cows weren't renowned for their brains or dexterity and the hay hadn't been there yesterday. This herd had been coaxed here.

Zoe was livid. Was this some kind of 'welcome to Kinloch' practical joke? These were killing machines! They weighed more than Siena. And they had bloody horns! How the hell was she going to get rid of them? She decided to make a run for it. Get to the truck, drive up the road until she found a signal, then ring Jamie to beg for help. She packed her bag, pulled on her boots and coat, and silently pushed the door open, gingerly lifting her foot to place one hundred and forty pounds of weight onto the ancient decking.

Creak! groaned the floorboard.

'Moo?' went a cow.

'Shit!' yelled Zoe.

'Moo!' went several happy cows, as the herd quickly made their way back to the porch.

Zoe rolled her eyes to the heavens and slumped her shoulders. This was not happening! The most she had blocking her path back home were old people wanting a chat with the bus driver, or the occasional drunk. Now she was confronted by the results of a gene-splicing experiment between a tank, a yak, and a Wookiee. Even Spanish bulls that gored men in sparkly outfits didn't have horns this big. This was it. Again. She was going to die. And this time, not mauled by a bear that wasn't a bear, but by thirty tonnes of shag pile carpet.

Two of the cows pushed forward and placed their front hooves on the bottom step. It gave way with an almighty crack. They stepped back in shock and Zoe walked forward, the sound of the breaking step being the last straw.

'Get off! Get back!' she cried, flailing her arms like a windmill in a hurricane. The cows nervously shifted back, allowing her space to descend the steps to the ground. She furiously pointed towards the track leading to the road.

'Bugger off! Shoo! That way!'

They looked blankly at her.

She stepped forward, gesticulating wildly. 'That way, you dozy fuckwits! Over there!'

'Moo?'

'Oh for fuck's sake!' Zoe muttered and strode on, the cows parting before her.

She got to the truck and opened the door, hyped on adrenaline. Before jumping in the cab, she turned. The cows had stopped and were looking expectantly at her. Could she lead them off her land? She slammed the door and set off walking up the track, her new friends patiently following behind.

Her heart was hammering in her chest, but with each step her confidence grew. They seemed calm enough, and she could see a breadcrumb trail of hay which would hopefully lead her back to where they had come from. She took out her phone and started filming. If she was going to die this morning, she wanted to make the news. When she reached the road she saw scraps of hay in the verge on its far side, leading to the right up the hill. Praying no cars were coming, she walked across and picked up the pace, checking they were all still following her. Ten minutes later, the trail turned left up a muddy track, and five minutes after that, she found a metal gate leading to an empty field. She opened the gate and they dutifully filed through. She shut it behind them and rested her feverish forehead on the cold metal of the top bar. She had done it.

BUOYED BY HER BOVINE SUCCESS, ZOE WENT INTO KINLOCH to check in with Morag and Fiona. The bell for the post office door tinkled happily as she walked in to be greeted by Morag, her face lighting up.

'Oh, there you are, love! Come in, come in. How did you sleep?'

Zoe's smile froze. The man-bear stood at the counter, a muscle in his jaw twitching, a German Shepherd at his heels. He looked away.

'You remember, erm.' Morag turned to him. 'What's your name, love?'

There was a pause as she watched the muscles in his face fighting with each other. Eventually enough tension was released for him to reply. 'Rory.'

Morag smiled. 'Nice to meet you, Rory. I'm Morag.' She turned to Zoe. 'You got your wood from him yesterday?'

The dog trotted forward, its tail wagging, pushing into her legs to say hello. She dropped to her knees, stroking it.

'Hello! And who are you? Aren't you gorgeous!'

The dog licked her face and she laughed. Rory whistled and it trotted back to sit at his side. Zoe stood, wiping her cheek. She turned to Morag.

'He wasn't in, so I had to drive to the garage on the road to Inverness and buy as much as I could from there.'

'Oh, love, that's daylight robbery!' Morag wailed. 'Anyway, this is Rory. Rory, Zoe; Zoe, Rory. Rory will sort you out now. Won't you, love?'

Rory swallowed and swivelled around mechanically to look at her. 'What do you need wood for?'

Zoe smiled beatifically at him. 'I've moved up to the cabin where Willie Laing used to live and I need wood for the Rayburn. I cleaned it out yesterday and it's running like a dream. I even made porridge on it this morning!' she said proudly before holding out her hand. 'I'm Zoe Maxwell,

Willie's great-niece. I now own the cabin. It's all mine. My property. Mine.'

There was a long pause. After an age, he stuck his hand out and gripped Zoe's.

Jesus! thought Zoe, as he gave her a death grip. Despite the pain, as he attempted to crush every bone in her hand, she smiled at him and pumped vigorously up and down, squeezing right back as hard as she could.

'So wonderful to meet you, can you bring a load up this afternoon? Do you need directions?'

Rory dropped her hand as if she had leprosy. 'I'm out of wood right now.'

Morag hooted. 'Mrs McCreedie told me you've got more trees up there than you can shake a stick at. I'm sure you can spare a bit for our Zoe?' She continued processing his letters, oblivious to the thunder rolling off him in waves.

The dog left his side again to make amends and Zoe dropped to her knees. 'You are so beautiful! What's your name?'

Rory cleared his throat. 'His name is Bandit.'

'Well, I think you're the most gorgeous male I've met since arriving in Kinloch.'

'What about our Jamie?' interjected Morag.

Zoe grinned and looked up at her. 'Okay, Bandit's the second most gorgeous male in Kinloch.' She sighed. 'I've always wanted a pet.' She looked at Bandit. 'Fancy a new home? Want to come live with me?'

Bandit barked his approval and Rory stood in front of him. 'He's not for sale.'

Zoe glanced at Rory's boots. A couple of tiny pieces of hay were stuck behind the laces. She frowned. Surely not? She straightened up and looked at him. An unwanted jolt of aware-ness shot through her. She stuck on a vacuous smile.

'Oh, I don't need a pet any more, I've got about thirty. Although I'm sending them off to market this afternoon. Possession being nine tenths of the law. Finders keepers and all that. I'll make enough to fix the cabin up good and proper. Might even put a hot tub on the deck.'

'Eh? What are you talking about love?' asked Morag.

Zoe's attention was all on Rory. His eyes widened and his jaw tightened. He pushed past her to the door, whistling for Bandit and walked out. 'See you later!' she called after him.

The only response was the tinkling of the bell as the door shut. Zoe turned back to Morag. 'Oh, I was just being silly. A load of cows got onto my land this morning but I walked them back up the road so they're safely home.'

'Well, that's good, love. Now, Jamie says it's not as bad as we all feared. Come and tell me all about it.'

Morag led the way out to the sitting room at the back, calling through as she went, 'Fi love, Zoe's here!'

ZOE SPENT THE MORNING BETWEEN MORAG'S AND THE library, making more plans for the cabin and juggling her budget. She may not have been paying rent any more, but the cabin was going to be a financial black hole if she wasn't careful. Even though she hadn't planned on doing any accountancy, Fiona was a mobile hairdresser and insisted Zoe do her books. The money wasn't going to stretch far and Zoe had a sinking feeling that sooner or later she'd have to get in her car every day and go to Inverness or further afield to find work.

It was drizzling by the time she drove up the track, making it slippery under the wheels of the truck. Thank god she had traded in Siena. The rain came down heavier as she ran for the cabin and she saw with dismay how churned up the ground was from the cattle earlier.

The Rayburn was running low so she fed it more logs. If she was going to keep this going through the winter, she couldn't leave it unattended during the day. She couldn't work in an office an hour's drive away. God, it just ate wood.

She felt a splash on her head. Looking up dubiously, she saw the roof was not as secure as she had led everyone to believe.

'Bollocks!' She dragged out some pots and pans, placing them below the drips and potential weak spots. The roof had to get fixed before winter set in. Jamie was coming around later with the sheep's wool for insulation. She would ask his advice.

❦

Rory sat in the truck, drumming his fingers impatiently on his rock-solid thighs in time with the rain on the roof. He was parked next to a field that contained thirty Highland cattle. Cattle that should still be at the cabin. How had they got back? And shut the gate behind them? Zoe couldn't have brought them here on her own. She didn't even know where they had come from. He brought out his phone to ring the tenant farmer, then paused and looked at Bandit.

'But what if she did bring them back?'

Bandit rested his head on his front paws. Rory banged his head back against the seat in frustration, then drove back into Kinloch. He needed to load the truck with wood for the interloper, then go to Inverness for a conversation with the estate's bank manager and its solicitors. But before all that, he needed to confront the most frightening part of his new job: paperwork.

5

The Kinloch estate office was ancient, and a mess. Big leather-bound volumes filled shelves that reached to the ceiling. The dust was thick, the paint was peeling, and cobwebs hung in every corner. It was a room where paper came to breed and die. Rory sat slumped behind a desk obscured by piles of the stuff, raked his hands through his hair and brooded.

On the table in front of him were letters from the bank. He had put off opening them until a call had come through that morning from the bank manager reminding him of his obligations. *Obligations*. His least favourite word. He'd spent most of his adult life running away from his particular ones, but now his father was dead and he had no choice but to face up to them. He knew he should have offloaded these tasks to someone far more competent than himself, but there just wasn't enough money to pay anyone. So, he ignored letters and emails, put off opening them, stupidly hoping they might disappear, or a solution might magically present itself.

Give him a tree to cut down, a fence to fix, a tangible and

practical problem to solve and he was the man for the job. Give him a balance sheet and he'd rather take a bullet. So now his problem chickens were coming home to roost, and it wasn't just him who would suffer, it would be his mother. After the death of his father, she relied on him completely. If he couldn't make the estate profitable then he would lose his job. What would happen to her then? He thought of them both resorting to stacking shelves in a supermarket and his head went from hurting to pounding.

By the time he arrived at the offices of the Kinloch estate lawyers, his brain was bursting out of his skull. Despite the sale of the estate's townhouse in the capital, the debt continued to mount and the castle continued to deteriorate. The bank manager hadn't sugar coated the situation. She'd told him there were limits to how big overdrafts could be and how long loans could last without repayment. Apparently, it was no longer acceptable that the ones for the Kinloch estate and the MacGinley family had begun in the time of Robert the Bruce and were due to be paid off when humans colonised Mars.

He now sat in a quiet room of MacLennan and McCarthy, the estate's solicitors, his socks sinking into the thick, pale blue carpet, his battered waxed jacket hung outside to dry. The staff had insisted he didn't need to remove his boots, but Rory could insist harder. His life was enough of a muddy, dishevelled mess without inflicting it on others.

He sat across from the latest McCarthy; acres of leather inlaid desk between them. The desk was polished, with a fountain pen stand, blotter pad and a brass desk calendar. In one corner was a crystal decanter of whisky and a couple of glasses. The old man's fingers had instinctively drifted towards it when they both sat down, but after an imperceptible shake of Rory's head, he called his assistant to bring them both a glass of Highland spring water instead.

Alastair McCarthy was of indeterminate age but clearly very old. His body had got to a point it was happy with, then stayed there, slowly desiccating. He was extremely thin, with sunken eyes, a shining skull, and a veneer of papery skin shrink-wrapped over his emaciated frame. He presented a visible anatomy lesson, and a study in stillness. It was only his habit of preceding every proclamation with a vigorous throat clearing exercise that reminded Rory he was, against all the odds, still alive.

Following enquiries after his mother, he placed a sheaf of papers in a brown folder down in front of him.

'Ahem. The papers you enquired about, containing the legal arrangement for the croft. The lease did not expire with the death of William Laing, so he was free to pass it on to whomever he chose. Here's the estate's copy you can take with you so you can see for yourself.'

Rory leafed through the papers, scowling at the name: Stuart MacGinley, Earl of Kinloch.

'The lease also includes access to the main road via the track, and it is recorded as having a dwelling, so the lady is, ahem, within her rights to reside there.'

'But he never paid the estate any money for it!'

The corners of Alastair's eyes softened. 'Ahem. He gave a lifetime of service essentially for free. Regardless, even if the land was still currently part of the estate, the sale of a new lease would make little difference to the present situation. Unless circumstances change, then the only course of action is to—'

'No.'

'Or fully embrace Colquhoun Asset Management's plans?'

'No,' replied Rory more forcefully.

'Have you spoken recently with the bank?'

'Just now.'

Alastair's shoulders sagged a little and he leaned against the back of his chair. 'Ahem. So you appreciate where we find ourselves...'

Rory's head sunk. This was all on him. The estate would go under and he had no one to blame but himself.

WALKING BACK THROUGH THE CENTRE OF INVERNESS, Bandit at his side, Rory fixated on the cabin. If only he was living there instead of this woman, he would have the headspace he needed to find the solution to an impossible problem. Alastair McCarthy's inference they should sell off more assets was the sign of ultimate failure. After the sale of the townhouse, the castle was about the only thing left of value, but still nobody wanted it. And as for the plans Colquhoun Asset Management had put forward? To develop the castle into a conference centre? He wanted that to be the last resort before repossession. His train of thought was interrupted by Bandit who had stopped outside a shop and was barking excitedly at the window.

Bandit had only been to Inverness a few times, but had decided that The Time is MEOW! was his favourite shop. He would pace up and down, tail wagging, barking hellos at all the pets on display. Rory didn't know whether his interest was friendship or food, and didn't want to take the risk of finding out, so outside the window was as far as he had ever got. He thought back to his encounter with Zoe that morning in the post office and his fingers curled possessively in Bandit's fur. She may have always wanted a pet, but she wasn't getting his. He zeroed in on a small cage in the window. He wanted her out of the cabin and she wanted a pet. Time to kill two birds with one stone.

A FEW MILES BACK DOWN THE ROAD TOWARDS KINLOCH, Rory realised he had made a terrible mistake. Bandit, usually the best-behaved dog in the world, was taking an unhealthy and overly excited interest in the cardboard box on the back seat. Rory was strong, but it was taking all his strength to keep the dog from leaping into the back. He drove with one hand gripping Bandit's collar and the other on the wheel to keep the truck on the road. Traffic was getting heavier and there was nowhere to stop and turn around.

What was I thinking? First the cows and now this? What the fuck is wrong with me? He glanced at the clock on the dashboard. He had just about enough time to get to the cabin, unload the logs currently filling the boot, put the box in their place away from Bandit, and drive back to the pet shop to return it. It would be tight, but if he was quick dumping the wood he could do it.

By the time he reached the track to the cabin he was sweating, and Bandit was beside himself with excitement. It was pouring with rain, and as he rounded the bend he saw how much the land had been churned up by the cows. *God, I'm an arsehole.* But that stopped here and now. He reversed the truck to get as close to the porch as possible and leapt out, dragging Bandit after him and dropping the tailgate. He then walked back and shut the driver's door before releasing his hold on Bandit's collar.

'Bandit, stay!'

But Bandit was having none of it, and careered around outside the truck, barking and whining. Exasperated, Rory threw the logs out of the back of the truck towards the porch. He didn't have time to carry them up, this would have to do.

Zoe rushed out of the cabin, pulling on her wellies. 'Hey, hey! What are you doing?' She ran down the steps into the rain. 'You can't do that, they'll get soaked!'

He kept throwing. Some of the logs thudded against the outside wall of the cabin, some hit her makeshift door, and most bounced back off the porch onto the muddy ground.

'Why are you being such a tool? What have I ever done to you?'

Bandit was now trying to get under the cabin, barking crazily. What was wrong with him? 'Bandit! Heel!' he yelled.

Bandit continued to ignore him. Now Zoe did too, grabbing the wet and muddy logs and throwing them onto the relative shelter of the decking. It became a race. Rory, with determination and urgency throwing the logs to the ground, and Zoe with fury and rage throwing them up onto the porch.

As soon as the back of the truck was empty, he ran to the cab to get the cardboard box to put it safely out of Bandit's reach. As he lifted it off the passenger seat, a trail of sawdust floated down. He saw with horror that a hole had been eaten into the side. He threw back the lid to confirm the worst had happened. The creature had escaped. Frantically he searched the cab. Nothing.

He ran back to the cabin, scanning the ground, calling for Bandit.

Zoe stomped up to him. 'What is your problem?' she yelled. Her wet T-shirt was clinging to her heaving chest. The rain had turned her hair into a river of red curls. She angrily swiped a long, wet strand from her face, smudging her flushed cheek with mud. Her eyes, framed by wet lashes, were glistening.

Rory's mind went blank, then his mouth unfortunately moved for him. 'That'll be one hundred pounds.'

Zoe's jaw dropped. 'Whaatttt? I'm not paying a hundred quid for sub-standard merchandise and shoddy service!'

Rory felt split in two. The better half of him was imprisoned inside someone who just shrugged in response.

She ran up the steps to the porch, kicking off her wellies and striding into the cabin. When she returned, she thrust three twenty-pound notes and a tenner towards him. 'That's all I've got,' she said quietly. Bandit called off his search and ran to her. She stroked him with her free hand. Rory took the money. 'I don't understand why you're being such an arse.' She held his gaze.

Rory turned away, whistling for Bandit, and got in his truck. As he drove down the track, he saw her walk back to the cabin, wiping her eyes with her sodden sleeve.

I DON'T UNDERSTAND WHY YOU'RE BEING SUCH AN ARSE. THE words went around his head as he drove along the road. *What have I ever done to you?*

He banged his fists on the steering wheel. 'Fuuuuuuuuuuuu-ucccccccccckkkkkkkkkkk!' The truck swerved and he pulled to the side of the road, killing the engine. 'Fuck, fuck, fuck, fuck, fuuuuuuuuuuuccccccckkkk!' Each word was punctuated by another bang of his fists against the wheel. Bandit began to whine, and he put his hand out to calm him.

He didn't recognise the person who had just behaved so badly. She didn't deserve to be treated like that; no one did. Zoe was right. He was an arse. He was an arsehole of the highest order. He ran his fingers through his hair, tugging it away from his scalp to relieve the tension. He relived the flash of pain that shot across her face as he asked for the money, her unshed tears glistening.

He dropped his hands and slumped back in the seat,

resting against the headrest. He let out a sigh. It was quiet now. The only sound the pitter-patter of raindrops on the windscreen and roof. What could he do? How could he make amends without fessing up to everything he had done?

In his mind he saw her deep dark eyes, her cascading curls of red hair, her luminous pale skin with its sprinkling of freckles. He saw her tall lithe frame, her perfect breasts revealed by the rain. God, she was beautiful.

He realised he had been holding his breath, tension thrumming through him. He let out another sigh, and stared out through the windscreen blurred with rain. He needed to stay away, leave her alone. Even if he hadn't just burned his bridges in a pyrotechnic display of stupidity, he'd never lay his heart on the line again. There was no space for romance in his life, and definitely no room for love. His mother and saving the estate had to come first.

ZOE STACKED THE LOGS AGAINST THE SIDE WALL OF THE cabin, her emotions radiating so much heat her clothes were beginning to dry. What was his problem? Even the worst of her London dates hadn't treated her with such harsh indifference. And to add insult to injury, why did he have to be so freaking gorgeous?

A shiver of goosebumps breezed over her skin. His cheeks were the same burnished bronze as yesterday. Water droplets had gathered in his hair like jewels. His eyes burned like silver stars. She had wanted to kiss him whilst simultaneously punching him in the face. Her heart thudded in her chest, hammering in a nail of frustration and anguish. He was a man of stone. Rock hard body and granite heart.

By the time Jamie rolled up the track, Zoe was sweeping

the deck. Jamie gave her a wave and pulled a bale of wool tied together with orange twine out of the boot of his car.

She plastered on a smile as he walked up to the porch. 'So, you got some insulation then?' she asked, eying the fleeces. They looked like they'd been sheared from the dirtiest sheep in the flock.

'Yeah, they're not in the best of nick but they'll do the job.' He rummaged in his pocket. 'And I got you these.' He pulled out a pair of voluminous tan women's tights. 'They're for the doorstop. I thought we could stuff the legs with some of the wool.'

Zoe took them from him and raised an eyebrow. 'Dare I ask where you got these, Jamie?'

The colour rose in his cheeks. 'I, er, borrowed them from Mum.'

Zoe clapped her hand over her mouth as a shocked giggle burst out. 'And when were you going to give them back?'

He blushed fiercely. 'You can't say anything.'

'James Robert MacDougall, I can't believe you went rummaging around in your mum's underwear drawer and stole her stockings!'

'Promise you won't tell?' he pleaded, sounding more and more like the little boy he once was.

Zoe laughed and put her hand to her chest. 'I promise. Hand on my heart, hope to die.'

Jamie joined in with 'stick a needle in my eye.'

They both smiled at the memories from long ago and Jamie deposited the fleeces on the porch.

'I'll tackle the door. There's no way I'm stuffing my mum's tights.'

For the next hour, they worked companionably together, Jamie unpicking one side of plastic sheeting and stuffing the inside before re-fixing it back, Zoe filling the tights along with a length of wood inside to keep the shape and the doorstop anchored to the floor. There was plenty of wool left over, so they went around the door and window frames, plugging any obvious gaps. As they worked, Zoe snapped photos; the contrast between the wool and the wood, Jamie's hands as he worked, his profile against the open door with the loch in the distance behind. Focusing on the beauty in the small details helped give the bigger picture a rosier glow.

She then followed him out, and drove up the road until she found a phone signal, spending a happy hour on Instagram, editing the images from the day. It was so beautiful here, even when it rained. She had messaged Sam who demanded to know why she was being 'chased by weird looking cows', and who the 'Scottie hottie' Jamie was. Zoe promised she would collect all the hotties in Kinloch for a non-specific day in the future when she was brave enough to come for a visit.

After speaking to Sam, Zoe rang home, sensing her mother's unease and worry crackling down the line, then returned to the cabin, to make herself more pasta for tea. As she ate, she wondered how she could run a small fridge. If she didn't get some vegetables into her diet soon, she was sure her mum would sense it and drive all the way up to force-feed her broccoli.

Without a TV or the Internet, and with her Kindle low on battery, there was nothing left to do in the long evening. She spent a couple of hours moving the old table around the cabin, balancing on it to clean the log walls of their prehistoric cobwebs, then rearranged her meagre possessions. She placed the bird's nest pride of place on top of one of the plastic boxes outside her tent door. Snuggled in her sleeping bag, under the twinkling of the battery-powered fairy lights she'd clipped inside the tent, she smiled. The unpleasantness with Rory seemed far away.

6

Zoe was not a morning person. It was at least an hour after waking before she was able to pass as a fully functioning human being, and the process had to involve a cup of tea. With her new front door up and running, she hadn't zipped her tent shut, and when the pale morning light hit her face she lay there, eye mask still on, checking all limbs were intact before she found the energy to move. It was ten minutes before she removed her mask and earplugs. She lay, gathering together her waking consciousness ready to deal with the day, listening to the birds outside.

There was another noise though, a scrabbling, scratching noise, closer to her. She corralled her brain into waking up, but no logical explanation came to mind. The noise was coming from right outside the tent. She opened her eyes looking at the plastic box with the bird's nest on top. Half-awake, her mind still not yet fully switched on, she stared at the nest. She felt detached, as if watching a TV show, as a cute little head poked out, with big round ears and whiskers. It looked at her, licking its paws, bringing them down over its face to clean it. It was so comfortable, so at ease in its surroundings, that Zoe could only stare. It looked like a cross between a fluffy hamster and a mouse. Was it some sort of rat?

Finishing its morning ablutions, it tentatively ventured out of the nest. It was large, with big, floppy ears, a glossy chocolate brown coat and fluffy white underbelly. The half-awake part of Zoe was telling her she should at least be screaming by now. The half-asleep part was telling her how utterly adorable it was.

Before her conscious mind could assert itself enough to create motor function, the creature had jumped out of the nest, off the box and onto Zoe's pillow, where it curled up next to her and fell asleep.

Was she still dreaming? She gingerly lifted her arm and gently stroked the soft warm body beside her. It opened its eyes, and nudged against her hand, as if wanting more attention. A half-laugh caught in her throat as she sat up, running her fingers over the silky fur. It was kind of rat shaped, but there was no way it was wild.

'Good morning to you,' she whispered. 'Why do I feel you're here to stay?'

Zoe took lots of pictures of her new friend while she made breakfast, as if recording the event made it somehow real rather than the invention of a scrambled mind. It was remarkably domesticated and ridiculously cute, sniffing the front of her phone as she snapped away. It wanted to be wherever Zoe was, and its favourite place was sitting on her shoulder, playing with her hair.

She had always wanted a pet as a child, but it had never happened. First her mother was ill, then they lost their house. Zoe stopped asking at that point, but would spend hours outside, trying to coax birds and squirrels into being her friend.

She wasn't so enamoured of her unexpected pet that she forgot it needed a toilet. She ripped up paper and placed it in the bird's nest, clapping like a proud parent when the creature she'd decided was a rat, immediately got the message.

'If you're going to stay then you need a home for when I'm not here,' she solemnly informed her new friend. 'Let's find a pet shop this morning.'

Zoe emptied a small plastic box she was using for storage and lined it with a towel to make a temporary home for the rat. She then took it, the bird's nest as a portable toilet, and her bag to the library in Kinloch. Ratty was asleep by the time she arrived, so she left him in the truck and went inside.

Sitting at a desk, she posted her latest photos to Instagram, including the ones from the morning, imagining the reaction that Sam would have to the rat. She charged her phones, Kindle and power packs, and continued her cabin renovation research.

Each time she added another line to her spreadsheet her heart sank. Why was it so expensive to renovate a cabin? Even the most basic essentials were going to max her out. The roof was the biggest unknown. If it needed a complete replacement it would make the whole project unworkable. She also had ongoing storage costs for her furniture and non-essential belongings. She didn't want to pick everything up only to put it in a house with a leaking roof.

She sat back, staring into the middle distance. She needed to see the roof, find out how bad it really was. But first, she either had to donate the rat to a pet shop or commit to looking after it. She gathered up her belongings and grinned. Life in Kinloch was proving far from boring.

Zoe stood outside the only pet shop in a fifty-mile radius

and tried not to giggle. The Time is MEOW! the sign pronounced, the windows full of fluffy little balls of cuteness; there wasn't an old or ugly creature in view. The interior was a pungent mix of animal feed and sawdust, softened by the warm greetings of an older couple. Their clothes were utilitarian, in nondescript browns and greens that hid a multitude of animal sins.

'Can we help you, lassie?' asked the man, smiling as Zoe gingerly brought out the rat.

The couple lit up and the woman exclaimed, 'Basil!' She nudged her husband. 'I just knew he would be going to a good home.' She stroked the rat, cooing. 'Hello, you little cutie! How are you enjoying your new human?'

'Err. You know this rat?' Zoe asked.

'Of course, my dear, we know all of our babies. This is Basil, he's a Dumbo rat. See his big ears. Aren't you gorgeous, my darling! And such a lovely present for a pretty girl! Your boyfriend came in yesterday to buy something special for you and decided it had to be a rat.'

'My boyfriend?'

'Oh aye, strapping fella, lovely hair and bright eyes. Good teeth too.'

Her husband turned to Zoe. 'Do you have everything you need? He said you had the essentials, but you might need a little more to get you going, and if you're going to be away from him a while then he needs a friend. Rats are sociable creatures you know.'

Zoe's jaw moved but no words came out. The lady stepped back and Basil scurried to Zoe's shoulder. The couple let out a collective happy sigh.

'Awwww. Friends for life!'

. . .

ZOE LEFT THE PET SHOP CONSIDERABLY LIGHTER IN THE pocket and heavier on unanticipated purchases. She hadn't budgeted for this. She sat back in her truck, Basil running happily back and forth along the dashboard in front of her.

Rory. Her mind hadn't left him since the pet shop. What in god's name was he up to? Did he think she would run back to London because of a rat? And did he think she was that much of an idiot she'd believe beautiful Basil was wild? Well, she had told him she thought he was a bear. She sighed. And he'd said she was his girlfriend? Fat chance of that. Not only did he despise her and want her out of the cabin, he obviously thought she was a half-wit as well.

Well, she would show him. She wasn't going anywhere and neither was Basil. She whistled to him as she fired up the truck and he leapt from the dashboard to her shoulder, chattering away.

ZOE STOOD IN FRONT OF THE TALL TREE SHE USED TO CLIMB with Jamie and Fiona when they were children. It was perfectly placed to offer a vantage point of the cabin's roof, and if there was phone signal up there, then so much the better.

However, the tree seemed to have grown far more than she had in the last nineteen years. She could touch the lowest branch but it was too high to haul herself onto it. Basil climbed to the top of her head as she contemplated it, as if a second pair of eyes would solve the problem.

'Right then, Basil, let's show them,' she said, as she strode confidently to the cabin, returning with the least rickety chair which she set against the trunk.

She made sure her phone was secure in a zipped pocket and lifted Basil down. 'Now then, you must keep still. I haven't done this since I was just a bit bigger than you, so you've got to be a help, not a hindrance. Okay?'

Basil twitched his nose in agreement and she placed him behind her, in the hood of her jacket. She stepped onto the seat. So far no broken bones. She reached her arms over the branch, lifted her right leg up and tried to swing it over, but it was too high.

'Come on, you can do this!' she told herself, bringing her right foot back onto the seat, then tentatively placing her left foot on the back of the chair.

It wobbled and she pushed it back against the trunk so the chair was now balancing on its back legs. Not wanting to take it past tolerance, she grasped the trunk securely with her arms, put her weight through her left leg, swung her right leg over the branch and heaved, just as the back bar of the chair snapped and the whole thing fell over. She was up!

'Yes!'

She punched the air at the small victory, then glanced at the broken chair. She turned to Basil who had worked his way to her shoulder.

'Come on now, that chair was knackered, I'm not that heavy. Now back into your seat and hold on tight.'

Basil scurried into her hair as she got to her feet on the branch and began her ascent.

The tree was a great one to climb once you got going. As a kid she'd never climbed that far but it still felt very high. As she reached each new branch, she took out her phone to check the signal. Nothing.

She paused on the seventh branch, high enough now to see the roof. She could see where a few of the shingles had come loose. It wasn't as bad as it could have been but it certainly wasn't pretty. She zoomed in with the camera on her phone to take photos. She could show them to someone who knew more than she did and make sure she only spent as much as she actually needed to.

Putting her phone back in her pocket, she heard a chattering noise above her and saw that Basil had gone exploring and was now perched above her, squeaking.

'Oh, what are you doing? Come back here! We've seen enough and there's no signal so we're going down now.'

Basil didn't budge.

'Are you stuck?!'

Basil continued his chattering and squeaking. Hadn't the lady in the pet shop told her that squeaking was a sign of stress?

'Don't worry, sweetheart,' she called up to him, 'Mummy's coming.'

She rolled her eyes at herself and the devotion she was showing to a rat that had been in her life less than twenty-four hours and hauled herself up the next two branches. Basil was higher but the next branch wasn't easy. It involved wedging her foot into a crack in the trunk as a step and she was beginning to realise she was higher up than she had ever been before.

'Do NOT look down now,' she said as she eyeballed Basil. 'You are in so much trouble, young man. Wait till I get you home. No TV tonight and only bread and water for tea.'

Basil was running back and forth excitedly, knowing she was nearly there. Zoe took a big breath in, wedged one foot into the crack, dug her fingers into the bark above and yanked herself up with all her might, swinging her other leg over the branch where Basil was perched and pulling herself up. She lay across the branch, eyes closed, heart thudding, whilst Basil sniffed about, making sure she was still alive.

A series of pings, dings and vibrations in her pocket alerted her that she had a phone signal at last. She sat up, checked her messages, then took photos from her vantage point and selfies of her and Basil. Thank god her parents didn't know what Instagram was.

With her back resting against the trunk and Basil wrapped around her neck, she posted the shots of them both up the tree, checked her bids on eBay, and read Sam's messages. She said Zoe had managed to go feral in less than a week and asked if Basil was a joke. Zoe replied that he was the cutest chap she'd met so far.

She then rang home. She knew both her parents would be busy at work but she left a message. Hearing her mum's voice on the answering machine sent a stab of pain to her chest. The last time she had been up this tree she hadn't even known she was going home to a mum. She was so grateful. She had wanted to break away from her parents, from their expectations of what they thought she should do with her life. But now she missed them terribly and they were very far away. She kept her message short and upbeat, injecting as much positivity into it as she could.

As soon as the cabin was as inhabitable as she had claimed, she would get them up. Just not before, or she knew they'd be taking her straight back down south, perhaps in a straightjacket.

Finishing her message, she had the urge to pee and realised she had been in the tree over an hour. She turned to Basil. 'Right, little monkey, we're getting out of here.' She secured her phone, stretched, then glanced down.

Big mistake.

Adrenaline had taken her up the last branch to get to Basil, but now adrenaline was showing her exactly how easy it would be to fall and end her life, thumping into every branch on the way down to the ground.

She groaned. 'Come on, come on, Zoe. You can do this.'

She felt sick. Dizzy.

'Come ON!'

Face down on the branch, she gripped it with her arms and right leg. Putting her left leg towards the trunk, she felt with the point of her boot for the crack.

Where had it gone?!

Her heart raced. Her muscles strained with the effort to keep herself on the branch whilst still reaching lower with her left foot.

Where was it?

She hauled herself back up fully onto the branch, feeling the bark against her face, and tried not to panic. Dammit. She was stuck up a tree. Like the idiot she knew she was. Why didn't she just buy a ladder and look at the roof a sensible way? She'd need one anyway to fix the bloody thing.

She brought herself back to a sitting position, then rang Jamie but it went to voicemail. He worked out of town as an electrician on new build projects and said he didn't always have a signal. The next call was to Morag, who thankfully picked up.

After Morag went through two minutes of worry, she reassured her she'd send someone out straight away. 'Don't worry, love, there's at least two people in the post office who could be your knight in shining armour. Sit tight, okay?'

Zoe thanked her and rang off. Her phone battery was now down to eighteen per cent, so she put it in her pocket and sat back to wait, wrapping her arms around herself to keep warm.

After ten minutes, the phone rang. Jamie?

It was Sam, who didn't even bother saying hello. 'A rat! You've got a frigging rat? As a pet? They carry the plague. You'll get boils, then die all alone in your Scottish shed and then your rat will EAT YOU!'

As an actress, Sam saw every situation as an opportunity to be dramatic. She called it 'expanding her range'. Zoe often asked why her range never included quiet, shy, retiring types, or nuns.

'I mean, for a rat, he is pretty cute but seriously, have you lost your mind? They piss over everything, all the time, and stink, then breed like fricking rabbits and chew through wires so you'll get electrocuted and die. Then they move onto chowing down on your hot, sizzling corpse.'

Zoe laughed. 'He's remarkably house-trained for a rat and so intelligent – I swear he can understand me.'

'O. M. G. That is it! You have got to get back to civilisation. I bet you haven't even had a bottle of Prosecco since you got there. You'll have swapped it for Irn-Bru.'

'Oh, I have, I drank a whole bottle on the first night and was convinced I was about to be attacked by a bear. So, when are you coming to visit?'

'You know how much I love you. But seriously? I am not spending any of my precious time re-enacting *Deliverance*. I'll see you when you've regained your senses and come home.'

'Not going to happen anytime soon, sweetpea, I'm falling in love with this place.'

'The place or a person? What's going on with Jamie? For a country boy he is proper hot!'

'Eww, no! He's like my brother! You can have him, although I think you might be too much for him to handle.'

Sam sighed theatrically. 'I'm *always* too much to handle. Ooh, hang on. Shit. Gotta go, agent on the other line.'

She hung up and Zoe rested back against the trunk. 'That was Sam. She sends her love and says she can't wait to meet you.'

Basil crawled out of her hair and ran along the branch, sniffing and moving his head.

'What is it? Can you hear something?' Zoe listened as the

sound of a car engine drifted towards them. 'It's someone come to save us. Now be as cute as possible. Okay?'

Zoe craned to see the track more clearly between the branches of the tree. The engine roared closer but she didn't see it until it rounded the bend. It was the filthy truck with the coat of arms she'd seen in the back courtyard of the castle.

She groaned. *Please, let this not be Rory.*

Zoe watched Rory swing out of the truck with ease and unstrap an extending ladder from the roof. He worked quickly and efficiently. Not once did he even glance in the direction of the tree where she sat, trying to make herself small and invisible.

Such a humiliation. Stuck up a tree like a sad cat, waiting to be rescued by the hunky fireman. He looked gorgeous, like a mountain lion crossed with a Chippendale. She thought of him stripping for cash in the local pubs on the weekend and couldn't help snorting with laughter. That would be something she would pay a lot of money to see.

On the ground, Rory paused. Zoe clamped her hand to her mouth. She needed to pee and didn't want him to leave her up there.

He moved the broken chair, put the ladder against the tree and kicked the feet into the soft earth at the base. Climbing up, he extended the ladder further until it reached the branch where Zoe was sitting. He climbed the ladder like a panther, light and lithe but all muscle and power. Zoe fixed her attention on his forearms; they were bigger than her calves. Did he possess *any* body fat at all? He got to the top of the ladder and met Zoe's eyes at last.

There was an uncomfortable silence.

'Er, hello,' she said finally.

Rory cleared his throat. 'I was in the post office at the wrong time.'

'Okay, that's great. If you could just move out of the way I'll shimmy down,' Zoe said brightly.

He didn't budge. Zoe lay on her front and swung one leg down towards the ladder.

'Stop!' His voice a command all sentient beings would have no choice but to obey.

'What is it?'

'It's too dangerous. You might slip and take both of us out at the same time.'

'It's fine! I got up here, didn't I?'

'Breaking a chair in the process and getting stuck. Sit back up and we'll do this my way.'

His way? Zoe took a big breath, drawing in the energy she needed to unleash a tirade, when he stopped her.

'Please?' The request was gentle, pouring oil on her troubled waters. She moved back up. 'Thank you.'

'Wow. Please and thank you back to back.'

He raised one eyebrow, sending a bolt of awareness through her. Holy crap was he hot. Oh my god, was he hot!

He climbed to the top rung of the ladder, his face now level with hers, just inches away. 'Now what we're going to do is—'

'WAIT! You have to rescue Basil first.'

'Basil?'

'Yes, Basil, my pet.'

As if on cue, Basil poked his head out from under her curls, checking out the person in front of him, his nose and whiskers twitching. Zoe bit the inside of her cheek. She couldn't laugh now, but she would piss herself later remembering the look on Rory's face.

He opened his mouth but no words came out. He cleared his throat again. 'That's a rat.'

'Oh yes, isn't he gorgeous! He's a wild Highland rat. He found his way into the cabin last night and we've become best friends.'

'Friends,' repeated Rory in a monotone.

'Oh yes,' her voice even more enthusiastic. 'He's going everywhere with me. Although rats are sociable creatures, so I'm going to buy him a girlfriend, and maybe,' Zoe crossed her fingers, looking earnestly at him, 'in a few months' time, if they get on, they might have a couple of babies so I can have a whole family!'

'A *couple* of babies...' If words were solid, Rory's were lumps of lead.

Inwardly, Zoe was doing cartwheels. Watching him squirm was the best revenge ever. If he thought she was stupid then she was going to play that role to perfection. She put her head to one side, looking at him as if *he* was the stupid one.

'Yes... If a boy rat and a girl rat like each other and the timing is right, then they can, erm, make ratty love, then after nine months, the girl rat has one or two ratty babies. It's biology. Science.'

Rory sighed. Zoe bit the insides of both cheeks. Rory extended his hand. 'Give me the rat.'

Zoe disentangled Basil from her hair and spoke to him. 'Now listen up, sweetie pie, this man is going to help you out of the tree first. I know you're scared, but Mummy's right behind you. Okay?'

Rory looked in pain. Zoe carefully handed over Basil. Who

bit Rory hard on the end of his thumb. 'Agghhh!' he cried, dropping him.

Zoe screamed. 'Basil!'

But he was off, jumping and scurrying down from branch to branch. He'd clearly had enough of this tree for one day.

'He bit me!'

'Yes, well he's a good judge of character,' retorted Zoe. 'You could have killed him. He doesn't know how to climb trees.'

'Really. So how come he's now on the ground?'

Zoe looked down. Basil was in the leaves beneath the tree, looking for something to play with, shag or eat. 'Oh. Well, if I had known that, I wouldn't have been stuck up here. I only came this high to rescue him.'

Rory sucked the end of his thumb, then took it out. 'What were you doing climbing the tree in the first place?'

'I needed to check out the roof and find a phone signal.'

Rory shook his head. 'I've had enough of your lunacy for one day.' He reached up, and in one fluid movement grabbed Zoe and flung her over his shoulder, holding her tightly with one arm, anchoring her legs to his chest.

She screamed. 'What are you doing?'

'Getting you down from this tree, going home, and removing this entire episode from my brain with a bottle of whisky.' He held the ladder with his free hand and began his descent. 'Now stop wriggling or you'll kill us both.'

Zoe kept as still as possible, her eyes tightly shut. If she opened them, she would have ringside seats to the rear of the year, but also to the exact distance she would plummet to her death if Rory lost his grip. She put her arms around his waist and held on. The loss of sight ramped up her other senses; he smelled divine. It was an intoxicating mix of soap, freshly cut wood, woodsmoke, and a musky essence that was all man. There was nothing artificial about him, no cloying aftershave, just pure, unadulterated masculinity. Zoe had never been so aware of a man before in her entire life. She wanted to press her face into his chest, breathe him in like he was the oxygen keeping her alive. She could feel his muscles moving as they descended the ladder, hot steel under her hands. Her pubic bone was resting on his shoulder, giving exquisite friction with every step. Her insides throbbed and her legs turned to jelly.

He stopped and Zoe looked to see grass under his feet. Neither of them moved. How could she prolong the connection? A squeaking sound finally broke the spell and Rory lowered Zoe gently to the ground, moving away.

She busied herself with Basil, hiding her burning cheeks. 'There you are, my darling, safe and sound.'

Rory went to the tree and took down the ladder.

Zoe spoke to the back of his head. 'Thank you.'

He stilled and nodded in response. Zoe felt reckless. Now she had him here, she wanted his knowledge. She knew after he left that would be it. Until the time he decided to gift her a snake. 'Can you stay for another five minutes, please? I could really do with some advice about the roof.'

Rory stopped, the ladder suspended in his hands. Then he appeared to come to a decision and snapped the final extension down, lifting it to put it back on the roof of his truck. 'I can't. I have to get back.'

'To visit your girlfriend?'

Rory turned abruptly. 'What?'

Zoe frowned and chewed her lip thoughtfully. 'Well, you told the owners of The Time is MEOW! Basil was a present for your girlfriend. And I'm *definitely* not your girlfriend, so I'm just a teeny tiny bit confused as to why he ended up with me. Unless as soon as you've hounded me out, you're going to install her here and turn my home into your love nest?'

Rory's cheeks flushed. He opened his mouth as if to speak, but Zoe cut him off.

'Oh, save your breath. Get your ladder and look at my roof. I have no idea why you hate me so much you resorted to buying a rat to get me out, but you could at least credit me with a modicum of intelligence. I mean, look at him. He's beautiful, house-trained and clearly comfortable around people. Anyone who thinks Basil could pass for a wild rat needs their eyes tested. Oh, and you also owe me a new step after you sent Clarrie the cow and her friends round for tea.'

Zoe could see embarrassment, guilt and rage fighting for supremacy across his face. She giggled. 'What's the matter? Rat got your tongue?' At her own joke, she guffawed with laughter until she snorted like a pig, which set her off even more, doubling over at her own hilarity.

Rory freed the ladder from the truck roof and walked it to the side of the cabin. 'What do you want?'

Zoe swallowed. What she wanted, what she really, *really* wanted, was for him to drop the ladder, throw her over his shoulder again, carry her into the cabin and lay her down on top of her sleeping bag. She wanted him to tear his shirt off and bring his body down over hers.

'Well?'

Zoe, flustered, quickly rallied. 'Erm, well, the roof is leaking and I need to know if I can just replace some of the shingles or if the whole roof has to go. I then need to know how much each shingle costs, where to get them, and if I can fix the roof myself. I also need to know about replacing the guttering and setting up a greywater system.'

Rory nodded, fixed the ladder against the side of the cabin and climbed up. She started running for the outhouse.

'Where are you going?' he called after her.

'I've been stuck up a tree for the last two hours. I need to pee!' she yelled back.

Rory was already up the ladder when she returned and had crawled to the top of the roof. She got her laptop out and stood with it wedged on a rung whilst he relayed how many shingles were loose or needed replacing. She then ordered an assessment of the guttering, firing out questions and tapping in the answers.

She'd twisted her curls to the top of her head and secured them with a pen, but one tight corkscrew had escaped and hung down by her neck, acting as a toy for Basil. She heard Rory sigh and looked up, to see his gaze flick away from her.

'What?'

'Nothing, just thinking about the state of your roof,' he replied.

Had he just said *your* roof rather than *the* roof? She felt light, like a fluffy pink marshmallow of happiness was expanding in her tummy.

'I know it's bad. I just didn't know how bad. I'll have to do the bare minimum to keep me watertight and warm until I can save up for extravagances, like a toilet or a chandelier.' She grinned up at him. He stared back at her, blankly. Her smile wavered. She turned back to her computer screen as he looked back to the roof.

Ten minutes later he was done. Zoe closed her laptop and graciously allowed him to step off the ladder. Rory indicated the computer. 'Can I see what you've been doing?'

Zoe stopped, surprised. 'Yes, yes of course. We can sit down and I'll go through it with you.'

She walked up the steps to the porch, hesitated about inviting him in, then sat on the top step, scooting her bottom to the far right-hand side as if she had to make room for a sumo wrestler next to her.

She cleared her throat, opened the laptop on her knees, and began. 'So, I've done a few simple spreadsheets to cover the renovation of the cabin and anything else I might need for my life here. I've created a pivot table so I can easily see which bits, for example, the roof or greywater system will cost, as well as some work on forecasting and allowing contingency of different percentages into each section, so the less I know about a job, the bigger the contingency. It's easy and quick to update and adapt and gives me a clear overview of exactly how I can't afford what I want to do.'

As she spoke, her fingers flew like startled birds across the keys, going from spreadsheet to table, to projection, showing him different views and calculations. He pinched the bridge of his nose. 'Are you all right?' she asked.

Rory nodded, let his hand drop and stared out into the distance at the loch. 'Numbers aren't my thing.' He stood abruptly. 'I've got to go.' He walked off to the truck.

Zoe called after him weakly, 'Okay, bye then.'

She closed the laptop and watched the truck drive off. What on earth had just happened? For a moment she actually thought they were getting on. He wanted to see what she was doing. He'd asked to see it. But then he shut down. She was well aware her job wasn't exactly synonymous with excitement. No little kid ever ran around their school playground pretending to be an accountant. But numbers helped you order the world, make sense of it. Without her spreadsheets, she wouldn't have a clue where she was with the cabin.

Was she that boring on top of every other negative emotion he had for her?

Zoe smiled, remembering his face in the tree when she'd played dumb, when she told him she knew he bought Basil, and when she blackmailed him into helping. His face had been a picture, so transparent. One day she was going to challenge him to a game of poker and fleece him for everything he owned. She'd even have the shirt off his back.

She let out a sigh. She would love to have the shirt off his back, and his trousers off too. When he sat next to her and leaned in to see the laptop screen, she could smell again the musky smell of man and woodsmoke, and feel the heat radiating off his body. She thought her heart was going to jump out of her chest. Her nervous excitement had made her speak faster than normal, move her fingers across the keys faster than normal. Was that it? Had she gone too fast for him to keep up?

'Agghhhhhhhhhhhhh!' She let out a cry of frustration and confusion and Basil squeaked. She stroked his soft brown body. 'Sorry, darling, I just can't work him out, and I doubt I ever will.'

She stared out at the loch under a darkening sky, then at her watch. Each day was getting noticeably shorter. And it was only going to get darker and colder as winter kicked in. She had chosen the worst time in the world to begin a renovation project.

She thought about driving up the road to get some phone signal and sighed again. It could wait till tomorrow.

༄

RORY ENTERED THE SMALL FLAT HE SHARED WITH HIS mother, oscillating between shame, frustration, rage, humiliation, and despair. He had never felt so impotent, so useless. He was someone who got the job done, who was reliable, who you could depend on in the worst possible situations. The kind of man every soldier wanted by his side. And now? How could he explain to his mother how bad things truly were? As he hung up his jacket his mother called out to him: 'I'm in the sitting room.'

He walked through and stood in the doorway, filling the space, not knowing what to do or say. His mother, Barbara, was reading a thick novel about medieval history. She inserted a bookmark and carefully put it down on a small side table, before pushing her reading glasses up into her impeccably styled blonde hair, and fixing him with her cornflower blue eyes. 'Oh dear. Is it really that bad?'

His mother was immaculate as always. Small, trim, and stunningly beautiful. He always thought he'd failed to do her genes justice. She was in her early fifties but could have easily passed for his older sister. He dragged his hands through his unkempt hair and sighed. 'I still can't find a way to make the estate profitable. It's going down the toilet. And fast.'

His mother arched a perfectly plucked eyebrow. 'There's no need for language like that, dear. And I wasn't talking about the estate, you know what to do. I was talking about the woman who's squatting in William's old cabin.'

Rory started.

'Oh, do close your mouth, you look like you're trying to catch flies. She must be a relative of his. It stands to reason. That family are always trying to take what isn't theirs. You can't keep secrets from me, darling. I know you were entertaining a wild notion you were going to live there, and you've been in an absolutely foul mood for the last two days; ergo, this woman. I bet she's as bad as Mary Laing'

'What?'

'William's niece. You know the sort. Flighty, untrustworthy, a *good time* girl if you know what I mean. Before I married your father, she set her cap at him. It was very distasteful. The whole village was relieved when she ran off with that English man.'

Rory sighed. *Not this again.* 'Dad married *you,* didn't he?'

'And she'll also have William's faulty genetics. A kind man I grant you, but not right in the head. And she's living in that hovel? I don't know what she thinks she's doing. She doesn't belong here. The land belongs to the estate.'

Rory let out a whoosh of air, releasing the pressure valve before he exploded at his mother. 'Mother, my mood is nothing to do with Zoe. I met with the bank manager and Alastair McCarthy today. The situation is serious.'

His mother stepped gracefully out of her chair and glided to the door. He moved out of her way and she passed through, patting his arm. He followed her into the kitchen and watched as she filled the kettle and switched it on.

'Darling, they're bank managers and lawyers. We've been here many times before. I have complete faith in you. The plans Colquhoun Asset Management have proposed are exciting, aren't they?'

She measured out tea leaves into a china teapot. Rory raised his hands, pushing his fists into his temples. 'Lucy is not the answer to our problems, Mum.'

The kettle came to the boil and Barbara switched it off. She pulled his arms away from his head and stared him down. 'Lucy and her family's company are precisely the answer to our problems. The sooner you set this in motion, the sooner we can leave this wretched place and get back to our lives in Edinburgh. The last thing anyone needs is a cheap little distraction veering you off course.' She dropped his hands and poured the boiling water into the teapot. 'Why don't you leave her to me?'

'Mum, no! Don't do anything. I've given her enough grief. She'll find out soon enough how hard winter is. She'll leave. They always leave.'

'Now, dear, you can't compare this woman to Lucy.'

'Her name is Zoe, Mother.'

Barbara fluttered her hand as if the name was irrelevant. 'Whatever her name is, she's not cut from the same cloth. Lucy is sophisticated, classy, socially adept, wealthy... The right kind of girl for you.'

'And she left. Remember?'

Barbara pointed a manicured finger at Rory. 'That was your doing, not hers. You didn't make the effort.' She squeezed the side of his arm, her voice softening. 'Darling. You didn't fight hard enough for her. I spoke to her the other day and she's not dating. You need to visit her, make an effort, tidy yourself up a bit.'

'Mother.' Rory's tone would have stopped a train, but Barbara was relentless and unbowed. She poured out a cup of tea.

'And whatever you do, don't get caught up in a web spun by that woman. She's a bad sort, a troublemaker.'

'Mother. I have no intention of being caught by Zoe, or anyone else for that matter. My priority right now is trying to keep a roof over our heads. And besides, she hates me.'

'Whatever do you mean? She's the type that's always throwing themselves at men in a very unseemly manner.'

'Rest assured, the only things she throws at me are tins of baked beans.' He walked out of the room before his mother could take the astonished look off her face and reply.

8

Zoe's plans for a quiet afternoon were ruined in the nicest possible way by the arrival of Fiona. She had left her car by the road and walked down the track to the cabin. She had a bag over her shoulder and was brandishing a bottle of wine and a bunch of flowers.

'Housewarming gifts,' she told Zoe as she stepped up onto the deck. 'Flowers for the house, and wine for you.'

Zoe hugged her tightly. 'Bless you, sweetheart, you don't know how much I need this right now. Do you want a glass?'

Fiona put her hand on the top of the bottle. 'No, save it for you. Duncan's coming home later today so I can't stay long. Mum's got Liam so I could come and see how you're getting on.'

'Come in. I'll put the kettle on.' Zoe pushed open the door and invited her in.

'Oh, Zoe, it's lovely. That Rayburn doesn't half kick out some heat. I love your tent. And the fairy lights – it's like something out of Narnia.'

Zoe put the kettle on to boil as Fiona walked around the cabin.

'Hang on, what's in the cage? Holy mother of god. Is that a rat?'

'Shhh... he's sleeping,' whispered Zoe.

'Why have you got a rat?' Fiona whispered back.

'It's a long story, but he's extremely cute and well trained. He's called Basil.'

Fiona looked dubiously at her. 'Jeez, you won't bring him tomorrow for Sunday lunch, will you? Mum hates rats. They give her the heebie-jeebies.'

Zoe grinned and spoke normally again. 'Oh, don't worry, I'll keep him here. Although I think I'm going to have to buy him a friend for when I'm out. I don't have any milk. Is that okay?'

'I'm happy with whatever you've got. You know, I should have brought you some chairs as a housewarming gift, you've only got one and I don't think it could support my post-baby weight.'

'That chair couldn't support Liam's weight, I think it's only good for kindling now. I've got some in storage I'll bring up when I've finished the roof.'

The kettle boiled and Zoe poured water into two mugs. 'We can sit on the deck, sorry I'm not more set up for visitors.'

Fiona waved her hand as if it was nothing. 'Zoe, you're doing grand.'

She took the big bag off her shoulder and emptied papers, files, and plastic envelopes full of receipts onto the table as Zoe finished making the tea.

'I forgot to say I've brought my accounts for you. I know it's not a big job, but Mum's spoken to Chantelle who runs the posh dress shop, and Sally who runs the cafe, and they say you can do their accounts. There's bound to be more work for you in the area. Mum just hasn't got around to bending everyone's ears yet. Oh, and as well as cash you get free haircuts for life from me.'

Zoe smiled and indicated her hair, currently making a bid for freedom from an unruly bun. 'Good luck with this mop. Seriously, Fi, I really appreciate it. It's going to cost me so much more than I thought to make this place a real home and my savings aren't going to cut it.'

The two women walked out to the deck and sat on the top of the steps, cradling hot mugs of tea in their hands. The sun was setting over a clear sky. Looking down the slope to the loch, lost in their memories, it was a few minutes before anyone spoke.

'Look at us, thinking about the past like we're two old biddies. We've got our whole lives ahead of us,' Fiona scolded. 'And you're young, free and single. What I wouldn't give to be where you are now.'

'Seriously? You'd rather be in this cabin on your own than have Duncan and Liam?'

Fiona let out a peal of laughter. 'God no, I can't think of anything worse than dating at my age and living somewhere I have to pee in a shed and can't have a shower. Dunc's the man of my dreams anyway. And you think the weather is always this nice? It's normally sheeting it down twenty-four seven. Nah, I was just trying to make you feel better.'

Zoe smiled. 'I think you'll always make me feel better.'

'And I doubt you'll be single for long. Mum's on a mission to marry you off to our Jamie.'

Zoe blushed. 'Fi, he's a handsome man, but I'll always see the eight-year-old I knew all those years ago. He's like a younger brother.'

Fiona snorted. 'He's still that eight-year-old! Liam's more

mature than he is. Mum's just desperate to get him out from under her feet, although the moment he does leave she'll immediately want him back. You're far too nice for him anyway. I'm on the hunt for a total cow bag so I can inflict him on them and ruin both their lives.'

Zoe giggled and they clinked their mugs of tea together. They lapsed into a companionable silence and watched the sun disappear behind the hills beyond the loch and the first stars twinkling above them. Fiona shivered. 'Full moon, and it's going to be a cold one too. Better bank the Rayburn well tonight.'

Zoe glanced sideways. 'Now who's sounding like an old biddy?'

By the time Fiona set off home, the moon was ascending in the night sky. Zoe made herself some food and brought Basil out to run around whilst she gingerly sat on the last chair standing and made sense of Fiona's books. She soon realised it wasn't going to take her long. Fiona was organised and her business was simple. Zoe wanted to get them done that evening and take them back tomorrow when she went for lunch. She wanted to show Fiona and her family how much she appreciated everything they were doing for her.

By eleven they were done, she had it all on a USB stick and the papers filed neatly away. She was ready for a good night's sleep. She brushed her teeth, banked the Rayburn, gave Basil a kiss and crawled into her sleeping bag ready for oblivion.

Oblivion did not come. She slept fitfully, tossing and turning. For hours she hovered, restless and agitated, on the edge of true sleep. She endlessly replayed Rory walking off, her spreadsheets, the warning from Fiona about the cold night, the Rayburn, and her parents. All her anxieties, confusions and fears stirred into an alphabet soup of sleep, as dreams morphed into waking thoughts, then back to dreams again.

Each time she rolled over, she would be awake enough to see the time, groaning as the hours limped by. By five o'clock she'd had enough. Her brain hurt and she wanted this night filed in the past. She got up, stretched, put on her coat and went outside onto the porch.

The moon was still high in the sky and the world was lit up before her, full of brilliant whites, deep blacks and shadowy greys. The light from the moon and the stars danced on the loch and shimmered across the frosty ground. She exhaled, watching her breath condensing out in front of her. It was indeed the first hard frost of the year. Winter was on its way.

She thought about Willie, spending his adult life here, watching the seasons unfolding, year after year. He took life in his stride, never fearing what winter might bring. Zoe had only ever known summer here, now she was about to meet its colder sister.

A memory came of one of her first nights in the cabin. She had missed home, was worried about her mother, and had woken herself calling out in her sleep. Willie had made a watery hot chocolate, poured it into a battered tartan thermos flask, and told her they were going to wake up the sun. Standing now, in the ice-still air, the memory seemed frozen in time, as if the adventure was about to unfold again. And all she needed to do was turn, and her great-uncle would be standing there beside her. She squared her shoulders. She would wake the sun once more and drink to his memory.

Ten minutes later, she was prepared with warm clothes, hot chocolate, her phone and a torch for good measure. Basil was sleeping so she let him be. She also didn't want to lose him so far from home. As she stepped off the porch onto the ground, her boots crunched on the frozen grass. The world was still, and sounds that would have been lost in the day were now audible. She could hear a dog barking in the distance, the sound of her trousers as they rubbed together with each step, and her breathing. She turned the torch on as she walked along the track to the road between the tall trees. However somehow that made everything scarier; the tiny point of light bobbing in front of her amplifying the blackness all around. She turned it off and let her eyes open to the shadows and subtleties of the night.

Crossing the road and leaving the tree line behind, the moon guided her way. It was utterly unchanged, the heather undulating on either side of her. The moon was just as bright above her, the path just as clear. She knew exactly where to go. As the path became steeper, she felt a stab in her heart and a memory in her palm remembering Willie holding her hand and leading her on. The cold air burned her lungs and stung the end of her nose. She paused a few times to blow it and catch her breath, but didn't look back. She wanted to save the view as the reward for her climb.

As a child she thought the walk went on all night, but now, after an hour of striding uphill, the path levelled off and she saw a dark shape growing out of the side of the glen in front of her. It was an abandoned bothy; a one-room house even smaller and more basic than the cabin. There was no glass in the one window, the roof was a bog and the whole place smelled damp and alive. As a child, she had refused to go further than the rotten door and Willie had laughed, laying an old blanket on a tussock outside, facing the view, and bringing out the thermos flask. They had sat together, drinking their hot chocolate whilst the world became lighter and opened out below them.

Zoe turned from the bothy to the view, finally getting to see just how high she had climbed. She sucked in a breath. It was as if she were suspended between heaven and earth. The glittering, undulating shape of the loch far below, the stars so close above she imagined she could reach out and pluck one out of the sky.

'You're the queen of the world,' Willie had told her. Despite being small and having big worries, seeing the landscape stretched out before her made things seem more manageable. She stood, taking everything in as her breathing quietened, feeling again like the queen of the world; a tiny figure in the landscape but able to hold it all within her vision.

Zoe sighed, exhaling a plume of mist to be lit up by the moonlight. She missed Willie and she missed her parents. Her heart swelled with love and she raised her eyes to the stars, sending out a prayer of thanks to her great-uncle for a new beginning in life, and a prayer of gratitude that her parents were still alive to see it.

She walked the last few steps to the bothy. Before she allowed herself the hot chocolate, she would take a peek to see if it really was as harmless as Willie had told her. It was exactly the same; dark and completely lifeless. She put her bag on the ground and took out her torch, pushing tentatively at the old wooden door which swung inwards. It was pitch black, and she shone the beam onto the far wall, highlighting bright green ferns growing out of the cracks. She crossed the threshold and flicked the torch to the right-hand wall. There was an open fireplace, empty and blackened with old soot. Clearly no one had lived here for a very long time.

She took a big, confident step further in, her torch moving along the back wall, then tripped over something large on the floor. She cried out, throwing up her arms to cushion the fall, the torch flying out of her hands, smashing against the wall and breaking, plunging the bothy into darkness.

Suddenly a figure was above her, pressing her to the

ground, one hand around her neck. She couldn't breathe, a loud barking filled her ears and panic shot through her. She frantically tried to tear the vice-like grip from her throat, her legs tried to free themselves from the weight above.

Zoe saw stars. This was it. She was going to die.

9

s soon as the nightmare had started, it stopped. The hand let go of her neck, the weight moved away, and she was licked all over.

'Bandit! Heel!'

The licking stopped and she brought her hands to her face, rolling to the side, wheezing and coughing.

'Oh god, Zoe, I'm so sorry. I'm so sorry. Are you okay?' Large, trembling hands stroked her hair. She heard Bandit whining. 'Shhh, it's okay, it's okay. It's only me, it's Rory.'

Zoe felt a total disconnection. She could feel his hand on her hair but was detached, as if watching a scene being played out on stage. Everything was unreal, not of this world.

'Talk to me, Zoe. Are you okay? What are you doing here?'

Slowly she drifted back into her body and took her hands away, staring dully at the dark wall and the rectangle of moonlight from the open door. Rory removed his hand from her hair.

'I came to wake up the sun,' she replied.

There was a long pause.

87

'I feel like we need hot chocolate,' said Rory.

'What?'

'I don't think you can wake up the sun without hot chocolate.'

Zoe slowly pushed herself up into a seated position and turned to face him. 'Did you know Willie— oh my god, you're naked!'

Only a square of light from the window and the opening of the door illuminated the inside of the bothy, but they cast a silvery glow over the marble perfection of Rory. He was completely unfazed.

'It would appear so.'

He was sitting cross-legged, his hands resting on his knees. His hair was almost white in the moonlight, waves of ancient light framing his powerful face. Shadows brought his cheekbones into starker definition, the bump on his nose, his full lips. His grey eyes were glowing. Zoe had never seen such perfection before. He was made by mountains, forged by fire, washed by the oceans and blessed by the gods. She ran her peripheral vision down the ridges in his chest to the darkness between his legs. She knew she had milliseconds to memorise this image before normal social rules compelled her to look away. She couldn't let him know how he made her feel. She put one hand over her face and stretched out the other, the palm facing upwards towards him. 'Jesus Christ! Put some clothes on, I've had enough trauma for one night.'

Bandit barked in agreement.

She heard a movement and peeked as Rory turned away to tug a shirt over his head.

Oh, my fricking god! He's going to have to stand up to put his trousers on, and then I'll get to see everything.

Rory turned back to her and she shut her fingers. 'No peeking now,' he rumbled.

'I have no intention of seeing any more than I already have, thank you very much,' replied Zoe as primly as she could. *Dammit!* 'It may be some poor fool's fantasy to be murdered in the middle of nowhere by a redneck-mutant-hobbit but it's certainly not mine. I've seen enough of you to last a lifetime, and if I fancy a repeat performance, I'll go to a mountain famous for rockfalls and avalanches and start yodelling.'

'You can stop talking now. There's only so much one man's ego can take.'

Zoe shut up, listening to the sounds of him moving about.

'You can open your eyes now. It's safe.' He was standing, unfortunately fully clothed, an old backpack on his shoulder with a bedroll and blankets slung underneath. Bandit stood by his side, tail wagging. Rory extended a hand to help her off the floor but she scrabbled backwards to avoid any contact with him. He moved it towards the door. 'After you.'

'I, I lost my torch.'

Rory brought it out of his trouser pocket. Zoe snatched it from him and walked out of the bothy.

৩৯৫৩

RORY FOLLOWED HER OUT, THE COLD AIR HITTING HIS cheeks. The moon was setting. It was the darkest hour before dawn. He stood beside her, looking down the glen towards the loch.

Zoe pulled the thermos out of her bag and held it up. 'How did you know about the hot chocolate?'

'If I get to try some, I might tell you.'

She frowned, took the blanket out of her bag, draped it over a tussock and sat down. Rory sat next to her and she shuffled to the far edge away from him.

'Very cosy.'

Zoe's eyes narrowed. 'Are you on drugs?'

What the fuck? 'Drugs?'

'Yes, you're being nice to me. My guess is ecstasy?'

His laugh burst out of him, before he could stop it. 'I had a black coffee yesterday morning. Does that count?'

Zoe unscrewed the lid of the thermos and poured some steaming hot chocolate into the mug. She handed it over and he breathed it in. It smelled of warmth, decadence, and long kisses by the fire.

'Are we sharing this?' he murmured.

Zoe's eyebrows shot up. 'Absolutely not! I'll wait till it's cooled down enough to drink from the flask. Now you've got your hot chocolate, you can talk.'

He inhaled the vapours and blew lightly over the top. *What to tell her?* He took a sip, feeling the heat slipping down to his knotted stomach and warming the cold memories. 'I spent a summer in Kinloch when I was nearly eight. My parents didn't care where I was, or what I did, so I spent my time with Willie. At the end of the holidays, I didn't want to leave. I didn't get on with my dad, and decided I was big enough and strong enough to fend for myself. So, on the last night I ran away to live with Willie. I was about a mile from the cabin when it started chucking it down. Within ten minutes I was soaked through, freezing cold and my sandwiches were soggy.' Zoe giggled. He raised an eyebrow. 'For a seven-year-old boy, soggy sandwiches are a very serious matter.'

'I apologise. Please continue.'

'Willie dried me out in front of the Rayburn. I begged him not to tell anyone he'd seen me, but he said no matter what I ever thought about my dad, I could never hurt my mum. He said I could stay the night and go back in the morning after we'd woken up the sun. We came up here when it was still dark with hot chocolate to watch the sunrise. He said I was the king of the world. By the time we walked back down, I knew something inside me had changed.'

'He did the same with me when I was a few years older. It really helped.'

'You ran away from home? You got a lot farther than I did.'

Zoe smiled. 'No, my father got made redundant, mum got cancer, and we had our house repossessed. Everything fell apart and they didn't want me to be around it all. Willie came down on the train and brought me here halfway through the summer term. I stayed until September.'

'Did she make it?'

'Yes, thank god. She's wonderful. In every way.'

Rory paused before he replied. How much more could he ask without cocking up? 'So, what made you want to come back?'

Zoe stuck her nose into the flask, inhaling before she spoke. 'When I came to live with Willie, it was the saddest and happiest time of my life. Knowing Mum might die made everything more urgent, more vivid. Those three months were the most important of my whole life. They shaped something deep within me. London never felt like home, but Kinloch always did, even though I was only here that once. For the last three years of his life, Willie lived with my parents. His mind wasn't really in the present, it was here, in the past. He remembered more about the time we spent together than I did, and it brought everything flooding back. When he died and gave the cabin to me, there was no questioning, no hesitation. I knew immediately I was going to come back here to live.'

'What do your parents think of you coming here? Your friends?'

'They all think I'm crazy, and I'll be back before Christmas.'

The moon had set and the world was still, holding its

breath for the arrival of the dawn. Rory felt as if they were in a liminal space, a space outside time, where he could be anyone he wanted to be. He wanted to know more about her.

'And your job? You're an accountant?'

Zoe let out a puff of air. 'Yes, I am. My parents wanted me to have a stable career after all they went through when Dad lost his job. I'm good at it, and Morag is helping me get work in the village, but it doesn't challenge or inspire me.'

'What *do* you want to do?'

'I don't know yet. I love photography. And in my last job, I was in charge of overseeing the rebranding of the company and the building of a new website. I loved that. Being in charge of a big project, creating something new, building something from scratch. It was amazing. What I did more than doubled the company's turnover.'

'That's incredible.' The words were out of Rory's mouth before he could stop them. She dipped her nose towards the flask.

'Can I ask you a question?'

Rory stiffened. 'That depends on what you want to ask.'

She didn't meet his gaze, apparently absorbed in her hot chocolate. The sky was getting lighter. Eventually she spoke. 'Why don't you have a Scottish accent?'

Tension shot through him. The box to his past was being opened. 'Not everyone born here speaks with an accent,' he said carefully. 'I've just spent a lot of time in England, that's all.'

'Why?'

Rory hesitated, unsure how much or what to tell her. 'I went to boarding school in England, then joined the army at seventeen. I've spent more of my life in England than I have here.'

'How old were you when you went to boarding school?'

'Seven.'

'Seven?' squeaked Zoe. 'Didn't your parents love you?'

An old wound tore open. He couldn't speak.

Zoe angled her body towards him, a frown puckering her forehead. 'Shit, I didn't mean it to come out like that, sorry.'

He looked into her deep dark eyes, pulling in his emotions. 'It's okay. My mother does love me but she always deferred to my father. I'm sure he loved me in his own way, but he had very clear ideas about how children should be raised.'

'Had?'

'He died a couple of years ago. I came out of the army and back to Edinburgh to be there for my mother.'

'I'm sorry.'

'Don't be. I'm glad you never met him.'

'Does your mum miss him?'

'Every minute of every day. If there was one good thing in his life, it was his relationship with her. He treated her like a queen and she worshipped him.' Rory tried to keep his voice calm but he recognised the edge of bitterness in it; the voice of a little boy whose mother always put him second.

'Do you have any siblings?'

'Nope. I think one was enough for my dad. Once my mother had produced me, that was it.'

Zoe took a breath in, as if to speak, then chewed her bottom lip. 'And now you're here, working for the estate?'

He managed to shrug, even though his muscles were strained with tension. He cleared his throat. 'Anyway, what about you? Brothers? Sisters? Apparently, your mother was a wild one who ran off with your dad.'

Zoe snorted. 'Wild? My mum? Her definition of wild is giving my dad pasta with pesto for his tea. The wildest thing she ever did was leaving Kinloch to marry him. She used up her lifetime's allowance on that one.'

'How did they meet?'

'My dad was on a walking holiday and got lost. Willie was out wandering, found him, and brought him back to my granny's house. When my parents saw each other it was love at first sight. In less than a week my mum had left with him. I don't think my granny ever got over the shock.'

'Did they have any other kids?'

'No, just me. Not through lack of trying though, I know they wanted more. But it's all good. They love each other and they love me. I know how lucky I am. I know what unconditional love is.'

Rory's heart expanded and contracted with every beat. Expanding with Zoe and contracting with memories and the knowledge he wasn't sure he'd ever known unconditional love. He needed to change the subject. 'Have you considered selling the cabin? Buying a small place in town? The estate would buy the lease back from you, turn it into a holiday let. It would be for the best.'

'Best for who? In what way exactly?'

Rory cringed. 'Don't you miss toilets, hot showers, a bed?' he mumbled.

Zoe rolled her eyes. 'There's more to life than modern plumbing. And I have a bed, it's just currently on the floor.'

She turned back to the loch as the sun rose. Her face flooded with golden light. Rory watched her. She was more beautiful than any sunrise or sunset could ever be. He thought back to what had happened in the bothy, the thought that he may have hurt her. 'I'm sorry, Zoe, god, I'm so sorry about earlier.'

Zoe put her hand to her throat and swallowed. 'Yes, about that.' Her voice rose with a crescendo. 'What the fucking fuck were you doing? I thought you were going to kill me!'

Rory put his head in his hands, running his fingers through

his hair and pulling at it. He dropped them into his lap as if they were toxic. 'I was in the military for years, and in some bad situations. I was asleep, but my subconscious took over when you fell on me... It won't happen again.'

She nodded. 'What were you doing here anyway?'

'I came up last night to get away from everything and wake up the sun. I just forgot the hot chocolate.'

Zoe held out the flask to refill his mug. 'Well, we managed it. We woke up the sun. Willie would be proud.'

Rory clinked the edge of his mug against the side of the thermos and they said 'cheers' in unison, as the sunlight crept towards the loch.

'King and queen of the world,' Zoe said, looking out.

'King and queen of the world,' repeated Rory, looking at her.

THEY WALKED BACK DOWN TO THE ROAD TOGETHER, BANDIT bounding ahead, walking side by side when the path was wide enough, and single file when it narrowed. When it got narrower, Rory would hang back, his palm outstretched, ladies first.

His actions might have appeared chivalrous but were entirely selfish. Walking behind, he could admire her, lust after her, without guarding his expression. But as they descended the glen, the reality of what he was going back to pricked at the tiny bubbles of happiness Zoe had brought fizzing into his heart, popping them with every step. By the time they reached the truck, he was beginning to think his mother might have been right. Zoe was trouble. Her very presence rocked the foundations of his carefully constructed life. He needed to avoid further involvement before her smile brought his walls tumbling down. However, he still needed to sort the shingles for her roof. It was the least he could do after the animals he had inflicted on her.

They stopped by the muddy estate truck.

'I know you don't have any signal at the cabin, but we might as well exchange numbers so I can text you when I've finished making the shingles,' he said, bringing out his battered phone. Zoe fished in her pocket, bringing out a phone with a pink glittery cover and a picture of a unicorn on the back. She ignored his raised brows, concentrating on the screen. When she finished tapping away, she handed it to him.

'You can put your number in now. I've created a contact for you.'

Rory took her phone. 'Man-bear, yeti, mutant-redneck-hobbit, hobo?'

'You should be pleased that I left off attempted murderer.'

Rory shook his head, and typed in his number before passing her phone back. He then made a big show of putting her contact details into his phone, occasionally pausing and pretending to think.

Zoe held her hand out to receive it, tapping her foot on the ground impatiently.

He eventually handed it over. He'd only typed one word – Zoe.

She looked up at him and he shrugged. For a moment she seemed disappointed. She put in her number, then handed it back.

'So, you'll message me when the shingles are done?' she asked briskly. He nodded. 'Okay, bye then, have a nice day.' She turned on her heel to walk back down the road towards the cabin.

Rory watched her go until she disappeared from sight.

10

Back at the cabin, Zoe let Basil out of his cage and checked on the Rayburn. The morning sun was melting the frost outside, but unless the clouds came back it would be sub-zero again that night. The logs were diminishing faster than she had anticipated and she mentally recalculated how much it would cost to live here through the winter.

With her back to the Rayburn, she stared at the inside of the cabin. She wanted to sit down on a sofa, put her feet up and read a book. Despite what she had told Rory earlier, she yearned for her bed. As soon as the roof was fixed, she was collecting her furniture.

She got out a bag and filled it with her dirty clothes. Morag had insisted she took her laundry to do at hers and Zoe wasn't going to argue. She was also going to go early for a big long soak in a bubble bath and to wash her hair before being fed. She was more excited about the bath than the food. She may have had a lot in common with her great-uncle, but did not share his scant regard for personal hygiene.

As she gathered up Fiona's finished accounts, Basil scampered onto her shoulder to play with her hair. She nuzzled him. 'I'm sorry, darling, but there are actually people in this world who are immune to your charms, so you can't come with me. I'll see what treats I can bring back, and I promise I'll get you a friend to play with. I know it isn't fair leaving you here on your own. Have a lovely sleep and I'll be back soon.'

A little later, Zoe knocked on the back door to Morag's house, loaded down with laundry, a bag of her toiletries, Fiona's accounts, and a bottle of Prosecco. She was enveloped in steam and the aroma of cabbage as a red-faced Morag opened the door and beckoned her in. 'Come in, love, I'm going to give you a feast! I hope you haven't had any breakfast?'

Zoe shook her head. 'Fi told me to come prepared.'

Morag laughed. 'Rightly so! Ah, you brought your dirties. Well done, lass, I'll pop them on now and have them clean and dry for you before you leave.'

'Oh, I can't have you sorting through it, Morag! I'll do it.'

But Morag was having none of it and grabbed the bag. 'Nonsense, love, it'll be roses compared to Liam's nappies, and besides, the machine is a bit temperamental. You have to have the knack and a strong right foot.' She exited the kitchen yelling into the passageway. 'Fi! Fi love, it's our Zoe, come through and give her something to drink.'

Fiona came into the kitchen and Zoe handed her the accounts and the Prosecco.

'What? You've finished them? Already? I only gave you them last night. And Prosecco. We are going up in the world.' She hugged Zoe. 'You're the absolute best. Thank you. I'll get you cash in a bit or do you want me to send it via bank transfer?'

'Either's fine, whatever's easier.'

'Let's get us both a drink, and you can meet Duncan. Jamie's not here but he'll be along in a bit.'

Fiona poured out three enormous glasses of Prosecco and handed the third one to her mother as she re-entered the kitchen. Morag took the glass and necked half of it. 'Woohoo! Now the party's started! Now off with you both.' She shooed them out of her kitchen. 'Go and chillax, or whatever it is young people do nowadays, and make sure Zoe gets the comfiest seat.'

Fiona led the way into the living room where a man with deep auburn hair was bouncing a delighted Liam up and down. He stood as Zoe entered, holding his free hand out to greet her. Fiona did the introductions, shining with pride. 'Duncan, this is Zoe. Zoe, Duncan.'

Zoe saw with relief her own open smile mirrored back at her from him. He took her hand and shook it firmly, as if a promise was being made. 'You won't believe it, but I've heard your name spoken for years. It's great to finally meet you, Zoe, and I'm happy for Fi's sake that you're back.'

Zoe felt a lump form in her throat. 'It's so lovely to meet you, Fi described you perfectly.'

Duncan looked at Fiona who blushed. He was tall, lean and handsome, with deep brown eyes that were full of love for his wife and son. But Zoe could also see shrewdness, a maturity, born from working offshore. She knew immediately this was a man who could be counted on, one who would always put Fiona and Liam first.

Fiona ushered Zoe into the biggest armchair and they chatted about the cabin, about Willie, and about Duncan's work on the rigs. He was an electrician and rope access special-ist, which meant he was the person hanging off the platform in the middle of the North Sea fixing things that no one else could get to. He downplayed the dangers, but Zoe could see Fiona's gaze drifting to the sideboard where an old photo was framed in pride of place. It was of a young and handsome man, a two-year-old girl held in one arm, the other wrapped proudly around his beaming pregnant wife. It was a photo Zoe knew as well as she knew this family. It was of Robert MacDougall, Morag's husband and Fiona and Jamie's dad, with the family he held in his arms all too briefly.

There had been a fire on the rig shortly after the photo was taken. A series of small and preventable errors had cascaded into one, fatal tipping point. Robert, an electrician, like Duncan and Jamie, had been one of three men to lose their lives that night. Zoe didn't need to ask to know that Jamie had not followed Duncan offshore because of his mum. The money was way better on the rigs, but he was too good a son to make his mother live out her nightmares each time the helicopter took off from Aberdeen with him in it.

Fiona shook herself as if to shrug off bad memories and fear fantasies. 'Zoe, your bath.'

Zoe turned to Duncan. 'Please excuse me whilst I make myself presentable. This will be the first bath I've had in four days.'

Duncan stood and offered her Liam. 'Fancy doing him whilst you're at it?'

Fiona thumped his arm. 'You daft bugger, you've only been back a few hours and you're already skipping out on the dirty jobs.'

Duncan kissed Fiona tenderly on the top of her head. 'Only playing, love, only playing.'

Zoe felt she was a witness to a private moment not meant for her. She grabbed her glass and went up the stairs to the bathroom. She was going to have a bath, and by god, was it going to be bubbly.

An hour later, the only thing that could be seen under a blanket of foam was her head. She'd washed her endless locks, put on a deep conditioning treatment and wrapped them up in a towel. She cut her nails, shaped her eyebrows, and let the hot water soak away all her cares. From downstairs, she could hear the crash of pots and pans from the kitchen and the sound of music. She couldn't work out what they were listening to, maybe an acoustic album, but it was beautiful.

After a while, Fiona knocked to give her a fifteen-minute warning. Zoe reluctantly sorted out her hair, got out of the bath, pink and glowing, and redressed, feeling much more human.

She followed Fiona into the small dining room, where the table was heaving with food. Apparently, Christmas dinner had married an all-you-can-eat buffet. Her eyes bulged. Jamie had arrived and gave her a hug. 'Zo, you've got to come around every Sunday if this is what Mum puts on.'

Zoe grinned. 'Are you up for the challenge?'

Jamie patted his stomach and pulled the waistband of his trousers away. 'Aye, I've got my fat pants on ready for some serious food action.'

Fiona shook her head as Zoe dissolved into giggles. Morag brought the last dish in, whipped off her pinny and ushered everyone to the table. They held hands as Morag said grace.

'Dear you upstairs. Bless this family and bless this meal. Thank you for bringing Zoe back to us and keep safe in your love the ones who are no longer with us. Amen.'

A squeeze ran through the hands around the table.

'Now then, girls, boys and babies, let's eat!' said Morag.

Zoe ate as she had never eaten before. There were two roast

chickens, a side of ham, roast potatoes and parsnips, carrots, and cabbage covered with at least half a pat of butter. Morag was a feeder, and the moment anyone's plate looked a bit empty she piled more food on, whilst fretting she hadn't cooked enough. After too many basic meals at the cabin, Zoe felt like she'd been dropped into the middle of Sunday lunch in heaven. Even though Morag and her mother had kept in touch sporadically over the years, it seemed there was a lifetime of catching up to do. Zoe was happy to talk about home, but the more she did, the more homesick she felt. She wanted to learn more about Kinloch, to immerse herself in the history and culture of her new home.

'So, the castle,' she asked. 'Does anyone live there?'

Morag shook her head. 'Not for decades. It gets opened up every summer to the public, but even that stopped a few years ago. It's such a shame.'

'Who owns it?'

Morag shrugged. 'We're not sure. It was for sale a while ago, but then the boards went down and we didn't hear anything. It might still belong to the current earl, Stuart MacGinley, but apparently he lives in London.'

'He's a wanker,' supplied Fiona.

Morag jerked her head towards Liam. 'Fi! The baby!'

Fiona rolled her eyes. 'Sorry, he's a *banker*.'

Zoe grinned. 'Don't worry, I know the type. So why doesn't he come back?'

'Why would he?' asked Jamie. 'Down south he's got a cushy life. If he came back, he'd have to spend time and money sorting it out. I'm sure he just wants to forget about it until he can find someone nuts enough to take it off his hands.'

'Is it really that bad?'

'Aye,' said Duncan. 'It's a mess. I think that's why they closed it to the public.'

. . .

WHEN PEOPLE COULDN'T EAT ANY MORE THE TABLE WAS cleared and dessert brought out. Jamie made a noise that sounded half joy, half fear as he confronted an enormous apple crumble with a jug of custard, and a tiramisu. By the end of death by food, Fiona was green, Jamie's trousers were completely unbuttoned and Duncan was breaking a sweat. Only Morag, Zoe and Liam were still going strong, although most of what went near Liam ended up on the floor.

When they finally conceded defeat, everyone staggered through into the living room. Morag flicked the TV on for background noise and they slumped in their chairs, unable to move. Zoe was the first to fall asleep, followed by Jamie. One by one they all dropped into a happy food coma.

It was over an hour before Zoe woke. The smell of coffee percolated through the air and the sounds of a guitar had replaced the TV. She opened her eyes to see Jamie gently strumming a tune. He grinned at her.

'I took it up after you left. The first tune I learned was *Joleen*, only I changed the lyrics,' he said. He sang in an atrocious American accent, changing the word *Joleen* to 'Zoe'.

Fiona threw a cushion at him. 'Yeah, you drove me and Mum mad.'

Jamie threw the cushion back at his sister, and went back to playing a melody that was familiar to Zoe.

'Earlier, that was you playing? It wasn't a recording?'

He nodded and started singing. Zoe let the music wash over her. She couldn't remember the last time she had been so content. She was full to the brim with food, love, and the sense that she had found her way home. Kinloch was where she belonged.

It was dark by the time she prepared to leave. Morag led her into the kitchen, handed her a pile of warm, clean and folded laundry and filled plastic boxes with the remains of the lunch. Morag was unusually quiet, a little hesitant, as if she wanted to say something but didn't know how.

'Is everything all right, Morag?' asked Zoe finally, when her nerves prompted her to speak.

Morag bit her lower lip. 'Love, I wanted to talk to you without the others around. I'm a bit embarrassed.'

Panic rose in Zoe's stomach, a fear that something could affect her magical relationship with this family. 'What is it? What's happened?'

Morag rested her hands on the outside of Zoe's arms. 'It's not that bad, sweetheart, we'll find a way around, it's just the businesses I had lined up for you to do their accounts have changed their minds.'

Zoe felt like she'd been punched in the stomach. 'What do you mean?' she stammered.

Morag looked embarrassed and troubled. 'I don't understand it, love. Yesterday, Chantelle and Sally told me they'd had second thoughts, and were going elsewhere. It's not like them to behave like this. I don't understand what's going on.'

Zoe's head was spinning. What had she done wrong? Why had they both backed out? She looked at Morag's anxious eyes and pasted on a smile. She would not allow Morag to see how badly this had affected her state of mind and the practicalities of being able to last the winter in the cabin.

'It's okay, these things happen. They don't know me from Adam. I'll find other work. It's okay, I'm fine.'

'I still haven't got to everyone in the village yet. I'll find work for you, I promise.'

Zoe needed to leave before she broke down. The bubble of warmth and security she had been encased in all afternoon had just been shattered by an ice pick and she felt cold and vulnerable. She called out to the others that she was leaving. They came through and hugged her with promises to see her in the next couple of days. Zoe knew it might be longer now Duncan was home and Jamie was back to work, so held them extra tightly. She could feel the tension radiating out of her. She saw Fiona give her mother a questioning glance. Morag shook her head, imperceptibly, as if to say, 'not now'.

As soon as Zoe was out and safely back in her truck, the smile fell off her face and she let out a sigh that was almost a sob. She wanted her mum. She brought out her phone to call home, then stopped. Her mother didn't need to hear this. It was possible she would take a couple of days off work and drive up. Zoe's resolve might break and she'd go home with them, her Scottish dream at an end.

No. She would not tell them. She was not going to be upset – she was going to be angry. The only explanation that made sense right now was that someone swayed their minds against hiring her. But who was desperate enough to get her out of Kinloch they could have convinced two important businesses to drop her before she'd even met them? She took a gamble, unlocked her phone and sent Rory a text.

Zoe: How could you stoop so low? Basil is one thing, but cutting off my livelihood? I will never forgive you for what you've done.

She put the phone down, and drove off. On the outskirts of Kinloch, it beeped a notification and she pulled over. Rory had replied.

Man-bear, yeti, mutant-redneck-hobbit, hobo: What have I done?

She rolled her eyes.

Zoe: You don't know? Pull the other one, it's got fucking bells on. The businesses Morag had lined me up to work for have changed their minds. There's only one person in this village who is so desperate for me to leave they would resort to this, and that's you.

Congratulations. Once again, you win arsehole of the year.

Once the text was sent, she switched her phone off, needing to get home. If she couldn't have her parents for comfort, Basil would have to do.

11

Rory stalked into the tiny kitchen where his mother was washing up. He loomed, his head almost grazing the ceiling. 'What have you done?'

His mother peered at him over the top of her glasses, then turned back to the dishes. 'Not a lot, dear, I didn't need to. I called upon an old acquaintance, Francesca Huntington-Smythe. I forgot her estate is only a few miles west of here. Her cleaner is from Kinloch. A frightful gossip, however terribly well informed. The squatter is indeed the progeny of Mary Laing. Apparently the cabin is even more dishevelled than her, and she can't afford to make the necessary repairs to survive the winter. The women who run the boutique and the cafe in Kinloch had rather ill-advisedly agreed to employ her, but it only took a few well-chosen words from Francesca to make them reconsider their decision.'

'I told you to leave her alone! What has she ever done to you?' Rory exploded.

His mother fixed him with a look. 'I'm more concerned about what she's done to you, dear.'

Rory ran his hands through his hair, tugging at the roots, looking around the kitchen for something he could break. When would she ever listen to him?

'Go and chop some wood, darling, that always helps you work off steam. As soon as she's back where she belongs, she'll be out of your head. It's Lucy you need to devote your attention to. Lucy and the estate. As soon as you've confirmed the agreement with Colquhoun Asset Management and set their plans in motion, we can get back to Edinburgh.'

'Mother! The decision hasn't been made. Even if it works, we'll never have enough money to return, unless you're happy to live in an ex-council flat in bloody Wester Hailes. Lucy and I are over. As for Zoe? I'm not interested in her and she's not interested in me.'

'Honestly, darling, disinterest is just a ploy to make you work harder. Now, go and throw an axe at something and you'll feel much better.'

Rory strode out, slamming the door behind him. She didn't care about what he wanted, she never had. He had to find a way to fix this.

🌺

ZOE CLOSED THE LID OF HER LAPTOP. SHE COULD DO THIS. As long as she had the roof secure, her furniture out of storage, and enough wood, she could last the winter. It wouldn't be pleasant, in fact without a proper front door it would be bloody miserable. But she could do it. Then, in the spring she could do without the Rayburn and find work in Inverness.

She sighed. Who was she kidding? As if on the first of May it suddenly became so tropical, she would no longer need heat or hot water? No, her savings wouldn't last that long. She needed a plan B. She absentmindedly stroked Basil who was investigating the new smells in her hair and ran through different scenarios, none of which were very practical.

The sound of a truck coming up the track brought her to her feet and she went out onto the porch. By now it was dark and she couldn't see who it was behind the glare of the headlights. They cut out and a figure emerged. Rory.

He strode purposefully up the steps to the porch and stood in front of her. 'It wasn't me.' Zoe snorted. 'I promise. The cows were stupid. Buying Basil was insane. Throwing your wood on the ground did indeed make me arsehole of the year. I'm sorry for all of those things. I've been a total dick. But I did not do this. You have every right to live here and I'm not going to try and stop you.'

'Then who did it?' When Rory hesitated, Zoe pounced. 'You know. Jesus Christ! What have I ever done to anyone here?'

'Nothing, you've done nothing. It's someone you don't know and are never going to meet. It won't happen again, I promise.'

'It's too bloody late!' Zoe cried. 'The damage is done. I've been rerunning the numbers, and even with the roof fixed I can't last the winter. I can't go to work in Inverness because I can't leave the sodding Rayburn without fuel all day, and without that, I'll freeze to death. And the rate at which I'm getting through the wood, I don't know if I can afford the fuel bill as it is. And that's without even addressing the water issue. If the stream or loch freezes then I'll be hauling chunks of frigging ice up here to melt!'

'Can I come in?'

'Why? No, you cannot.'

'I have a suggestion that could help.'

Zoe fumed, eyeballing him.

'It would solve most of your immediate problems and wouldn't cost you a penny. Please, just hear me out.'

Zoe turned. 'This had better be good. And take your boots off.'

Rory followed her in, putting his boots by the flimsy door. Zoe took the only chair and sat down, the table between her and Rory. She picked Basil up, holding him to her as if for protection. Rory stood on the other side of the table

'Well?' said Zoe archly.

Rory swallowed. 'I, I'm not very good at my job.'

His face was taut with tension.

'And what exactly *is* your job?'

Rory paused, and stared at the floor. Zoe could see his hands opening and closing into fists by his sides, muscles working in his jaw, his body primed to fight or flee. He took a big breath. 'I've just started working on the Kinloch estate. It's big and complicated. There's only me, and I don't know what I'm doing. Chopping wood, mending fences, herding cattle, I can do all that. But the admin just fries my brain. If I can't find a way forward, the castle will have to be sold.'

'What about your boss?'

'The estate is still in the possession of the Earl of Kinloch.'

'Stuart MacGinley? Isn't he a wanker banker in London?'

Rory glanced up. 'Wanker banker?'

Zoe shrugged. 'Typical toff. Born with every advantage in the world, but still wants to make more money off the backs of ordinary people by playing fast and loose with their pensions, before becoming a Tory MP. Why isn't he doing anything to help?'

Rory dropped his head again. His hands contracted back into fists. He hesitated. 'He's as clueless as me. There's a proposal by a big asset management company on the table, but it's not right. It's not right for the castle.'

'And what has any of this got to do with me?'

Rory fixed her with his luminous eyes. 'You're clever. You rebranded the last company you worked for, did their new website, doubled their turnover. And you're good with numbers. If there's an answer to be found then you'll find it.'

'And is the estate going to pay me for this?'

'No.'

'Then we're done here. I'm not doing a favour for someone with a silver spoon up their backside.' Zoe rose to her feet, Basil scrabbling for her shoulder.

'Wait, just listen.' Rory raised his hands in supplication. Zoe lowered herself back down, folding her arms in front of her. 'The estate can't give you money, but it can give you wood. And me.'

Zoe fought with all her might to control her features. He was offering her his body, his wood. She must not laugh. She must not ask him to undress. She coughed. 'Please elaborate.'

Rory took another big breath.

God, he was gorgeous. Heart-stoppingly beautiful. She could stare at him forever.

'The estate doesn't have money but it does have wood,' he said. 'I can bring you more than enough to last the winter for free. I'll provide the materials to mend the roof and replace it entirely next summer. Again, for free. I'll install your back boiler, a greywater system and make you a bathroom and a kitchen. I can install solar panels and a wind turbine if you get them so you'll have power. I can make new windows and a new front door. None of that will cost you anything.'

Zoe kept a straight face, but inside she was at the Rio carnival, on the top of a float, sambaing away in sequins. She was getting his wood and then some. Not only would she get everything she needed for the cabin FOR FREE! but she would get to ogle Rory. She'd have to crank the Rayburn up to full blast when he was around. She had to make sure his top came off again. The only issue was making her side of the bargain take longer. She reckoned she could get the website sorted within a few weeks, so she'd have to work super slowly, something she wasn't used to doing.

'If I can get the small quarry on the estate reopened then you can have as much hardcore as you like for the track,' he said. 'And I'll see what I can do to get the telephone line extended down from the road. Whatever you want I'll try and make it happen.'

Zoe stood up, loving how insecure he looked. She held out her hand. 'Deal.'

Rory took her hand, then dropped it like it was on fire. He moved towards the door.

'Wait!' commanded Zoe. He stopped.

'You need to shake Basil's hand too.' She held out Basil towards him and lifted one of his paws. Rory tentatively extended a finger, allowing Basil to sniff at it, then put it gently under his paw, lifting it up and down a couple of times. Zoe's heart expanded. Rory dropped his hand, moved to the door, and put on his boots without doing up the laces.

'I'll be back.'

What was he up to now? Zoe gave Basil her best Arnold Schwarzenegger impression.

'I'll be baaaaahhhhhk,' she whispered to him as they waited.

He soon reappeared, an enormous bin bag slung over his shoulder, like a Pound Shop Santa. He kicked off his boots and brought the bag to the table, lifting the contents out.

'You knew I'd say yes?'

'I hoped.'

Zoe leafed through A2 sized leather-bound tomes, as Rory shook out loose sheets of paper and leaflets advertising the castle. They fell to the table like confetti and Basil promptly started tearing them to pieces. Zoe lifted him off to put him in his cage.

'This is a joke, right? Where are the actual accounts? I need a USB stick with them on.'

'This is all I've got for now.'

'No wonder the estate's in trouble if this is how it's being run.'

Colour flushed across his cheekbones. 'I told you I'm not good at this.'

'Well, I like a challenge. I'll start in the morning.'

Rory's shoulders relaxed. He looked intently at her. 'Thank you.'

Zoe nodded and immediately turned away. She would be undone if he looked at her like that again. Her insides were melting, pooling into hot lava between her legs. Fuck! Get him out of here. Now!

She shooed him away. 'Right then, I've had quite enough of you for one day. Bugger off and I'll see you when you've made the shingles for the roof.'

Rory put his boots on and hesitated. Zoe didn't meet his gaze. 'Okay, bye then.'

He walked out the door.

Zoe looked to the heavens and let out a long slow breath. He was killing her and he had no idea. She turned back to the table. She wanted to let Basil out of his cage so this mess needed to be out of his reach. She put the leaflets and pieces of paper in neat piles, anchored down by saucepans. The leather-bound books she arranged on the desk. She would attack it when she was fresh in the morning.

She idly picked out a trifold leaflet. The first page was filled with an imposing image of the castle. It could have been a prison; threatening and austere. She opened the leaflet to see more uninspiring photos, including one of the great hall, filled with dark and gloomy portraits of miserable people. She shuddered. If this was meant to attract visitors, it would undoubtedly have the opposite effect. She put the leaflet down, let Basil out and grabbed the bottle of wine Fiona had given her. She poured some into a mug and leafed through the papers and books Rory had brought her. She rolled her eyes every time she saw the name Stuart MacGinley, Earl of Kinloch. Here she was, just another peasant sorting out his problems for him.

By two o'clock the bottle of wine was finished, along with a third of a bottle of whisky, but Zoe was not. Her laptop battery had died, so she worked with a camping light and pen, scrawling notes manically on the books and on the backs of invoices. She was pissed, her mind possessed with possibilities, and loving every minute of it.

WHAT SHE DIDN'T LOVE WAS WAKING UP AT NINE, HER mouth drier than the desert and her bladder fuller than the sea. She'd crashed out in the tent fully clothed but had at least remembered her eye mask and earplugs. She had no time to get up leisurely. If she didn't make it to the outhouse immediately, she was going to have an accident that would put Basil to shame. Her head was pounding and the daylight outside of the mask was too bright so she kept it on, navigating by the narrow view out the bottom. Earplugs could also wait to be removed. The last thing she wanted was to have birdsong hammering into her skull.

She got to the front door, managed to get one boot on, then tried to put on the other. Unfortunately, there was something wrong with her balance. She made the critical mistake of leaning against the flimsy door as she pulled at the boot, finally yanking it on as the door gave way. She fell through, arms flailing, crashing into an object. Something hard and heavy that slowly moved out of her way. Behind the muffling of her earplugs she heard a yell, and pushed the eye mask up, in time to see an extremely large man fall out of the sky and land with a thump on the ground in front of the porch.

She saw with blinding clarity she had fallen into a ladder. A ladder that had been supporting the weight of Rory. A ladder she had pushed over. In front of her, both it and Rory were now lying immobile on the ground. She could see Bandit leaping out of his truck and coming to see what was going on.

She stumbled off the deck into the cold morning and ran to him, kneeling on the frosty ground, placing her hands on his shoulders and yelling his name.

'Rory! Rory! Oh my god! Are you okay? Rory!'

She couldn't hear a thing. He wasn't moving. She straddled him for balance and put her ear to his lips to see if she could hear him breathing, and her hand under his jaw, frantically searching for a pulse. His skin was like burning silk with a faint prickling of stubble, but in her panic, she could feel nothing, hear nothing. Bandit was alternating between licking his face and hers, not sure who needed his attention more.

She tried to remember her last CPR course and knew she had to get help. But there was no bloody phone signal. Then she had to get his airways open, start chest compressions. She clumsily tugged at the buttons of his jacket. She was going to have to give him mouth to mouth. Oh god, with her hungover breath? Wasn't it preferable to just let him die?

What is wrong with these bloody buttons! She tried to rip them but they were sewn on with steel. She was near tears, her bladder screaming, her stomach wanting to vomit its contents over the man below her. She saw his eyes open. His mouth moved, but no words were coming out.

'Oh my god! Rory! You're alive!'

He mouthed more words.

'What? I can't hear you. Speak to me. Are you okay?'

Rory reached up, and with exquisite delicacy for such huge hands, located an earplug and popped it out, presenting it to her. With his other hand he gently pushed Bandit away.

'I was just asking why you were shouting so loudly.'

Zoe grabbed the earplug from him and pulled out the other, pocketed them and clamped her hands over her mouth. He was alive. And that meant he could smell how rancid she was.

'Are you okay? I'm so sorry, I didn't see you, I didn't know you were here.'

His hand dropped weakly, and landed on her thigh. 'Why do you have your hands over your mouth?' he asked feebly.

'Because I stink, and if I haven't killed you with the fall, I'll definitely do it with my breath.'

Rory tried to laugh but it turned into a wheezy cough. Zoe dropped her hands to hold onto his arms.

'Oh god, don't move! You might have punctured a lung or something.'

Zoe started to move off him, but his hand clamped down on her thigh. 'Wait,' he croaked pathetically. 'I need to check if everything's still in place.' Zoe went stock still.

She was hit with a wave of guilty pleasure feeling him between her legs. It was better than any fantasy. He was so broad and solid. His hand was so high up her thigh he was practically cupping her bum. He had one of those big thick Maglite torches in his trouser pocket, and she briefly entertained the fantasy it was him, before discounting her wishful thinking. Nothing human could be that big, that hard, and he'd made it abundantly clear he found her about as appealing as a hole in the head. Her bladder screamed and she wiggled her hips. If she didn't get to the outhouse soon then it was going to explode. Rory looked in extreme pain.

'What are you doing?' he hissed at her through gritted teeth.

'I'm absolutely desperate to pee, and if I don't jiggle, I'll have an accident.'

'Just go,' he yelled hoarsely. 'Now!'

Zoe leapt off him and ran.

Rory didn't move. Feeling the weight of her still on him, her thigh beneath his hand, the pounding desire filling every part of him till he thought he might burst. Straddled by legs he had only dreamed of and staring up into the anxious eyes of the most beautiful woman in the world, he couldn't remember the last time he'd felt so alive. He may have fallen the best part of twelve feet off a ladder onto frozen ground, but he had enjoyed the experience immensely. She had been made especially adorable by her pink fluffy eye mask, the word 'Princess' embroidered on it, which had been perched askance in her wild curly hair.

'What am I going to do, buddy?' he asked Bandit. 'She's going to be the death of me.'

Bandit lay down, placing his head on Rory's chest. Rory stroked him distractedly. The safest thing for his sanity was to walk away from Zoe and not look back. But he might as well try and defy gravity. He sighed. Despite all the longing, his feelings were not reciprocated. He sat, and listened to her puking her guts up in the outhouse. However good he felt, he knew she must be feeling equally terrible. He wanted to go to her, comfort her, bring her a glass of water. But that was not his place, so he got off the ground, picked up the ladder and went back to work on the roof.

He looked away when she walked back up the slope to the cabin. After ten minutes, she came out onto the porch and called up.

'Er, hi.'

He stopped hammering and stepped down the ladder to stand in front of her. Bandit went to her side and she scratched behind his ears.

'How are you feeling?' he asked.

'Like crap. I've got to check a few things online so I'm popping to the library. I'll be back in a couple of hours, I expect you'll be gone by then.'

Rory shrugged. 'I need to take some measurements. Do you mind if I go into the cabin?'

Zoe shook her head. 'No, do what you need to do. Just let Basil out if he wakes up and make sure he's got enough food and water.'

'Will do. Are you okay to drive?'

Zoe frowned. 'Yes, I'm fine, I'll try not to run anything over.' She turned on her heels and strode to her truck, driving off so fast the wheels spun.

❧

AT THE LIBRARY, ZOE SET HER DEVICES AND BATTERY PACKS to charge, then slumped back into her seat. What had she done? She could have killed him. She allowed herself a wry smirk. At least they were now even. Shit, she felt terrible. Her head throbbed despite the paracetamol she had taken at the cabin. Ugh. She was never going to drink again.

Whilst she waited for the water and painkillers to take effect, she flipped between chatting to Sam and Instagram. She then emailed her parents a long description of Sunday lunch at Morag's and updated her spreadsheets to reflect what she could now get for free. She wanted to know if she could afford solar panels and a small wind turbine with enough power to give her light and a fridge. When she was up to date with everything and felt more human, she searched for the castle online.

She finally found a website which had been started in the nineties and never finished. It was a holding page with a flashing sign saying 'our website is coming soon!' and a tally at the bottom of the screen that showed a grand total of four hundred and sixty-three visitors to the page since it was built.

Zoe tried to find mentions of the castle as a tourist attraction on other websites but could only find one, which described it as 'worth a visit if you want to make sure you've visited every castle in Scotland, but you'll be lucky to find it open'. There was no social media presence at all.

She sighed. At least she knew the size of the mountain she had to climb. Land rents were static and couldn't be increased enough, and there was a limit to how much wood they could sell. There had been a recent cash injection from a property sale, but it didn't make a dent in their position. The estate was losing money and had no way of repaying the loans they had taken out. Not unless they changed their business model and hopefully made a profit. The only way to generate new income was through tourism. She couldn't remember much about the castle other than it was dark and grim. She'd need another visit to know what she was dealing with.

She packed her bag back up, left the library and went to the main castle entrance. It had a faded and peeling sign outside announcing it was closed, so she walked around the exterior, taking photos, then sat in her truck, uploading them to Instagram with as many Scottish themed hashtags as she could think up. Her tummy rumbled loudly, reminding her she hadn't even had breakfast yet. She glanced at her watch. Twelve-thirty. Good. It meant Rory would be long gone by the time she got back. She couldn't face him again until she'd had time to recover from the embarrassment of the morning. He didn't much like her at her best, and this morning she'd gifted him with her at her worst.

SHE DROVE DOWN THE TRACK TO THE CABIN, ROUNDED THE final bend, and saw with a sinking heart he was still there. She checked her appearance in the mirror, pinched her cheeks to get some colour into them and got out. He wasn't on the roof and the new shingles were all in place. *Jeez, he works fast*.

She pushed the door open and saw him in front of the Rayburn boiling the kettle. He moved stiffly as if he had injured himself. Had he fallen off the roof again? Maybe he hadn't realised how hurt he was from the morning?

'Hi, I'm back. Are you okay?'

He moved slowly around, and she saw with delight that Basil was perched on his shoulder playing with his hair.

'He forgives you!'

'He doesn't want to come down. I can't do anything with him up here.'

Zoe disentangled Basil and gave him a kiss. 'You gorgeous little rat! Come to Mummy and leave the big man to do his work.' She glanced around. 'Where's Bandit?'

'He's sleeping in the truck. I didn't want to risk him meeting Basil without you here.' The kettle came to the boil and he made Zoe a mug of tea. 'Milk?'

Zoe shook her head. 'Until I get a fridge, it's a no. How did you get on?'

Rory gave her the mug, and their fingers briefly touched. A shock went through Zoe's hand and she snatched the mug from him. Rory turned away. 'Good. The roof will do you till next year, although I'd like to batten in sheep's wool for extra insulation. I've taken measurements for the door and windows and I've made a plan for the bathroom and kitchen, although I need to go through it with you first.'

'Can you show me now?'

He brought an envelope out of his pocket where he had sketched out the floor plan of the cabin. He'd drawn a bathroom in the far right-hand corner, and a kitchen running down the rest of the right side around the Rayburn.

He took a piece of chalk out of his pocket and drew lines along the floor to show where the units would be and the space for the bathroom. Zoe put her mug of tea on the table, and Basil on the floor, and followed him, keen for any excuse to be close to him, to smell that intoxicating scent of man and wood.

'So, you'd come through the bathroom door here, then we've got a toilet, which will be compostable but built-in, so will appear like a normal plumbed in one, and a sink here. I don't think there's room enough for a bath, but instead I can build you a larger shower here.' Rory sketched the outline on the floor and stood in it. Zoe joined him.

They were facing each other in the space he had drawn. Her heart raced. They may have been standing in a chalk rectangle, but in Zoe's mind they were already in the shower: wet, naked, their bodies entwined.

'It'll be big enough for two,' he said gruffly.

'Two?' she questioned faintly.

Rory swallowed. 'Basil has to wash sometimes, doesn't he?' He smiled tightly and stepped away from her. 'I was also thinking I could put a sleeping platform in the roof for you which would free up more room. But before that, I want to take up the floorboards and insulate underneath.'

Zoe wasn't listening. He could have suggested installing a nuclear reactor and spinning the cabin upside down and she would have nodded in agreement. Having him so close had dissolved her cognitive function to mush.

'And there's the greywater system to install, but I want to see if you can afford a UV filter so you can drink it too. You can take the water from the roof and also from the stream. If you get a big enough tank, it will last all year with the amount of rain we get.'

Zoe was happy not to talk. She was utterly absorbed in staring at his back, his arms, his tousled hair, as he talked through his plans. Heat had gathered between her legs and made her restless. Her body was craving release. She hadn't had an orgasm for months. Her libido had been extinguished by her London dating experiences but it hadn't bothered her. She wasn't interested in men any more. However, Rory wasn't a man, he was a god. Her desire had woken with a vengeance, like a lioness waking from sleep, stretching her limbs and flexing her claws.

Rory finished talking, and saw her scribbled notes on the table. 'You've started already?'

Zoe glanced up, then down at the table again. She couldn't look at him and use her brain at the same time. His eyes were arctic, shining with glacial light, silver stars shooting out through the irises. When she stared into them she was lost in a blizzard, her body dissipating into a storm of snowflakes till she was no longer there.

'Yes. I didn't mean to, but I made the mistake of going through everything you gave me last night along with a bottle of wine and, erm a little whisky, and got a bit carried away. It was three before I ran out of light and paper and had to go to bed.'

'You worked on this till three?'

Zoe couldn't work out if he was impressed or derisive. 'Yes,' she said defensively. 'It's a bloody mess. I mean,' she lifted one of the A2 leather books, 'this belongs in a museum. No one has been using books like this for over a hundred years. I can't believe you can even buy these any more.'

He shrugged. 'They're there, so they might as well be used.'

'The best use for these is in the firebox. Give me a new one to photograph, then I'm eBaying the lot.'

Rory swallowed and Zoe looked at him. Her heart was stuttering wildly, pounding up into her throat. She had to find an outlet for her energy so channelled it into indignation. 'You've got a problem with that? Finding it hard to stop using the swan-feather quill? Still got a stream of peasants wanting to donate their blood for ink?'

'N-no,' he stuttered. 'It's just going to be a lot of changes, that's all.'

Zoe's jaw dropped open. She lifted the chair and brought it to his side of the table, placing it beside him. 'I think you'd better sit.' She guided him to the chair, any excuse to touch him. He sat down heavily and it collapsed, sending him sprawling on the floor and Basil running for cover.

'Oh, for fuck's sake! That was my last one!'

Rory got to his feet, the remains of the chair in his enormous hands, his cheeks flushed. Zoe tipped her head back and slumped her shoulders. 'Put what you can in the firebox and take the rest away. I'll drive out to the storage unit where my furniture is this afternoon. If I leave now, I'll be back by tonight.'

'I'm sorry.' He put the pieces of wood in the Rayburn.

'It was going to happen sooner or later. I'm just glad you

did it, not me. There's a limit to how many chairs I can destroy without getting a complex. Now lean against the Rayburn for support and if you feel dizzy, breathe out slowly through your mouth, I'm out of paper bags right now.'

She saw a glint of amusement flash across his face, and his lips twitch. Her tummy sparkled. She moved away from him.

'Okay, listen up, Stone Age Sam. I've checked out the castle's "website" and it's edged in front of that god-awful leaflet in the running for the 'thing most likely to put people off visiting Kinloch castle' award. All copies of the leaflet need to be chucked, and you only get another one designed when you've got more cash. Anyway, most information is online now. People have the attention span of a gnat so will never pick up, let alone read, a leaflet. Everything is on their phone. If you want people to come to the castle and spend money, you need to have a functioning website, and be on all the social channels. You need to create a brand, an identity, a hook, tell people why they have to schlep all the way out here for a few dark rooms and a leaking roof. Call to something in their soul, make them feel special they came. Then fleece them in the tea room and the gift shop. That's where you'll really make your money.'

Rory seemed lost, as if she'd told him he had a couple of months to learn Mandarin and become a world-class chess player. Zoe brought out her phone. 'You know Instagram, right?' Rory shrugged non-committedly. She walked over to him and showed him her screen, hyper aware of his body next to hers. 'So, this is my Instagram account. I opened it a couple of weeks ago for my friends to see my life here.'

'Is that the castle?'

'Yes, I took some shots this morning.'

She scrolled down and he pointed at the selfie of her and Basil in the tree. 'Was that when you were stuck?'

'I was on a rat rescue mission that went awry. I was not stuck.' With no connection, she couldn't load more images. 'Dammit! There's no signal, I can't show you any more.'

She went to close the phone, but Rory put his hand over hers. 'Can I see them again?' Zoe passed him the phone and stepped away. His touch was like fire.

She went back to the table, watching him holding the pink glittery phone. He was scrolling through every photo, his face inscrutable. He finally spoke.

'These are incredible. They're better than anything a professional could take. The castle looks amazing.'

Zoe blushed. 'It's not me, it's the filters. I'll show you.' She extended her arm and he gave her the phone. She opened the camera. 'Okay, I want you to take a picture of me and Basil. I'll show you what I want the composition to be by taking a picture of you first. So, go stand by the window over there.' Rory awkwardly complied. 'Now, put your right hand up to your shoulder, as if you're holding Basil. Good, now drop your chin a bit. Hang on.' She moved forward and brushed a curl of hair away from his face. It didn't need moving but she couldn't resist. Rory flinched, and a little piece of her heart broke off. He really didn't like her.

She moved back and took a few photos.

'There. All done. Now see the composition.' He stared at the photo, as if seeing himself for the first time. She passed him the phone and went to pick up Basil. 'You have a go.'

She stood by the window, Basil on her shoulder. 'Come on, you little monkey, it's time to perform. You need to look cute for your fans.' For a second he stayed still, then clambered onto the top of her head. 'Basil!' She lifted him back down, then turned to Rory. 'Did you manage to get anything?'

He gave the phone back to her and she flicked through. He had taken photos the moment she'd put Basil on her shoulder and there were some amazing shots, far better than she had anticipated.

'Oh, these are great!'

He seemed relieved.

Zoe selected one of her laughing at Basil and applied filters. When she'd finished, she showed him the difference between the original photo and the edited one. 'You can see how much better this one is. I'll drive out later and post it online.'

Rory looked between the two photos, then at her. A crackle of electricity passed between them and Zoe swallowed, moving away from him.

'So, I need you to give me a tour of the castle, tell me what makes it special. And I'll need to get photos of the earl to use as publicity.'

'No,' said Rory immediately.

'Why not?'

Rory turned away and ran his fingers through his hair, pulling at it. 'He won't want anything to do with this.'

Zoe rolled her eyes. 'Typical toff.'

He didn't meet her gaze, just walked to the door and put his boots on. 'I'll let you know when you can look around. Don't drive all afternoon to get your chairs, I'll bring some from the castle no one will miss. I'll see you later.'

He walked out without a second glance.

13

Zoe let out a huff of frustration. He was more hot and cold than an erratic Icelandic volcano. She wanted to sit and think, but there were no chairs left, so she crawled into her tent and lay down.

Her heart was still thumping. She couldn't be around him. But then she couldn't *not* be around him. If she couldn't have him then she wanted to photograph him, so she could always have a piece of him with her. A wave of tiredness rolled through her and she yawned. She'd have a quick nap, then she'd get up and have something to eat.

Three hours later, she was woken by the smell of brewing tea. She grunted in confusion and saw Rory, standing a few feet away, holding out a mug.

'How long have you been standing there?' she asked, her speech still thick with sleep.

'Only a couple of minutes. I've been back for nearly an hour but wanted to wake you gently before I brought in the scaffolding.'

'The what?' Zoe scrambled into a seated position and Rory passed her the mug of tea. It was strong and milky. 'There's milk!' She looked up in surprise as if he had manifested a miracle.

'Yes, I got a pint from the shop. It will last fine outside until tomorrow. Now, can I get back to work?'

Zoe saw a glint of humour in his eyes. 'Yes, stop slacking and get on with it.'

Rory walked out and immediately returned with scaffolding poles, pushing the door open with his backside. Zoe stood up. What was going on? In the far corner of the cabin was a gigantic pile of fleeces, a stack of wooden battens next to them, and six scaffolding boards propped against the wall.

'Did you bring all that in while I was sleeping?'

Rory nodded and went back out the door for more. Zoe watched him go, noticing four chairs next to the table. They were ornate and carved out of dark wood. One of them was like a throne on top of a wooden box. She went to inspect it. There was a hinge on the back of the seat. She lifted it up as Rory clanked back into the cabin.

'Ahh, I see you've found the commode.' He put the poles on the floor and came over to show her how it worked. 'You've got a porcelain potty in the box underneath. When you need the loo, you lift the lid, and do what you need to do. Then, when you're done, you pull down the front panel like this, and take out the pot.'

'I am not using that!'

'Would you prefer to get up in the middle of the night and traipse down to the outhouse for a wee or use this? Besides, I got it for me, not you.'

'This is for you to use?'

'I'm not going to piss in it. I mean I got it for you, so you didn't need to knock me off a ladder every morning.'

'Oh.' She pointed to the scaffolding poles. 'What are they for?'

Rory wasn't someone who wasted time. He began connecting them together. 'I need to make a moveable tower to put the wool under the roof. You can help me in a bit if you don't mind.'

'Can I eat something first? I'm starving.'

Rory smiled. 'Carry on, I don't need you yet.'

Zoe filled the firebox with wood and opened the Rayburn up. She wasn't going to cook, but if she could warm Rory up then maybe some of his clothes would come off. She went outside to collect the leftovers from the porch and brought them in to eat straight from the boxes.

It was a luxury to sit on a chair at the table, a mug of tea in her hand, good food in her belly, and a view to die for in front of her eyes. Watching Rory work was like the beginning of a porn film from the seventies. A hunk doing manual labour before the action started.

As she tucked into her food, she got out her phone and surreptitiously took photos of him, feeling a little sordid, but not enough to make her stop.

'Do you want anything to eat? It's leftovers from Morag's.'

'Got any meat?'

'None left I'm afraid, but I can offer you a traditional Scottish dessert of tiramisu apple crumble. It's an unusual combination I admit, but very nice.'

'Thanks, but no thanks, I'll eat later when I get home. Let me know when you're finished, I'm ready for you now.'

If he was ready for her then she was definitely finished. She gulped the dregs of her tea, snapped the lids back on the boxes, put them outside, and came back to stand by the half-completed tower. A thought came to her, too delicious not to share. 'I like your erection,' she said, lifting an eyebrow.

Rory stepped back in shock, his mouth open. Zoe couldn't hold it together and spat out a laugh that didn't stop. She doubled over, gasping for breath. 'I'm sorry! But the look on your face. Priceless! Oh my god, that was our favourite joke from Design and Technology classes at school, I haven't used it in years.'

'Have you quite finished?'

Zoe tried to calm herself, but was in the middle of a tiramisu crumble sugar rush. She reached towards the pile of scaffolding on the floor. 'I just need to get a good grip on your pole.' With that double entendre she fell about again, howling with laughter.

Rory stepped off the tower, grabbed a pole and climbed back up. Zoe was trying and failing to get herself under control. She was hysterical after the last few days. She'd moved house, got a pet rat, been strangled, got stuck up a tree, drank too much alcohol, thrown up, and been gifted a commode. And throughout all of this, she had fallen in lust with someone who thought she was at best repulsive, at worst a simpleton.

She wanted her friends, she wanted her parents. But most of all she wanted to stop laughing.

The thought of her parents helped calm her down. She wiped her eyes and blew her nose. 'I apologise. I've had too little sleep and too much sugar. My comments were inappropriate and unprofessional. I want to assure you the only erection I am interested in is this,' she slapped the side of the tower with her hand, 'and I am now here to assist you.'

Rory didn't say anything, just pointed at the scaffolding poles on the ground. Zoe picked one up and passed it to him, followed by a clamp. They continued to work in silence.

After a couple of minutes she decided there was nothing more erotic than the sight of a man doing physical labour. She needed both arms and all her strength to lift the poles up to him. In contrast, he reached down and casually grabbed them from her, lifting them with ease. Zoe could see the muscles working under the skin of his large forearms, but it appeared effortless. She usually felt tall around men, bigger than most of them. But around Rory, it was as if she could be lost within the expanse of his arms.

She had each pole and clamp ready before he asked for it and the tower was quickly finished. She passed up a few wooden battens and he attached them in rows to the underside of the roof with a nail gun. After he'd done a section, he asked for the first fleece and pushed handfuls under the battens.

He looked down from the scaffolding.

'It's not pretty but it should make a big difference.'

Zoe was entranced. 'I think it's beautiful. I'm going to climb up later and take loads of photos.'

'Don't get stuck. Again.'

Zoe passed him another couple of battens. 'Oh, ha ha ha. Now crack on, I want a quarter of this done by the time we go to bed.'

By the time we go to bed... Zoe cringed inwardly at her inner thoughts becoming outer. Her comment was the last word spoken for the next hour as they both worked in silence until they had run out of wood. Nearly a third of the underside of the roof was now fluffy and warm. Rory swung himself from the top of the tower and landed, almost silently, on the floor. He didn't look at Zoe, just tidied his tools.

'I'll come back tomorrow morning and keep going. I'll have it finished by the end of the day, then move on to the door. I think that's a bigger priority than insulating under the floor.'

'Can I help?'

'No. This is grunt work. Any idiot can do it. I need you using your brain.'

'Can I visit the castle tomorrow? I need to see it as soon as possible.'

Rory hesitated. 'Yep, we can go tomorrow.' He slung his tool bag over his shoulder. 'What time will you be up? I'll start on the roof as soon as you're ready.'

'Whenever you like, I'm always up early,' Zoe lied, eager to have as much time with him as possible. Why wouldn't he look at her?

He nodded and walked to the door, putting on his boots. 'See you then.'

He put his hand on the flimsy door and shook his head as he pushed it open. Then he was gone.

Zoe didn't move until she heard the truck drive off, then allowed herself a loud and frustrated yell. He wanted her brain? It was currently filled almost entirely with him, leaving only a tiny amount of room left for basic bodily functions, like walking. It was nearly nine but she needed someone to talk to. She grabbed Basil, her phone and keys and went out to drive up the road.

Her mum picked up after five rings. Zoe saw this as a good sign.

'Darling! Is everything all right? Are you okay? ARNOLD! IT'S ZOE! SHE'S STILL ALIVE! Hang on love, let me put you on speaker.'

'Yeah, I'm great. How are things with you?'

Zoe kept the conversation light. She nearly told them about Basil but then decided they weren't quite ready for that, so told them more about Sunday lunch and Jamie's music. She wanted to tell them about Rory, to unburden herself, but knew if she started, she wouldn't stop. So instead, she reassured them everything was great and rang off.

On Instagram, she posted a few of the pictures Rory had

taken of her and Basil, itching to post the one she had taken of him. God, he was gorgeous. She could look at him forever.

She stopped herself, but couldn't resist sending it to Sam. She captioned it 'my builder'. It took less than twenty seconds for her phone to ring. Zoe laughed till her cheeks hurt listening to Sam losing her mind.

'WTAF! He's your BUILDER? Can he come and shore up my retaining wall?'

Zoe told her about the ignoble rescue from the tree and pushing him off a ladder. Sam shrieked and made her promise to 'act a bit more normal' so she could ensnare him. Zoe informed her she was the last woman on the planet he was interested in, and that he was responsible for Basil and the cows. She didn't mention the bothy. That would have completely freaked her out. She promised Sam she would take more photos of Rory for her, but didn't tell her about the ones she'd surreptitiously snapped of him assembling the scaffolding tower. If she did that, she'd never get off the phone. So she promised she would see what she could do and rang off, her heart full of love for her amazing friend. She gave Basil a kiss.

'Come on, darling, time for bed. Mummy's got to be up early tomorrow.'

Zoe had formulated a cunning plan for the next morning. She would set her alarm for seven, get up, put on make-up, then make porridge and tea so when Rory arrived he would be greeted by a domestic goddess and fall instantly in love.

Instead, she woke at half eight and crawled out her tent door, hair defying gravity, eye mask still half on, to see a pair of stockinged feet standing in front of her. Rory crouched down and held out a mug of tea.

She pulled out her earplugs and pushed the mask to the top of her head but didn't look up.

'Good morning, Princess. How was your beauty sleep?'

Zoe ripped the mask off, took the tea and glowered at him. 'What time is it?'

'Half eight. I've just brought the second load in. I was about to move a few things so I can reposition the tower.'

'I set my alarm for seven.'

'I know, I could hear it from outside. When you didn't shut it off, I got concerned you were stuck up something else so I poked my head around the door. Luckily, your snoring reassured me you were fine, so I unloaded the truck, then went back for more wood and some breakfast.'

Zoe dropped her head, utterly mortified. 'Did I really snore?'

'To be fair, it was more of a snuffle, I thought it was Basil at first.'

'Go away,' she mumbled.

Rory grinned, stood up, walked to the table, lifted it up, and moved it across the room. He then came back for the chairs.

'No! Stop!'

Zoe was on her feet, stumbling towards him, hot tea slopping everywhere. She put her free hand on the back of the commode. 'Don't touch it!'

'Why not? There's nothing inside, is there?' he asked, innocently. 'Let me just take a look.'

Zoe sat down on the seat and glared at him.

'Well, I'm glad it's been useful for you.' He started laughing, face lighting up, the sound resonating through the floor and sending a tingle up through her legs. 'Do you want me to empty it?'

Zoe pointed to the door. 'Out! Get out! I've had just about enough embarrassment for one morning. Give me five minutes, then you can come back and pretend you've just arrived and none of this ever happened.'

Rory gave her a salute and walked out, still chuckling quietly.

Five minutes later, Zoe emerged with the potty to find Rory lounging against the wall of the cabin, his thumbs hooked into the belt of his trousers. He was so devastatingly gorgeous she let out a moan which she disguised with a cough.

'You may go in now,' she said, with as much dignity as she could muster whilst holding a container of her own wee, and hurried off to the outhouse.

When she reappeared, Rory was nailing in battens with practised efficiency. She opened the Rayburn to put more logs in, only to find he had already done it. She hadn't the energy for porridge so finished off the last of Sunday's leftovers, then stood at the bottom of the tower.

'What time can I visit the castle?'

'Meet me in the back courtyard at two. That should give me enough time to finish this.'

'You sure I can't help you here?'

'Yep, go make an Instagram or whatever you need to do. I'll take care of Basil and the Rayburn. I'm better off on my own.'

His words stung. She knew how he felt, but to hear it vocalised still hurt. 'Yep, me too,' she replied brightly, then packed her bag and left him to it.

BACK AT HER USUAL SEAT IN THE LIBRARY, ZOE ARRANGED TO pick up the back boiler for the Rayburn, ordered a water tank, and set to work on the castle's website. She bought a new domain, wrote a website brief and chose a WordPress theme. She then went to an online jobs site to put out a tender for a developer and fleshed out her ideas for the menus and content.

Her tummy rumbling made her realise how much time had

gone by. She went to the post office to give back the empty Tupperware and hopefully cadge a sandwich.

Morag was about to close for lunch and told her it was perfect timing. Fiona and Liam were off with Duncan, and Jamie was out at work so she was glad of the company. The two of them sat around the small kitchen table and chatted as Morag plied Zoe with soup so thick you could stand a spoon up in it. Morag was still fretting about the businesses who had let her down but Zoe reassured her.

'It's fine, I'm doing a job swap with Rory. He's helping me do up the cabin in exchange for me helping him sort out the castle accounts and designing them a website.'

'Has he said anything about the earl? Is he coming back?'

Zoe shook her head. 'I don't think so. He's just left other people to sort out the mess.'

'Well, if you find anything out, let me know. It would be nice to have it open again. It's been shut for too long.'

Zoe let Morag's happy chatter wash over her, and ruminated about the best marketing approach for the castle. It was hard to be inspired about a cold dead building, when images of a man who was the embodiment of life kept pushing their way into her thoughts. As she let her unconscious mind sift through ideas, she turned over a magazine on the table. It was last month's copy of *Vanity Fair* and on the cover, smouldering out at her, was her first love.

Morag paused her stream of consciousness and let out a sigh.

'Oh, Zoe, what a dreamboat, eh? That's going to be my bedtime reading for quite a while.'

Brad Bauer: Hollywood superstar and power player. He began his career as an actor, then moved into producing blockbusters with his name on the top of the poster and his face in every scene. Not content with dominating at the box office, he also wanted recognition, and once a year took on smaller, indie projects, this time his focus on a different kind of prize. The roles he played involved angst, injustice, and disability, and were set against the backdrop of slavery, poverty, or any war starring Americans. They were Oscar catnip, and he'd finally hit the jackpot playing a one-legged, gay, French–American Jew who became a spy, stealing Hitler's secrets out of Germany hidden in his prosthesis.

'Have you ever seen anyone more gorgeous than that? Apart from our Jamie of course.' Morag swooned.

Brad stared out at Zoe from the front cover. He was classically and conventionally good looking. High cheekbones, long dark lashes, tanned skin with a hint of swarthiness from day old stubble, and thick black hair cut short. He was responsible for kickstarting Zoe's puberty with a film called *The Boyfriend Plan*, in which he played a small-town bad boy, who pretends to be dating a pastor's daughter to help keep him out of a juvenile correction facility. The pastor's daughter agrees to his idea as a form of rebellion against her domineering father, and to gain acceptance from the cool kids at high school. The film was everything you expected: racy enough to earn it a 15 certificate, but with a suitably moral ending, and innocent enough for parents to allow their kids to see it. The film had changed Zoe's life, and she watched it over and over again, especially the scenes where the heroine locked lips with Brad.

Morag snatched the magazine from Zoe and thumbed through it. 'You'll never guess, but he's Scottish!' She reached the interview and photoshoot, cracked the spine of the magazine, and laid it down in front of her with a flourish. 'Get a load of that braw man. I've never wanted to be a kilt so bad, I can tell you.'

Zoe's eyes widened as she took in the image of Brad Bauer, lying back on a four-poster bed, naked except for a length of tartan material. His hair was tousled, a faint sheen of sweat caressed his chest, and he was staring directly out at Zoe. The tagline read 'My Scottish Dream'. She swallowed.

'Good grief, Morag, this is, er, um—'

Morag let out a hoot. 'Aye, it's pretty racy stuff, I nearly put it on the top shelf.'

Zoe tore her gaze from Brad's body to skim through the article, quickly getting the gist that he saw himself as the next Braveheart. She turned the page, then the next, then the next; photo after photo of Brad Bauer draped in tartan fabric and little else. If he'd intended to cause a storm then he had succeeded. This was gale force filth. Zoe sat back. If only she could use these on the castle website, they'd have no issues attracting visitors.

There was a faint knocking on the post office door and Morag glanced at her watch. 'Got to open up, love, you stay out here as long as you like. Fancy another bath?'

'Could I possibly have a quick shower? That would be amazing.'

'Of course, love, help yourself, and take the magazine. It's not good for my health having him around.'

Twenty minutes later, a clean and rosy Zoe left Morag's with Brad Bauer in her bag. She could continue working on content for the new site offline, and now she felt more presentable she wanted to see Rory. She walked quickly up the road towards the castle, her feet and heart tripping over themselves in their haste to see him. She shook her head. Did she really have it that bad? However, rounding the castle wall and stepping into the courtyard to be greeted by him, she knew it was far worse than she could have possibly imagined.

14

Rory stepped out of a door to a long, low building at the side of the courtyard, brushing sawdust and wood shavings off his clothes and stood in front of her.

He was devastating. It had only been a few hours since she'd seen him, but he appeared even bigger, even stronger than she remembered. A thick shirt and old trousers did nothing to disguise the power of his body. His eyes were pools of endless darkness and blue fire, drawing her to her doom.

He stared at her blankly, as if he had forgotten who she was and was trying to place her, then opened his mouth to speak and coughed.

Zoe could see wood shavings in his hair. *He must have sawdust in his throat.* Her feet walked her forward before her brain caught up to the fact she was moving. He stepped back but stopped when she reached out, plucked a delicate curl of wood and dropped it to the cobbles.

He bent his head for her and, with trembling fingers, she picked through his hair to remove the rest. The heat from his scalp radiated out through the dark gold waves. She wanted to feel that heat warming through to her bones, filling every part of her. Her need for him was getting so strong, so deep, her hands shook visibly with the desire to grab him and pull his mouth to hers.

He tossed his head like an angry bull and stepped back, striding towards the castle. Zoe followed him, desire, hurt and embarrassment scorching through her. Why was he so cross? She wanted to say something to break the ice, but didn't know what or how.

He opened a small, unassuming door in the back of the castle and led Zoe along a rabbit warren of stone-flagged corridors. The floor was worn down in the middle by hundreds of years of footsteps. She could see other rooms off the corridors, piled high with dusty boxes, furniture and accumulated junk. These were the rooms the servants used. Functional and utilitarian, no need for comfort or grandeur. The ceilings were low and Rory had to dip his head. He filled the corridor, blocking out the light. Eventually, he rounded a corner and passed through a fire door into the main body of the castle.

The ceilings were at least twice the height of the corridors they had just walked through. From her research, she knew the estate was an earldom and had been in the hands of the MacGinley family for generations. The front of house rooms were built for status; for proclaiming wealth and power. Zoe followed Rory into the great hall and stared up at the portraits lining the walls. They were hung four metres from the ground, hundreds of years of inbreeding and entitlement sneering down on those below them.

She shivered. 'Why can't they have been painted smiling? They were the ones with all the money but they look bloody miserable. Typical upper-class nobs. Turning their noses up at everyone and never having to work a day in their lives. They weren't the peasants hauling wood, herding cattle and shovelling shit.'

Rory's cheeks flushed and Zoe winced. 'Oh god, sorry, I didn't mean to imply you're a peasant.'

Rory raised an eyebrow, and gave a wry smile. The sun came out in Zoe's heart. 'There's nothing wrong with shovelling shit. It's very Zen, and it keeps you fit. Anyway, I'd rather be a peasant than one of them.' He looked at the portraits and continued. 'They didn't have to empty their own commodes, but it didn't mean life was easy. The women were treated like property, married off by their fathers to benefit the estate, and the men were unlikely to live to a ripe old age. They were either killed in battle, executed for choosing the wrong side, or murdered by a younger brother.'

Zoe shrugged. 'Maybe, but not any more. It's just their inbuilt sense of superiority that gets me, and how they treat people. Willie worked for the estate his whole life and I don't think they ever paid him a penny. He was happy as Larry but it wasn't right. They took advantage of him.'

There was a pause, then Rory spoke. 'He got the cabin and the land. It's worth quite a bit. He could have sold it.'

Was he trying to bait her? His face was blank, she couldn't read him. 'Leasehold. He got the cabin *leasehold* remember? And Willie would never have sold. He didn't want to live anywhere else. Mum says he was little more than a slave for an entitled bully.' She shook her head. 'Sorry. I'm not a fan of the MacGinleys, or hereditary peerage, but it's not going to stop me doing my job. I promise.' She walked to one of the tall windows, shaded by blinds. 'Can I open them?'

Rory nodded. She pulled on the rope: light flooded in. The room was now much less foreboding and she walked around, imagining the potential beyond a few day-trippers. There were spaces on the wall at the far end of the hall. Faint outlines where two paintings had hung.

She gestured to them. 'What used to hang there?'

Rory's face was shuttered. 'A couple of portraits that got water damage. They're being sent for restoration.'

He walked out of the room. Zoe sighed. His moods were like the Scottish weather: ever changeable. But she did just throw his boss under the bus. She followed him through the castle on a whistle-stop tour from room to room: library, study, billiard room, dining room. On and on through rooms trapped in time. Rooms that hadn't seen life for years. Dusty and tattered around the edges, smelling of age and neglect.

She made notes and snapped photos as they went.

'Can I see the kitchens and below stairs rooms? There could be hidden treasures we could use to help the castle make money.'

'Not likely.'

He led her to the basement where one of the wine cellars had been converted into a tea room, but it was dark and damp and there was no gift shop. They climbed the main stairs to the upper floors and the multitude of bedrooms. Zoe didn't want to stay long. Being in a room alone with Rory and a four-poster bed was a torture too far. After an hour of traipsing up and down stairs, he led the way to the great hall, drew the blind, and returned her to the back door. Rain was hammering down. They stood in the entrance.

'Have you seen enough?'

'I think so. I'll need to come back with my bigger camera and take proper photos for the website as soon as possible. Where's Bandit?'

Rory gestured to the single-storey building running along the side of the courtyard, the one he had come out of as she arrived.

'Is that your workshop?'

He nodded.

'Can I see it? See how the front door's coming along?'

He hesitated and Zoe saw a muscle twitch in his jaw. His internal argument seemed to reach a conclusion and he held out his arm, gesturing her towards the building. She dashed across the cobbles through the rain, pushed open the door and ran in.

The smell of freshly cut wood travelled up her nostrils and fired her pleasure centres. She knew she would forever find this smell erotic, as it was one of the notes that made up the incredible man who had entered the building behind her.

Before her stretched a winter wonderland of wood, with drifts of sawdust covering the floor like a blanket of snow. The building was the old stable block, with a cobbled floor and pitched timber-framed roof. She could see indentations in the walls along the far side where the stalls used to be, round metal baskets for holding hay still attached to the walls. The horses were long gone. Now planks and blocks occupied every available space, propped up or piled in heaps, and work-benches, bandsaws and circular saws were dotted around. A large dog bed lay off to one side containing Bandit, who pricked up his ears as they entered, and trotted over to say hello. Zoe scratched behind his ears as he pushed against her leg.

On the largest workbench in the centre of the room was a heavy oak door, the door she presumed he was making for the cabin. She walked over with Bandit by her side. The wood was already thick, but she could see he was making it double skinned to maximise the insulation. It was a door that mirrored its creator. Built to withstand everything from the weather to invading Viking hordes.

She marvelled at how quickly he had made it. She ran her

fingers across the surface. It was as smooth as glass, like silky skin.

'It'll be ready soon.'

Zoe jumped at the sound of his voice behind her, her breath quickening.

'I'm going to put in a triple glazed panel to give you more light.'

She scooted away from the bench with the pretence of looking around the rest of the workshop at the half-finished projects. Rory followed her, keeping his body between Zoe and his work, preventing her getting too close. She got to the far end of the building and noticed something. Unconsciously she pushed past him and knelt down.

'This is incredible!'

There were big carved pieces of dark wood resting against the wall. She pulled them out, propping them next to each other so she could see them better. 'Did you make this?'

Rory nodded, his features hard.

'It's unbelievable,' she said. 'I've never seen anything like it. It's a bedframe?'

She felt over the wood, as if reading braille. It was carved like a tree in the landscape, with the four legs as thick trunks, the branches weaving up along the sides of the bed. There was a footboard, which depicted grassland, heather and animals, with the loch in the distance. The animals seemed suspended in the moment, ready to go back to their day when she looked away. She traced the outline of a powerful stag, its head raised and alert, and the tiny bodies of field mice nibbling at wheat kernels. The headboard was fit for a woodland king, the branches of the tree bursting with leaves and life. Each leaf, each twig, a work of art. There were birds hidden amongst the leaves, a nest with baby chicks, a delicately carved worm held between the beak of a parent, butterflies and insects. It was a carving of constant discovery and wonder. In the centre, in the tree canopy was a round plain space, about the size of a dinner plate, still uncarved, with pencil markings on it, unfinished and waiting.

It was the most beautiful thing Zoe had ever seen, created by the most beautiful man she had ever met. She saw the mastery of his craft, the care he had put in, his humour, his mind, his soul. Her feelings ran so deep for a man she would never have. She stood up, facing away from him, her eyes compressed tightly shut. She wouldn't cry, she just couldn't.

'Zoe?' His voice was right behind her, deep and soft. He sounded concerned. She held her breath, trying to stem the tide of her emotions until she couldn't hold it any more and the dam burst. She shuddered out a sob. His hands came to her shoulders, turning her towards him. She stared at the floor, violently shaking her head, shedding more tears.

He drew her into him, stroking her back and nuzzling her hair. 'Shhh. Shhh now, it's okay.'

Through the fog of her emotions, she felt him kissing the top of her head. She was cocooned within his arms, warm and safe, her insides a jumbled mess of adrenaline and emotion.

'It's only a bit of wood,' he said. 'No need to cry.'

'I'm so sorry, it's just so beautiful,' Zoe hiccupped into his chest.

He breathed out into her hair. 'Take it.'

Zoe lifted her tear-streaked face. 'What?'

His eyes were light. 'I want you to have it. I'll finish it off and bring it to the cabin. I've got a mattress too that's brand new. Take them both.'

'But isn't it yours? I—'

He brought his lips down to her forehead. 'Shhh. I made it for someone who didn't like it or want it.'

Zoe looked at him in astonishment. 'They didn't like it? What's wrong with them?'

He smiled. 'And that's why you have to have it. I want to know it's gone to someone who will love it.'

'Thank you,' replied Zoe faintly, her mind lost in his arms. 'I'll think of you every time I go to bed.'

She saw Rory's eyes change, the pupils overrunning the irises with darkness. She froze, flushing with horrified embarrassment. Then it started. The nervous hysteria that hurt her cheeks and stabbed her stomach.

He stepped back.

'I'm so sorry,' Zoe spluttered. 'It's not you. When I say something stupid it happens.'

The corners of his mouth turned up in a tight-lipped smile that didn't reach his eyes. 'I expect nothing less from you.' He walked back to the workbench, took up the plane and continued to work on the side of the door.

Zoe held her sides. It wasn't funny, it was painful. The sound tore at her throat, still raw from crying and knifed her in the guts. She'd laughed at him again. And she'd also seen his horror at the thought of the two of them in bed. She'd hurt both of them.

By stuttering degrees, she got control of herself. The room was silent except for the rhythmic sound of the plane on wood. She had to find a way to make amends, to make him understand. She walked to the workbench and stood in front of him.

He ignored her and carried on with his work, warm shavings dancing up into the air, then falling to the floor. She placed her hand on his and he stopped dead.

'I want to apologise,' she said unsteadily. 'I need you to understand that when I am nervous, or upset, or embarrassed, I start laughing. It's like a nervous tic. Mum thinks I have a form of Tourette's. I try to control it, but the more I try, the worse it gets. And the more upset or agitated I am, the more impossible it becomes to stop.'

Rory didn't move.

She squeezed his hand, willing him to listen. Her voice wobbled. 'I laughed at Willie's funeral. My mum was so upset, then she had to deal with me as well. She was so understanding, but to me, it doesn't make it right. If I laugh when you are around it has nothing to do with you, it's just the faulty wiring in my brain.' Rory was silent. She put her hands to her forehead. 'This is one of those moments when I really don't like myself. I'm so sorry you've had to see this. I'm so much more than just Mad Willie's crazy great-niece. I'll leave you to it for a couple of days. I've got masses I need to do anyway, and I think you could do with some time off from the Zoe experience.'

She hurried out of the workshop before he could reply.

RORY WATCHED HER LEAVE. THE LAST HOUR HAD BEEN excruciating. He'd almost convinced himself that she meant little to him. That the stress he laboured under was searching for an outlet, and by fantasising about her he could escape the reality of his situation. But when she'd entered the courtyard, he'd known he was lost. He tried to speak but no words had come, just a cough in his constricted throat. And then she'd touched him.

The muscles of his arms had strained against the desire to reach out to her. Standing unmoving, whilst she had picked the curls of wood out of his hair, was worse than crawling over hot coals, or being thrown into a pit of snakes. It was unbearable. Then she'd invited herself into his workshop, his most private space, the only place he felt truly himself since the move to

Kinloch. He walked back to the bedframe, his feet dragging through the sawdust as if drawn to a magnet against their will. He remembered the hundreds of hours of love he'd poured into it, only to have it, and him, rejected.

He'd had enough of Lucy's ghost in the last week. The memories he'd fought so hard to suppress had crawled out of their graves to stalk him. Zoe had unconsciously reanimated them with her very presence, and by finding the bedframe he'd created for Lucy as a wedding present. And now his mother was mentioning her daily, unwilling to let go of her as he had done.

He remembered her sleek brown hair, always perfectly in place. Her artfully shaped brows framing pale blue eyes, and her nose wrinkling at the sight of him whenever they were in public together. Lucy was sophisticated, cultured, charming; a perfectly groomed social animal. Rory sighed. He was just an animal. Despite nearly a year together, and her best efforts, even she couldn't polish a turd. What had she seen in him? He walked to the back wall of the workshop, and tugged a large tarpaulin off the two paintings he had taken down earlier from the great hall. They showed exactly what Lucy had seen in him. It was what everyone saw in him.

The faces of a man and woman stared out from the canvases. The man was in his mid-forties, tall, haughty, domineering. He was wearing a kilt and a tweed jacket, and resting his arm on the butt of a shotgun. Behind him was painted an idealised version of the glen, and on the ground beside him lay a magnificent stag, its breast bright crimson with blood. The man's head was tilted back as he looked out of the frame, condescending down to the viewer. He knew his place in life, and that place was above everyone else.

The portrait of the woman was in marked contrast. She was young, barely out of her teens, slim and beautiful. She was wearing a long gown, and seated in an ornate chair in one of the castle's drawing rooms. Light from the window glinted off an enormous diamond ring on her ring finger. Her expression was victorious and bright. At such a young age, she'd achieved everything she'd always dreamed of. She was poised, in control and ready to take on the world.

The Earl and Countess of Kinloch: His mother and father.

As far back as he could remember he knew his life was mapped out for him. He was never given a choice, only expectations and obligations as constraining as a straightjacket. His father had been a brute. The only bad thing about his death was it forced Rory to take on the life he had spent years running away from. He loved his mother and he felt obligated to the job he was born to, but the estate was crumbling and so was he. Maybe it had been denial that had kept him and his mother in Edinburgh for so long after his father died. But when the castle didn't sell, it was the townhouse that had to go, and they had no choice but to return to Kinloch. It had been mortifying for his mother to leave her carefully cultivated life with her rich and aristocratic friends for a backwater village she'd spent her life disassociating herself from. And as for him? The responsibility of the estate, his name, and his title were dead weights hanging around his neck. He didn't want any of them. He didn't want to be the earl, he didn't want to have to sort out the mess his father had made, and he didn't want to be known as Stuart MacGinley. Until he came to Kinloch, everyone knew who he was. Even in the army, when he started calling himself Rory, his parentage was something he could never truly escape from.

And as for women... At least Lucy was the daughter of his mother's best friend. He had known her all his life, and their family had more money than he would ever see in a lifetime. His title and her money. What a perfect combination that should have been. But even the prospect of being the Countess of Kinloch wasn't enough to make Lucy stay.

Now Zoe had exploded into his life and set him on fire. He wanted her but she clearly didn't want him, and to top it off, she hated the MacGinleys and the peerage. He shook his head. He had so fucked this up. If she didn't want him now, when she found out who he really was she'd want him even less. He'd thought he'd found freedom in Kinloch by hiding who he was, but he'd just created a prison he had no idea how to escape from.

15

Over the next few days, Zoe began to suspect Rory had placed a tracking device on her in order to avoid spending any time in her company. Each day she would wait at the cabin, working offline on her plans for the website until her batteries died, then she would dash into town for electricity, Wi-Fi, and food and company with Morag and Fiona. She left a spare key outside for him, and by the time she returned to the cabin she would discover he had been and gone. The firebox of the Rayburn would be filled with wood, the floor swept, and her milk supply replenished. No matter how she switched her day around, she always managed to miss him. By the end of the week, the windows had been replaced with wooden frames and triple glazing, she had an insulated box behind the cabin to use as a temporary fridge, and a new front door. The cabin was finally warm and weathertight and felt like heaven.

The next priority was getting a water supply and connecting it to the Rayburn. She'd spent a day driving to pick up the back boiler she'd won on eBay, and the water tank had arrived, but rigging it all up and diverting the water from the stream was a big job, and not one Rory could do hidden away in his workshop. In preparation for this, Zoe had bought extra battery packs so had enough power to last her laptop all day. He couldn't avoid her forever, even if he wanted to.

With a never-ending supply of fuel, and the new windows and door, it was easy to get the cabin warm and toasty. She allowed herself a little luxury and cranked the Rayburn up to eleven, stripping off her eternal layers of jumpers until she was down to the Precambrian layer of a thin T-shirt. She'd texted Rory telling him she now had the back boiler. If she wanted to see him, she just needed to wait.

Finally, at lunchtime the following day, the time she was usually out, he rounded the bend. Her heart accelerated as she saw him look from her truck to the window, staring at her impassively as she gave a wave. He nodded in response, then got out to unstrap a ladder from the roof, Bandit by his side. She sighed. How could anyone so big be so graceful? As he moved, the air seemed to part in front of him, shimmering as he passed, before coalescing again behind him. He was so solid, part of the landscape itself, and yet at the same time not truly mortal. He was a Norse god, or a kind of fairy king.

Basil was on her shoulder. 'Oh, darling, what am I to do? I can't get him out of my head.' He snuffled into her ear, trying to impart some ratty wisdom. 'I left London wanting to be by myself. Now I'm scared I'll always be alone because no one else will ever compare.'

Her feet moved of their own accord to take her out of the cabin onto the porch. The cold air hit her, sending goose-bumps rippling across her skin and hardening her nipples. 'Can I help?' Rory was absorbed in hefting the ladder against the

side of the cabin. 'I can hold the ladder for you? Make it safer?'
Or just spend a couple of hours ogling your backside?

He glanced at her, then immediately away, shaking his head. 'Not now. I want to get the gutters up and the water butt attached.'

He walked towards his truck and Zoe's gaze slid down his back. 'What a butt...'

Rory turned, his eyes wide. 'What?'

Shit! She had spoken out loud. 'Water butt, you said you were going to attach it?' she replied, her voice going higher.

Rory flushed. 'Yes, if you'll leave me in peace, I can get on with it.'

Zoe fled back into the cabin, shut the door and sank to the floor, her hands clamped over her mouth to stop her giggles. This was too embarrassing. She couldn't trust her unconscious mind to stay quiet. Why couldn't she be more normal? Maybe if she had straighter hair and a straighter mind he might be interested. Being an accountant was the most normal thing about her but it wasn't exactly a sexy job. She got off the floor, got out her phone, opened the camera and stared at her reflection, trying to find some redeeming features. Crazy hair, bonkers freckles, nondescript brown eyes. She pulled back her lips. At least her teeth were straight. She huffed. It was hopeless. She was never going to make a silk purse out of a sow's ear. She stuck her tongue out at herself, gave up, and went to fetch her computer.

Sitting at the battered oak table, she thought about how best to promote the castle. It needed a hook, a USP, and at the moment it didn't have one. Actually, she mused, that wasn't quite true. She knew exactly what made the estate so special, and that was Rory, but she couldn't exactly attract the tourists with the promise of seeing a hot estate worker chopping wood in the back courtyard. She grinned to herself imagining a busload of Japanese tourists being led in by a tour guide to gawp at him. She thought of suggesting the idea, if only just to see his reaction.

She shook her head. The last thing she wanted was to cause him more discomfort, and she also didn't need any more confirmation of how little he thought of her. She moved the table to position it so she could see his ladder from the window, tuning the TV window to channel Rory. It was like watching an old black and white movie, where the action was a little too fast. He was literally running up and down the ladder. After five minutes, she heard a loud thud and looked up to see he had decided to dispense entirely with a normal descent and was simply leaping from the top of the ladder back to the ground, holding a drill, screws clamped between his lips.

How could she concentrate on writing whilst this was going on? There was no leisurely sound of precise and measured hammering, just the whine of the drill as if a plague of enormous mosquitos were taking it in turns to land on the roof before being slapped into submission by one of Rory's powerful hands. What was he trying to achieve by working like a lunatic hyped up on amphetamines? He had at least four hours before it got too dark to see, he didn't need to work like the devil was at his heels. Zoe moved the table away from the window and put her earplugs in. This was the only way she would ever be able to concentrate.

She stared back at the screen. Writing about the castle was easy. All she had to do was replace the word 'castle' with 'Rory' and she could wax lyrical for hours. Words like 'rugged', 'imposing', 'dramatic', 'majestic', 'stunning' flew out as she hid her feelings in plain sight. Now she needed images to match the words. Having flicked through the *Vanity Fair* photoshoot with Brad Bauer looking like a Scottish strippagram, she knew what she wanted, but whether Rory went along with her plans was a different matter altogether.

❧

UP ON THE ROOF RORY PUMMELLED THE GUTTERS INTO submission. The harder he made the job and the quicker he pushed himself to complete it, the better. He could have easily done with Zoe's help, but if she was anywhere near him he'd either grab her or do himself an injury with a power tool because he was so distracted.

He hadn't had a good night's sleep since she arrived. From that first night when he'd found her at the cabin his mind had been scattered, his body restless. He wanted the cabin and now he wanted her. Neither of which he was going to get now. And when he finally fell into a fitful sleep, his dreams of her were nightmares. She was always out of reach, slipping from him like smoke. She was laughing at him, kissing other men, undoing the buttons on their jeans. His unconscious mind always woke him at this point, aware this was torture too far. Then he would lay awake for hours, his body on fire.

And now she filled his every waking thought. Her smile, which set off flashes of light inside him, the smattering of tiny freckles across the bridge of her nose and her high cheek-bones, her glorious hair, as bright and vibrant as a shepherd's sunset. He wanted her smiles to belong to him. He wanted to kiss every freckle, name each one like a star. He wanted to bury his head in her hair, breathe in the essence of her. His fingers were itchy, sensitive, hyperaware. All the nerve endings in his hands calling out for her.

She utterly bewitched him, and she had no idea who he was. Finally, he could be himself. Truly himself. Only he'd been a dick and it was clear she didn't like what she saw. The fact she found him repulsive was in an odd way refreshing. She flinched when he went near her, she moved when he sat next to her, she laughed at the sight of him shirtless. There was no pretence. He knew exactly which dung heap he was sitting on.

And yet...

He could have sworn she'd said *what a butt*, not water butt. He wasn't the sharpest tool in the box but he wasn't deaf. *Did* she like him? Or was she taking the piss? He cursed himself for the umpteenth time and dealt with the fact that now the gutters were finished and the water butt attached, he had to continue working inside the cabin.

RORY KNOCKED ON THE DOOR, THEN WALKED IN WHEN ZOE called to him, recoiling from the wall of heat that hit him like a tropical summer. She was working at the table, the thin white T-shirt clinging to her body and leaving nothing to his imagination.

'Are you trying to recreate the surface of the sun?'

She grinned at him and stretched her arms over her head, the T-shirt framing her breasts. 'It's all thanks to you. How did you get on with the gutters?'

'Fine,' Rory muttered, going to inspect the back boiler on the floor beside the Rayburn. The back of his neck prickled with sweat. He wanted the Rayburn off and the temperature down by fifty degrees. He needed Zoe wearing so many clothes she became indistinguishable from a sofa. He lifted the back boiler to inspect it.

'I've been thinking,' said Rory.

'Hmmm?'

'Water and power are your biggest priorities right now. I've done the gutters and the water butt but I need to hire a digger to get the water tank in the ground. And once the back boiler is in, you need power to run a proper fridge and the pumps. I also want to clear out under the porch so I can fit more wood there. I want you to be able to last at least a week here without being able to get out.'

'A week?' cried Zoe. 'Does the main road often get blocked?'

'Not often and usually not for long, but I want you to be prepared.'

'There's so much to do.'

'Yes. Why couldn't you have come here in the spring? Why choose November?'

'The rental period was coming up on my flat and I couldn't bear the thought of another six months when I knew this was here. It's easier to ignore the potential difficulties when you're fantasising about it while sitting in a hot bubble bath with candles and a glass of Prosecco.'

As Rory's mind slipped into the bath with her, the back boiler fell out of his grasp, landing on his foot with an almighty crash and a blinding flash of pain. 'Fuck!'

Zoe dashed over, dragging the boiler away and guiding him to sit down. 'Oh my god, that must have hurt. Are you okay?'

Rory closed his eyes tightly, holding his foot and using the agony to detract from her hands fluttering over him. If he had been wearing his boots then the metal would have bounced off the steel toe caps. Stockinged feet were no match however against fifty kilos of boiler, and this hurt like a bastard. Zoe knelt on the floor beside him. 'Can I take a look at it?'

Rory released his foot and felt her carefully take off his sock. He heard her sharp intake of breath as she shuffled closer. He opened his eyes to see her sitting on the floor between his legs, inspecting his swelling foot and chewing her bottom lip. She looked up and opened her mouth as if to speak. He stared at the full, lush softness of her lips.

She darted her tongue out, moistening them, then swallowed. 'Do you want some ice for the swelling?'

Jesus Christ, she would be the death of him. He needed ice all right, just not for his foot.

'Do you have any?' His voice was low and husky. She shook her head. Silence crackled between them. 'Can you go to the truck and get the first aid kit out the back?' he asked, trying to keep his voice level.

Zoe nodded, leapt up and ran out of the cabin. Rory hung his head, holding his breath, willing his erection to subside. He couldn't be around her. He was turning into an animal. Despite being seated, he had loomed over her, power and desire radiating out of him. He knew in terms of size alone he was a man and a half, and right now he had the libido of twenty. He needed to get away from her, and fast. By the time she got back, he had already hobbled to the door and pulled on his boots. Confusion and worry played across her face.

'Are you okay? Are you sure you don't want me to strap it up or anything? Can I help?' She put her arm out for him but he shrugged her off.

'The truck's automatic and my right foot's fine. I just need to get home and ice it. I'll see how it is in the morning and let you know. I've also got lots of other jobs to do for the estate I can't put off any longer.'

She nodded. 'Sorry, I know how much you've been doing up here.'

His shoulders slumped. Had he upset her? Again? 'It's fine. I'd rather be here than at the castle. It's just... If there's anything I can to do to help you, ask, okay?'

Zoe looked up. 'I need to get back to the castle to do a

photoshoot for the website as soon as possible. Will you let me know when?'

'Will do,' he replied, limping off to the truck.

He reversed out down the track, throbbing with pain and desire. He needed this arrangement with her over sooner rather than later.

ZOE WAITED FIVE MINUTES, THEN DROVE UP THE ROAD TO find a signal. She needed to talk to a friend; someone who knew her and didn't know Rory. Sam picked up after one ring.

'Babe! Oh my god, I can't believe your timing, it's perfect. We've just wrapped my scenes for today. Tell me everything, beginning with when the fucking fuck you're coming home, and moving swiftly onto my favourite hot Scot, your brother-from-another-mother, Jamie.'

Zoe giggled. 'You have no idea how much I need you right now. I need to talk to you about Rory. I'm totally in lust with him but I'm pretty sure he can't stand me and thinks I'm a nutjob,' she moaned.

'Oh, babe, being a nutjob is what makes you so utterly adorable. Have you laughed at him shirtless again? Got stuck up any more trees?'

'Ugh... Yes, after he gave me a bed and kissed me on the head. And I also told him he had an awesome water butt.'

'Whaaaaat? He gave you a bed? With him in it? And he kissed you on your head? Where? Did he miss your mouth? Did he try and tongue your ear? WTAF is going on?'

Zoe snorted. 'Oh god, Sam, it's such a mess. Sometimes I think he might actually like me, but it's either that or he wants to murder me. If there's a fine line between love and hate then he's walking it, and I don't know which way he's going to fall.'

'Well, if you're near a bed then make sure he falls on you. Have you got any condoms?'

'What? God no.'

'Right, I'm going to send you some as I'm sure the locals just use sheep guts. What's your address again? Creepy cabin, Deliverance-ville, East Bumfuck, Scotland? That'll get to you right?'

Zoe really missed her friend. 'You are a very bad person. Tell me what to do. You're so good when it comes to men and I'm bloody clueless.'

'Ha! The only advice I have is to leap on him. Always works for me.'

TWO DAYS LATER, WHILST SITTING IN HER FAVOURITE plastic chair in the library, she received a text from Rory.

Man-bear, yeti, mutant-redneck-hobbit, hobo: You can get into the castle tomorrow to take photos if that works for you. Let me know if you need anything. Rory.

A thrill of excitement ran through her. Her fantasies, well, some of them, were about to be fulfilled. She replied.

Zoe: Awesome! What time? Do you have a kilt?

Man-bear, yeti, mutant-redneck-hobbit, hobo: Why?

Zoe: Oh, and a sword. Cheers.

Man-bear, yeti, mutant-redneck-hobbit, hobo: What?

Zoe: Long, pointy thing, made of metal.

Man-bear, yeti, mutant-redneck-hobbit, hobo: I know what a sword is. Why do you need one?

Zoe: I've got a few ideas for the photos you can help me with. I just need you and a few props. Can you get them? What time tomorrow? Cheers.

Man-bear, yeti, mutant-redneck-hobbit, hobo: Where are you?

Zoe sighed. This had been a gamble and it wasn't about to pay off.

Zoe: At the cabin. What time tomorrow?

Man-bear, yeti, mutant-redneck-hobbit, hobo: Great phone signal you've suddenly got. Where are you?

Should she reply?

Man-bear, yeti, mutant-redneck-hobbit, hobo: Zoe?

She tossed the phone on the desk and dropped her chin. She wasn't going to see him until he'd had a chance to calm down. She had work to do.

꧁꧂

FIVE MINUTES LATER RORY STALKED INTO THE LIBRARY. Thank god it was empty. He walked through to the back, where hidden behind a wall of bookshelves was a row of tables and computers. There she sat, bent over a magazine, her corkscrew curls tied up but grazing her exquisite neck. God she was beautiful. She was concentrating so hard on what she was reading, she didn't hear him. He looked at what she was engrossed in and his heart sank. Brad bloody Bauer.

Rory believed a special circle of hell should be created for wife beaters, child abusers, and Brad Bauer. He was Lucy's celebrity crush, and she'd made Rory agree she was allowed to snog him if they ever met. In return, she magnanimously offered him a free pass to kiss the celebrity of his choice. Rory told her the only person he wanted to kiss was her and she got annoyed with him, telling him he just didn't get it. She said that to him a lot.

So, he was forced to endure viewings of Brad's films, whilst calculating what else he could have done in the hours he was wasting. One of the last films he had watched with her, *Death Party*, had been set during the Afghanistan conflict and bore as much resemblance to reality as *Alice in Wonderland*. Lucy, keen to find a commonality between her fiancé and her fantasy boyfriend, told Rory about the Special Forces training Brad had received and how many stunts he'd done himself. Rory thought the only stunt Brad had pulled was getting anyone to believe he could hold his own in a fight that involved anything more than pillows.

Rory stared at the image of Brad having sex with a kilt, and his blood went from boiling to thermonuclear. This was a man? An overly manicured pretty boy who spent his time in front of a camera, a mirror or in the pants of reality TV stars.

'Please tell me you aren't expecting me to recreate this?' he hissed.

Zoe leapt around, her hand clutching her chest. 'Jesus fucking Christ!' she whispered. 'How long have you been standing there?'

'Long enough. Is this what you find attractive?' he asked with thinly veiled contempt, indicating the magazine. Zoe became very interested in the carpet, scuffing at it with the toe of her boots. 'Zoe?'

'He was my first ever crush,' she mumbled. 'He's super hot. I mean, he's been voted the world's sexiest man more than anyone else. But I'm only using it as inspiration. I don't expect you to get naked or anything.'

Rory tried to hold it together. Now he knew for certain he didn't have a chance with her. Her ideal man was a dark haired, perfectly formed fop like Brad Bauer, not an oversized scruff-bag like himself. He stared at her, still apparently obsessed with the library floor.

'So, let me get this straight. You want me to put on a kilt

and ponce about the castle, while you take photos then put them on the Internet?'

Zoe glanced up and blushed.

Rory shook his head. 'I'm surprised you haven't thought to ask me to take my top off and brandish a sword whilst yelling "freedom!"'

Zoe flushed even redder and looked away.

'Jesus!' said Rory. 'You have!'

Zoe snapped her head back. 'Shush! We're in a library. And I didn't think about the freedom part.'

'No. This is not happening,' he hissed through clenched teeth.

Zoe stood. 'Listen to me. Please,' she whispered urgently. 'The whole point of the website is to sell the castle to tourists. Most of the people who visit are not from Scotland. They're here to experience something different from what they get at home, and that means kilts, shortbread, haggis, castles and bagpipes. It means Ben Nevis and Glen Coe, the Loch Ness Monster and whisky. It can't be sold through photos of a stately home that could be any old National Trust pile. We have to sell a story, a dream, and that involves people. I can't photograph Lord Kinloch, and I bet he's too stuffy anyway. You look right.'

'What do you mean? Doesn't Morag have a son? Why can't you use him?'

Zoe smiled. 'Jamie is a handsome man but he's too shy to be a Scottish warrior. You look timeless, strong, wild. The kind of man that built the castle. The kind of man that other men want to be and, er.' She looked away. 'Some women want to have.'

'So not a man-bear, yeti, hobbit, thingymajig then?'

'Only a little bit, and only to me,' she muttered.

Rory felt like he was on shifting sand, everything was

unstable. 'I'm not a performing monkey. I'll be a laughing stock,' he said quietly.

'You won't. I promise. Who cares what anyone thinks? People are only jealous they don't look like you. These photos are going to make all the difference. I promise.'

Rory sighed. 'What other plans did you have for me?'

Zoe passed her notepad to him and took a step back. He scanned the page, then his head shot up. 'Marriage shots? Who the hell am I meant to be marrying? You?' Heat scorched across his face. Hers was on fire.

'God no,' she replied. 'Fiona, Morag's daughter.'

He dropped the notepad onto the desk. 'Morag's daughter? Jesus!'

His skull was about to shatter. Keeping a low profile didn't involve getting his kit off on the battlements. Soon the whole village would be speculating about who he was.

'She's going to bring clothes and hold lights for me. And I want her help with your hair, as she's a hairdresser. She won't tell anyone, I promise.'

Rory fixed her with a stare. He saw her swallow. 'She's the postmistress's bloody daughter! I bet she could walk on water sooner than keep a frigging secret. I give it ten minutes before the whole of Kinloch knows what you've planned.'

'I don't know why you won't trust me. I'm not the devil incarnate.'

He gave her a look that suggested he thought otherwise.

'How about this,' Zoe ploughed on. 'Let me take the photos I know will work. And if you don't like them, we won't use them. You'll have a veto. Deal?'

He glared at her. She chewed on her bottom lip and he looked away. Fuck! He would do anything for her. 'Deal,' he said in a flat tone.

Zoe gave a little jump. 'This is going to be incredible!' She picked up her notebook, ripped out a page and passed it to him. 'This is a list of things I need that I think you should have. What time can we start?'

He stuffed it in his pocket. 'Eleven. I'll meet you out the back.'

He walked out.

16

The next morning, Zoe went to Morag's to collect a massive Scottish flag she had earlier bought online. Fiona had brought a bag of clothes, plastic flowers, her hairdressing supplies, and Liam.

'I'm so sorry, Zoe, Duncan had to go for a meeting and couldn't take him, and Mum's working so he's stuck with us.'

'It's okay, photos are silent so it doesn't matter what noise he makes,' Zoe reassured her, whilst worrying about Rory's reaction.

They walked around to the back of the castle just before eleven, bags hanging off their shoulders and carrying the flag. Rory stalked out of his workshop to stand in front of them. His face was grim. Half executioner, half condemned man. He stared at them.

'Hi, er, I'm Fiona. And this is Liam.'

Silence echoed around the courtyard.

'I'm Rory.'

'Morning, Rory!' Zoe trilled like a bird on amphetamines.

Rory walked forward. 'Can I help with your bags?'

Fiona handed him a bag and they followed him into the castle. When they reached the great hall, they dumped everything on a folding table next to a wall. Rory stood back as if the contents might explode at any point. A broadsword was propped against the wall next to three lights on stands.

Zoe was well aware he was here under duress, so quickly got her camera out and attached the lens she wanted.

'Okay, first I want to get lots of shots of each of the rooms, so wides, mids and close-ups. Fi, can you take my notebook and tick off when I've got the photos I need? We'll then come back here and do the ones involving, er, people.'

She risked a quick glance at Rory. He was looking away. 'Rory, please can you bring two of the lights?'

He nodded. 'Where do you want to go first?'

'I thought we would start upstairs and work our way down.' She looked at Liam asleep in his buggy. 'Is there a lift?'

Rory shook his head and took the notebook from Fiona. 'I can multitask.' He walked off and Zoe hurriedly followed, mouthing 'sorry' back to Fiona who waved at her to go.

Zoe usually liked to take her time composing shots. She loved shooting landscapes because they didn't move. This, however, was different. Rory was in no mood for artistic faffing. She had to get in, get the photos she needed and get out.

Most of the rooms had enough natural light to illuminate them, so she focused on making the old and tired spaces come alive again. Rory ticked off her shot list and they went through the castle in silence except for the sound of the shutter clicking away. Whenever the room was too dark, Rory added background light. They worked easily together as a team, and in an hour they were back in the great hall to find Fiona trying to entertain a wide awake Liam.

'Sorry, Zo,' she said, bouncing him up and down. 'He wouldn't sleep any longer.'

'It's okay, I can hold him.' She looked at Rory. 'Um, could you possibly, erm, get changed now?' she asked, her face reddening.

'Can we get the worst of your ideas over and done with first?'

Zoe swallowed. 'Er, the ones with the erm, sword and er, kilt?'

'Yes, them.'

Zoe nodded.

He picked up a suit carrier and walked to a door leading off from the great hall. 'I'll get changed in here.' He walked in, closing the door behind him.

Zoe turned away from Fiona, under the pretext of checking through the photos on her camera. She needn't have worried as Fiona's attention was caught up with a fractious Liam.

After a couple of minutes, the door reopened and Rory emerged. He was wearing a dark green kilt and a loose white dress shirt that was half unbuttoned. His legs were bare and his feet were back in his work boots. He had a sporran dangling from one hand.

Zoe looked up, then down again immediately, the heat blooming in her cheeks and rushing through her body. The back of her neck prickled, and she tugged at the front of her top to let in some air. She rolled up her sleeves to try and cool down and attached a different lens to the camera.

The brief glance had burned his image into her retinas. He was pure power and sex. His calves were big and strong, almost as bronzed as his arms and covered in light brown hair she felt compelled to feel against her skin. The kilt was slung low on his hips, the white shirt unbuttoned enough to get another glimpse at the expanse of his chest.

His wavy dark gold hair grazed his shoulders, framing his broad face. His full lips were closed and Zoe longed to bring hers to his and run the tip of her tongue between them, loosening them, claiming him. The pupils of his eyes were big and dark, the blue-grey irises lit up from within.

'Sporran or no sporran?'

Zoe didn't raise her head. 'None, please. I want to start with shots at the window, a bit like what we were doing in the cabin.'

He threw the sporran onto the table, stalked to the window and stared out. The two women followed. Zoe put her camera over her shoulder and took Liam from Fiona.

'What do you want me to do, Zo?'

'I don't want it tamed, but I do want separation to get more graduation and depth.'

'It?' asked Rory.

'Your hair!' said Zoe, flushing to her roots.

Fiona grabbed a chair and Rory sat down with a thump.

'I don't think even I could tame this,' she said, spraying on water, then deftly arranging his hair with a wide comb, whilst he sat woodenly, staring out into the middle distance. 'He's all yours, Zoe,' said Fiona, stepping back and taking Liam off her.

Rory stood. 'Right. Let's get this over and done with.'

Zoe looked at her camera for moral support. 'Okay. Let's begin by having you by the window.'

His features beat any landscape hands down. The cool north light coming in from outside accentuated the sweep of his strong jaw, the bump on the bridge of his nose, the long lashes framing his luminous eyes. Every line, every curl, every part of him was a work of savage art, the imperfections creating a perfect whole. The more photos she took of him, the more she knew this was right. He personified the castle.

She moved him to one of the thrones at the end of the hall,

removing the second one and placing him in the middle of the dais. She had him sit, his legs apart, the fabric of the kilt resting between his enormous thighs. The look she was going for was undiluted confidence and power. The fact his shirt was undone and he had work boots on only added an extra layer of sex. She knew the images were pure filth. If he saw them as she did then he would never allow her to use them, but she was going to take the chance anyway.

She moved him into different poses and got Fiona to bring up the sword. When Rory took it and pointed the blade into the floor, casually resting his hand on the hilt, Zoe let out a squeak, unable to contain her visceral reaction. 'Watch the floor!' she said breathlessly.

She took more photos, then the three of them climbed up to the castle tower, Rory carrying the flag and the sword, Fiona carrying Liam. At the foot of the tower the steps got older, narrower and more uneven.

Fiona stopped. 'You two go on, I don't want to take Liam up there.'

'Okay, we won't be long,' said Zoe and she made her way up the tower after Rory, holding the cold stonework for support.

They exited through a trap door onto the flat roof of the turret. A pole was the only decoration, a tattered flag with the MacGinley coat of arms at the top, fluttering in the breeze.

'Okay, what now?' Rory sighed.

'I want to do similar shots to what we did in the hall, then we'll bring the flag out and have a play around with that.'

Despite his grim expression he was the perfect model, anticipating what Zoe might need and improvising when she wasn't sure. She unfurled the flag and had him standing, looking out over the battlements, holding it in one hand, the sword in the other. The breeze lifted the flag and his curls, giving life to a man who was so strong he could have been part of the tower.

Zoe put her camera down and paused.

'Do you want me to take off my shirt?' he asked.

Zoe dropped her head. 'Only if you don't mind,' she said in a small voice.

'Are you going to laugh again if I do?'

Zoe nodded. 'Probably. It's nothing to do with you, it's just the stress of the situation. You're a very, er, fine example of a man,' she muttered to her feet.

Rory grinned. 'I'll take that. Coming from you, fine is the best compliment I could ever hope for. It's a big step up from hobo.'

In her peripheral vision she saw a white shirt land on the ground and her heart sped up so fast the pounding in her ears was deafening. She willed her shaking fingers to be still and brought the camera up, only looking through the lens, never at Rory directly.

Even through the tiny viewfinder, he was larger than life. No classical statue could ever compete with the godlike perfection of his body. At the base of his torso, indentations ran from each side to vanish into the top of the kilt, a small line of brown hair following them down from his navel.

Zoe's breathing became more uneven and a hiccup burst out of her.

Rory raised his head to the clouds. 'Come on,' he said, resignedly. 'Let it all out.'

Zoe began wheezing as she inhaled, trying to get air in when all she wanted to do was laugh till she collapsed. She bent over, trying to protect the camera. Rory stepped forward, taking it from her and pulling the strap gently off her curls.

She dropped to her knees, clasping her sides as if trying to relieve a stitch. Rory crouched down beside her and touched her shoulder. 'You okay?'

She shook her head violently and put her hand out to signal him to go away. He stepped back to give her space. Eventually, the laughter petered out, and her breathing slowed. 'It's gone now. I'm sorry.'

Rory looked at her wryly. 'I've never had this effect on a woman before, but now I'm kind of used to it.'

She wiped her eyes. 'Thank you for being so understanding.'

He passed her camera back to her. 'Shall we have a go at giving Brad Bauer a run for his money?'

Zoe smiled shyly back at him and nodded, getting to her feet and lifting up the camera.

As she snapped away, she thought that Rory actually appeared to be enjoying himself. He loosened up, swinging the sword above his head, roaring like a lion. In between poses that promised death and retribution, his face relaxed into smiles, as they imagined what an American tourist would want to see. They spent longer than planned, and when they got back to the great hall Fiona was feeding puree to Liam from a glass jar.

'Did it go okay? Get what you wanted?'

'Yes,' replied Zoe. 'It was perfect.'

'So, according to your notes, you want to get shots that look like they're from a wedding?' Fiona asked.

'Yes, details of the happy couple, sitting on the thrones, standing lovingly by the window, that kind of thing. When you've finished feeding Liam you can get changed.'

Fiona nearly dropped the jar. 'Me?'

'Yes, that's why I got you to bring your wedding dress.'

'You have got to be joking! I've just had a bloody baby! I dieted for six months before the wedding and now all I eat is cake and biscuits! There's no way I'd fit into it now, and besides, I had three hours sleep last night and look like shit.'

'But who can I get to wear it?'

'You, you daft bugger. You'll look stunning in it.'

'But I need to take the pictures.'

'I'll do it. Set the shot up how you want it and I'll press the button. If it's a bit wonky then you can straighten it out on your computer.'

'But...'

'How does it feel to be on the other side of the camera?' Rory asked.

Zoe gave him a murderous glance, took the bag containing the dress and walked to the door where Rory had changed, opening it and slamming it shut behind her.

The room was now used for storage. It was small but filled with plastic folding tables against the walls, and piles of stacked chairs. There was a big industrial floor cleaner, cleaning products and rolls of blue paper towels. Draped over a chair in the middle of the tiny floor space were his work shirt and trousers.

Zoe pulled another chair off a pile and laid the bag containing the dress on it. She looked at the door, then back to the chair where Rory's clothes lay. She tried to memorise their exact position then lifted them up to her face. She breathed hungrily, inhaling his incredible scent. She couldn't get enough; it was a thirst that could never be quenched.

She knew if she didn't hurry then Fiona would come searching for her, so she reluctantly put his clothes back and lifted the bag containing the dress. She heard a knock at the door.

'Are you okay, Zoe? Do you want some help?' Fiona called through.

'I'm fine, just give me a second.'

She hastily unzipped the bag, took the dress off the hanger and slipped it on. It fit like a glove. It was made from cream satin, strapless, fitting tightly around the bodice, skimming down the hips, then flaring out into a fishtail to the floor over layers of net. It was simple and beautiful, the kind of dress that would make anyone feel like a princess.

Zoe couldn't manage to do the back up so called out to Fiona. 'Could you help me with the zip?'

Fiona entered without Liam and her jaw dropped. 'Oh my god, Zoe, you're beautiful! If only Mum and Jamie could see you now.'

'It's an incredible dress, Fi, you must have looked a picture.'

Fiona zipped the dress up, then anchored the veil in the back of Zoe's hair with the attached comb. 'I scrubbed up well. But you. Oh, my lord, you're stunning.' Zoe blushed as Fiona steered her out of the room. 'That Rory won't be able to keep his eyes off you!'

As they re-entered the great hall Rory gave them a quick glance then turned away, letting a chortling Liam shove his tiny fist into his mouth.

He gently pulled out Liam's hand. 'What shots do you want then?'

Fiona strode up to him, taking Liam out of his arms. 'Isn't she beautiful?'

Rory gave Zoe a perfunctory glance up and down, then shrugged his shoulders.

Fiona walked back to Zoe, shaking her head. 'Well, I think you look incredible. Now, what do you want the shots to be?'

Zoe stood silent, lost in thought. She knew she looked nice in the dress. It would have suited just about anyone. When she'd entered the hall, she noticed Rory's eyes widening, his lips parting, and his cheeks burning. Even now, she could see a muscle twitching in his jaw and his hands balling into fists at his sides.

Had his behaviour simply been his attempt to keep her at arm's length? She thought of Sam's advice to leap on him. Easier said than done with Fiona and Liam around, but what she could do instead was a bit of scientific investigating. Playing the role of the happy couple would give her the perfect opportunity to find out what he really thought of her.

She turned to Fiona. 'The castle is the perfect place for weddings, so I want to get a few shots that look like they could be from a real wedding. I want to keep them mid length and close up so we don't get our shoes in. I saw a fantastic location upstairs so I thought we could start there.'

She picked up her camera and sashayed off across the hall without waiting for a reply, deliberately undulating her hips. She was going to find out the truth from Rory's body even if his mouth remained closed. They made their way up the main staircase, and Zoe opened the door to the grandest of bedrooms. In the centre was a huge four-poster bed, the mattress so far off the ground it was at the height of her hips. The window was a three-sided alcove, a wooden window seat running along the sides. It was intimate, a place for private conversations and leisurely kisses.

'Okay,' said Zoe. 'We'll begin by the window. We need to make sure you can't see our left hands as we don't have any rings on.'

'You can take mine,' said Fiona. 'If I can get them off that is.' She put Liam in the middle of the four-poster bed, twisted them off and passed them to Zoe who put them on.

'Oh, they're beautiful, Fi! What do you think, Rory?'

He shrugged. 'Can we get on with this so I can go back to work?'

'Yes of course,' said Zoe sweetly. 'Now if you could sit

there.' She indicated the window seat and he sat down stiffly. 'Now I'm going to sit on your lap.' She turned her bottom towards him.

He stood back up immediately, bumping into her and sending her tripping forward into Fiona. 'No,' he said, his face red. 'We need to stand.'

Zoe kept composed and noncommittal. 'Okay, that's fine, you stay there, let me just readjust my dress.' Facing him, she reached down inside the front of the gown and lifted her breasts a little higher. 'That's better,' she sighed.

She glanced up to see Rory staring at the front of her gown, his mouth open. He looked in agony. Zoe gave her camera to Fiona, delirious with excitement, and turned back to face him. 'I've been chatting to Fi about what I want,' she said casually. 'I've put the camera on automatic, so instead of setting up each shot, we'll just get into various poses and she'll snap away. Okay?'

Rory nodded, fixing on a point an inch above her head. Zoe chewed her bottom lip. Rory swallowed.

'Okay, so you stand there,' she said. She brought herself up to him, her right hand resting on his heart, her left tucked around his waist. 'If you could put your arms around me and look at me that would be perfect,' she said cheerfully.

He slowly brought his arms around her as if she were the finest porcelain, and looked down into her eyes.

The rest of the world dropped away.

Zoe felt the heat from his chest under her palm, the thudding of his heartbeat. The muscles of his back tensed underneath her fingers. She breathed in the scent of woodsmoke, soap, and aroused male. She lost herself in the blackness of his dilated pupils, the irises a nebula of silver light and blue fire. Her lips parted and she licked them.

He tensed and she shifted closer, pressing herself along the length of him. There was something big, long and hard underneath his kilt, digging into her tummy. Oh my god, it hadn't been a Maglite that day she'd pushed him off the ladder. It had been him. He hadn't been in pain, he'd been aroused.

By her.

Rory's cheeks were flushed, his breathing unsteady. She angled her body to his, his lips tantalisingly close. His grip tightened. He slowly brought his mouth down towards hers.

Holy crap. She wasn't imagining what was under his kilt or his feelings for her. This incredible man was about to kiss her.

'Keep it up! This is amazing, you guys. It looks like you're about to kiss,' yelled Fiona in excitement.

Rory dropped Zoe as if she was on fire and stepped away. Zoe stumbled and reached out to the window for support. There was a deafening silence, broken only by the sudden, terrifying sound of a red-faced Liam unleashing an apoocalypse into his nappy.

'Shit, Liam, no!' yelled Fiona, thrusting the camera at Zoe, scooping him off the bed and lifting him into the air to check for leakage.

'Sorry! If I could control him I would. Give me five minutes, back in a bit.' Fiona ran out of the room, Liam in her arms, and slammed the door behind her.

Zoe was left alone with a one hundred per cent aroused Rory and a four-poster bed.

Time to leap.

❧ 17 ❧

Zoe put her camera down on a small table. Rory was facing away from her, his hands squeezed so tightly into fists the knuckles were white. She walked to his side.

'Rory?' He continued to stare out of the window, his body tensed. She swallowed. 'Can you look at me?' He ignored her, but she could see a pulse beating wildly in his neck. She touched his arm. He flinched and shrugged her off.

'Don't you like me?' she asked.

Rory turned towards her. His eyes were burning. She stepped back, her breath stuck in her throat. Silence stretched out, waiting to snap.

'No, Zoe, I don't like you.' His voice was strained; the voice of a man pushed to the edge of reason, then kicked off into the abyss. 'I'm overwhelmed by you. My head is so full of you there's no room for anything else.'

He pressed his fists into his temples.

'My life was simple before you showed up, and now it's a car crash. I can't think straight. Fuck, I can't even think at all when you're around. I might as well try to count all the stars in the universe than make it through a day without a raging hard-on or dropping a boiler on my foot.'

He advanced on her. She backed away until she bumped into the edge of the bed. She leaned back against it and he leaned forward, towering over her.

'So no, I don't like you. I want you. I crave you. I hunger for you. Everything you are, and everything you do drives me crazy. Like doesn't even begin to cover it.' He closed his eyes. 'I can't be here. I can't—'

Zoe put her arms around his neck and stopped his mouth with a kiss.

Their lips touched with a tingle of electricity, a fizzing plea-sure that spread through her chest and ran down her spine with a shiver. She moulded herself to his rigid body, stroking the back of his neck with her fingertips, coaxing him to respond. His lips were shut but soft and warm. She kissed around his mouth, the prickle of his stubble thrilling her nerve endings.

He reached back behind his neck, grabbed her wrists and slowly pulled them away from him, breaking the connection. 'What are you doing?' he asked, his tone harsh but his breathing ragged, as if he had just run for miles.

'I'm kissing you.'

'Why?'

'Because I don't like you either.' She saw confusion, uncer-tainty, doubt, disbelief and hope flash across his face like a summer storm.

'You don't?'

She shook her head, then rewound her arms around his neck and brought her mouth back to his, running the tip of her tongue between his lips, willing him to open to her. As she scraped her nails up into his hair, he broke, groaning and wrapping her in his arms, meeting her passion with his own. He kissed her like a man lost in the desert being given a cool glass of water, holding her tightly, possessing her, running his tongue into her mouth, drinking her in. Zoe gasped, relief and desire coursing through her. She clung to him, a throbbing heat urging her closer.

He broke the kiss and stared at her, blinking as if he couldn't believe what was happening. 'You're so beautiful. Jesus, Zoe.' He lay her back on the bed, his left hand cradling her head, and sunk his face into her curls, kissing her, inhaling her, growling with desire. 'You're so fucking beautiful.' He buried through her hair to the sensitive skin of her neck; kissing, nipping, licking whilst she writhed beneath him.

'Oh god, Rory.' She bit her lip to stop it trembling.

She reached towards his kilt, needing to feel him. He shot back as if scorched, pinning her hand to her side. He lay his forehead on hers.

'Fuck no, Zoe. You can't touch me or I'll explode.'

She felt his hot breath on her face, and lifted her lips to his burning cheek, kissing her way up to his ear. 'But I want to,' she whispered.

She gently tugged on his earlobe with her teeth. It was like pouring gasoline on an inferno. He took her mouth with his, devouring her, as he pushed past layers of satin and net to find her leg, running his hand up her skin, dragging her bottom towards him. He bent his right leg and pushed his thigh between hers as she writhed to get closer, grabbing at his glorious mane, pulling at his arms, frantic with need. He slipped his hand under the cotton of her pants, cupping her bottom, the calluses on his palm sending shivers across her silky skin.

'God, Zoe. It's, it's...'

She bucked her hips against him, desperately seeking relief.

He released the pressure of his leg between hers and she tried to open for him against the confines of the dress, shifting her hips, encouraging him to move. As she twisted he let go of her bottom, and slowly slid his hand around to her front, sinking a thick finger into her wet heat. She cried out and he growled in response, sucking at her bottom lip and her tongue, feasting on her.

He circled around her clitoris, zeroing in on the source of her pleasure. Flashes of fire shot through her, ricocheting back and forth, colliding and multiplying, as she began to shake. She was imprisoned by the dress, his mouth, his caress, and the only escape was up. He stroked her higher and higher. She wanted to touch him, to give him the same pleasure he was giving her, but she was lost, disorientated, her breathing fitful and frantic.

'Yes, Zoe, yes,' he breathed between deep, frenzied kisses. He held her tightly, relentlessly driving her on. His fingers were flames, filling her with light and heat as she blazed in his arms. She felt the pressure building, saw stars behind her eyes, heard a ringing in her ears as he rocketed her into a blinding climax. She detonated with a scream, her body pulsing with spasms of searing pleasure, looping and radiating through her.

He swallowed her cries, holding her, riding out the overwhelming sensations that throbbed and burned, the aftershocks darting over her skin. Eventually, she went limp in his arms with a soft sigh, her eyes open but unseeing. She was vaguely aware of Rory gently kissing her forehead, but she was scattered, lost across multiple dimensions of space and time.

He stopped kissing her. 'Get up,' he whispered urgently. He leapt off, strode to the door and was gone.

The high-pitched wail of a baby could be heard echoing down the corridor, getting closer and closer. Reality hit her like a cold bucket of water. She was lying across a four-poster bed.

Wearing Fiona's wedding dress. Having just experienced the most intense orgasm of her life. From the sexiest man she had ever met. Who apparently liked her. Really liked her.

She shot off the bed, her hands smoothing the dress down, then fluttering to her hair. The comb holding the veil had fallen out to the floor and she snatched it up, jamming it back into her curls. The ornate counterpane covering the bed was in disarray so she pulled it straight, then looked frantically around the room for more evidence of carnal carnage. She found her reflection in a gilt mirror and stared at herself in horror. Liam's screams were right outside the door but coming no further. Was Rory keeping Fiona talking? How could it not be obvious what had gone on?

As the door opened, she went to the table where her camera lay.

'Shit, Zo, I'm so sorry, he's shat over everything and upchucked cottage pie. He's in a state; I've got to get him back to Mum's,' Fiona rattled out over Liam's cries. 'I'm so sorry to let you down, but Rory told me he's got to get back to work so can we finish this another day? I'm so sorry, love. Who'd have a bloody baby, eh?'

Fiona was frowning with anxious worry, holding Liam wrapped in a blanket as he attempted to throw himself out of her arms, beetroot red with rage.

'God, Fi, no worries, let me get this dress off, then I'll help you get him home,' she replied, bustling them both out of the room.

TWO HOURS LATER SHE WAS BACK AT THE CABIN, HOLDING A small package that had arrived at the post office addressed to her. It was from Sam, and she knew exactly what the contents would be. She tossed it unopened into one of the boxes containing her clothes, checked on a sleeping Basil, filled the firebox of the Rayburn with wood and made herself a cup of tea.

Sitting at the table, she switched on her camera and went through the photos from the shoot. The pictures from around the castle were good and definitely showed it at its best. The photos of Rory however, were incendiary. Her gaze roamed lasciviously over his body, remembering how his lips had felt on hers, the hot warmth of his tongue, his voice in her ear telling her how beautiful she was, his finger sinking deep inside her. She gasped out loud, her head spinning, her heart pounding in her chest. What had he done to her?

She felt utterly changed by what had happened. As if she had been unpicked, turned inside out and stitched back together with threads of light. Her internal landscape had been transformed into something deeper, more primeval, more powerful. Nothing would ever be the same again.

What would happen when she next saw him? Should she drive up the road and message him? And if she did, what should she say? Hi, Rory, thanks for the earth-shattering orgasm. Fancy giving me another? Cheers, Zoe. Ugh. She sank her head in her hands. She'd made the first move. She would wait for him to make the second.

Seventeen hours later, she was still waiting. She had hoped he would pop around, come to see her after their abrupt parting, but he hadn't, and now she was convinced she had dreamt it all. She packed her bag and drove to the library to work.

SHE SAT AT HER DESK IN THE LIBRARY AND TOOK OUT HER laptop, chargers, notebook and phone. She had a new text message and feverishly opened it up.

Man-bear, yeti, mutant-redneck-hobbit, hobo: I've

finished your bed and borrowed a van. I can bring it to yours after lunch and we can drive to the storage place and collect your things. Rory.

She nearly dropped her phone. He had finished the bed. And now all she could think of was christening it with him. Shit. How could she reply without sounding crazy and desperate? Another message pinged through.

Man-bear, yeti, mutant-redneck-hobbit, hobo: If that's okay with you?

Is that okay? Hell yes! She was shaking as she typed back.

Zoe: Yes please. What time?

Man-bear, yeti, mutant-redneck-hobbit, hobo: What time is good for you?

She looked at her watch. Was nine o'clock in the morning after lunch? Could she pretend Kinloch was on Dubai time?

Zoe: Whenever, I'm easy.

I'm easy. Gah! Unsend! Undo! Nooooooo! Her phone pinged again.

Man-bear, yeti, mutant-redneck-hobbit, hobo: I wouldn't say that...

She dropped her head to the desk with a thump. This was mortifying. There was only one thing for it. She would have to leave Scotland immediately. Forever. Right now.

Man-bear, yeti, mutant-redneck-hobbit, hobo: I'll see you at one.

Okay, so maybe she'd leave tomorrow... Three hours and fifty-five minutes till she saw him. Not that she was counting or anything. She glanced over her shoulder to make sure the coast was clear, and sniffed her armpit. It smelled okay but she wanted to shower again before she saw him. She'd work for the next couple of hours on the website, then go to Morag's.

. . .

AT HALF PAST TWELVE A SQUEAKY-CLEAN ZOE DROVE UP THE track to the cabin, knowing she had half an hour left to put on some make-up. She rounded the track and saw a huge white van parked up. Her stomach did several backflips and heat rose up through her body. She had to hold it together. She parked to the side so he could get out, and got out to face him.

He was on the porch, stacking the long pieces of the bed, wrapped in packing blankets, his tool belt slung low on his hips. An enormous mattress, wrapped in plastic, was leaning against the outside wall. Zoe's heart hammered in her throat. She stopped at the bottom of the steps, unsure about going any further. Rory turned.

'I was going to let myself in and make you a cup of tea, but you'd locked the door,' he said in a conversational tone.

Zoe looked away. 'Yes. I was trying to keep out undesirables.'

Rory gave a low chuckle which sent shivers of delight down to her toes. 'I'm definitely that.' He stepped off the porch and came to stand in front of her. 'Do you know where we're going?' he asked softly.

'What?'

'The storage unit. Where your furniture is.'

She looked blankly at him, her brain attempting to sort out the true meaning of his words. She fumbled in her pocket and passed him a piece of paper.

'I know roughly where it is,' Rory said. 'You can give me directions for the last bit. Do you need anything from the cabin before we leave?'

She shook her head.

'Zoe?'

She looked up at him through her lashes. He seemed nervous, unsure. Was he regretting what happened yesterday?

Oh god, was he about to let her down gently? Tell her it had been a mistake?

He swallowed. 'I, er. About yesterday... I can't...' he began uncertainly.

Tears pricked at her eyes. Shit! She couldn't cry. She blinked furiously.

'God, Zoe. What's wrong?' He brought his arms up, as if to touch her, then hesitated.

'It's fine. You don't need to say it. It was a mistake. Let's forget it ever happened and move on.'

'What? You think it was a mistake? Jesus, Zoe, not for me. It was fucking mind-blowing. I was just trying to say I can't stop thinking about it, about you.'

She stared at him.

'Do you think it was a mistake?' he asked again.

She shook her head and the tension left his face. He looked at her as if she was a dream.

'You're so beautiful,' he murmured.

She reached forward and he caught her hand in his, rubbing his thumb in slow circles on her palm. 'We'd better go,' he said quietly. Zoe opened her mouth to speak but only a whimper came out. 'If we don't go now, then I'll carry you into the cabin and we'll never leave. I can't touch you without wanting all of you.'

He let go of her and walked stiffly away towards the truck, stopping halfway to adjust himself. He glanced over his shoulder at her balefully and she giggled.

The cab of the truck felt small with Rory in it. On the passenger side were two seats and she sat in the one by the window, her bag on the seat between them. He looked at her. 'Wise decision. I need you out of reach.'

Her heart was still thumping. 'Where's Bandit?'

Rory drove slowly down the track. 'He's at home. It's not

safe to have him up here for such a long journey, and I don't want to have to fight him for your attention.' He stopped at the end of the track and signalled right. 'What was it you said? "He's the most gorgeous male in Kinloch"?'

'After Morag's son, Jamie,' she replied with a smirk.

Rory fixed her with a look. A bolt of desire shot through her body. 'I guess I'll have to work harder on changing your mind then,' he said, his expression glowing with promise as he eased the van out onto the main road to Inverness.

They didn't speak for the first few miles. In Zoe's head, however, there was constant chatter as she tried out conversation starters and found them all lacking. She sneaked glances across at him, so comfortable in his own skin. His shirt sleeves were rolled up and she had unfettered access to drool over his powerful forearms, tanned by his work outside. When the road was straight he let his left hand rest casually on his solid thigh, and when they rounded corners he turned the wheel with the heel of his right. His strength and self-assurance were the most powerful aphrodisiac she had ever experienced. She wanted to touch his arms, his legs, to feel the latent power. She wanted to get closer to him, breathe him in, taste him. She shifted in her seat; hot and bothered.

'You okay? Do you want to stop?' he asked.

'I'm fine,' she said. 'This is way more comfortable than The Beast.'

Rory glanced at her. 'You called your truck The Beast? I'd thought you'd have reserved that name for my collection.'

'Gotta share the love. Besides, after my last car, it is a beast. I keep thinking I'm going to take someone out in it.'

'So do I.' Rory smirked.

'Oi! I'm used to London driving. It's hard to adapt to the pace of the countryside.'

'It won't take long. Soon you'll be saying "och aye the noo" and eating haggis like the rest of us.'

'I don't have that stereotyped a view!'

'Kilts, shortbread and bagpipes? Isn't that what you said the website should have?' Rory asked with a grin.

Zoe blushed. 'Gotta give the tourists what they expect.'

They rounded a corner and a loud ping came from Rory's phone, lying on the seat between them. Zoe took advantage of his attention on the road to look at it. It was a text from someone named Lucy. She could read the beginning of it: *Hi, I saw your mum yesterday.*

Zoe looked left out of the window as the road straightened and Rory glanced down. She was itching to ask who Lucy was.

They continued to drive in silence for a few seconds, then another ping came through. Zoe couldn't help herself. She zeroed in on the phone in time to see another message. *I've missed your kisses.*

Rory lifted the phone and threw it on the floor by his feet.

'Do you need to get that?'

'No,' he replied curtly.

Zoe knew something was up but thought it best to stay silent. One minute he'd been fine and the next minute thunder clouds had rolled in. She was not going to ask who Lucy was. Not yet anyway. She stifled a yawn, settled herself into the seat and closed her eyes. She was going to allow herself time to fantasise.

As they ate up the miles, her mind had them married. They were driving along, her right hand resting on his thigh. Occasionally he would glance from the road to her, looking at her with smouldering intent. Sleeping in the back were their golden-haired children, William and Shona. Everything was perfect, everything was complete.

❧ 18 ❧

Rory stood in the queue to pay for petrol, looking out of the window at Zoe asleep in the van. He never knew joy and pain could be so intimately bound together. The joy of being around her, and the pain of knowing it was all going to come crashing down. Being with her was like a dream, a fantasy, something outside normal space and time. He couldn't remember the last time he'd felt so alive. But for each high there was a gut-churning low. How could he tell her who he was now? That he'd lied to her? Every moment he kept quiet only made it worse. He felt sick to his stomach. He'd do it today. He'd try to find the right words, and hope for the best.

'Hello? Earth to loverboy?' The cashier was calling out to him.

He walked forward to the counter. 'That obvious?'

The older woman gave a knowing smile. 'Love's young dream. You're a lucky man. She's a beautiful lass.'

Rory nodded his head in agreement. He saw her waking up and flipping down the sun visor to check her face. She was adorable. She was as strong as acid, etching herself onto the steel plate of his heart, condemning him to a lifetime of printing out the same image, over and over again, a portrait of a woman of fire and light named Zoe.

He paid for the fuel, strode back to the van and climbed in. She turned to him, uncertain.

'Did I...?'

He leaned back against the headrest, closed his eyes, opened his mouth, and began a pantomime snore.

She let out a wail. 'Noooooooo!'

He stopped snoring and chuckled.

She poked him in the ribs. 'It's not funny.'

He tried to evade her pokes. 'You didn't snore, you just drooled.'

Zoe moved her bag off the seat between them and prodded him with both hands. His laugh went up an octave. 'I did not. I checked,' she said with conviction. 'Are you ticklish?' He shook his head, but his face was contorted with giggles. 'Oh my god, you are!' she squealed with glee.

She climbed on top of him and attempted to wreak her revenge. He was gasping now, tears squeezing out of the corners of his eyes. He pinned her arms to her sides. She was straddling him in the front seat of the van, still fighting to free her arms. He got his breathing under control and looked at her. There was a moment of stillness, then he released her arms and pulled her mouth down to his.

Their kiss was frenzied, torrid, a tangle of tongues and need. She wound her fingers up into his hair and he dropped his hands to her bottom, grabbing it and pulling her towards his cock. She ground her hips into him, finding his hard length and circling into it. It was like he'd crashed into the surface of the sun. Light and heat ripped through him. He slid one hand under her clothes, over the silky softness of her skin, found her bra strap and unfastened it. She moaned and rocked her hips over his cock. Each time she rocked back, her bottom bashed against the steering wheel, setting off the horn.

Rory could hear beeping, people calling out, but nothing could stop Zoe overwhelming every one of his senses. He needed her naked, he needed to be inside her, he needed—

'Hey! Romeo and Juliet! Yous two in tha' white van!'

Zoe jerked her mouth away from his. She stared out of the front windscreen to the glass wall of the forecourt shop. The cashier was using the tannoy to address them, as well as anyone else within a five-mile radius.

'Aha! So yer not deaf then? Jolly good. Hows about yous take yer little love-in somewhere more private, eh?'

They looked with dawning horror at the punters standing around laughing. Zoe scrambled off him and sank down to hide in the footwell as Rory started the engine.

'Don't forget your seatbelt, lassie!' boomed the cashier.

Zoe's arm snaked up from the floor to pull it down, and Rory drove out to a chorus of claps, cheers and whistles. Zoe sat back in her seat, head in her hands. 'That was mortifying,' she mumbled.

Rory chuckled. 'Not from my perspective. It was insanely hot, and now everyone is wondering what I did to deserve you.' He smiled at her. 'We're nearly there. Can you direct me the rest of the way? The satnav lady sounds like she's channelling my old drill sergeant and I'd rather listen to you.'

Five minutes later, they drove into an industrial estate to the end where a security guard opened a gate to a yard holding shipping containers of various sizes. Zoe handed him her paperwork and he unlocked her container as Rory backed up the van. They both got out and stood looking at her life in objects.

'Is that a sun parasol?' Rory asked. 'You're a little optimistic. Have you got a bikini to match?'

'I downsized!' Zoe wailed. 'And now it looks like I'm a hoarder. We're never going to get it in the van. We'll have to come back,' she said glumly.

Rory was undaunted. He was used to thinking spatially, working in three dimensions. Here was a problem he knew he could solve. After an hour, the storage unit was empty and the van was full. He'd performed the miracle of the loaves and the fishes in reverse.

'I can't believe you got it all in,' said Zoe, shaking her head.

'I knew the hours playing Tetris as a kid were worth it. Shall we get going?'

Anticipation crackled in the air between them. Zoe nodded, blushing. They got into the van in silence and drove off, the security guard shutting the gate behind them.

BY THE TIME THEY ROUNDED THE BEND IN THE TRACK TO SEE the cabin once more, neither of them had uttered a word for nearly an hour. All Rory could think about was getting the bed made and her in it, preferably naked. He wondered if she was thinking the same thing, as she was out the van as soon as he cut the engine, dashing to the front door of the cabin to prop it open.

He jumped out and opened the back of the van, grabbing the first few boxes, stacking them high, then jogging to the cabin. As he hefted furniture and her other belongings, he thought back to the obstacle courses he did in the army. Pulling himself and others over high walls, crawling through mud under netting, swimming through pipes of black water, bursting to breathe, trying to better the time he had set before. He approached unpacking the van in the same way:

focused intensity, efficiency of movement, controlled power and speed.

In twenty minutes everything that was staying in the cabin was in, and her tent was packed away. She asked to keep the chairs and the commode, so he kept the ones she had brought from London in the van to store in the workshop, along with the sun parasol and other things she had no room or use for. He then carried in the pieces of the bed and began unwrapping them.

As soon as the first one was on the floor in the far corner of the cabin, Zoe knelt down and ran her fingers over the intricate carvings. 'It's so beautiful. Are you sure I can have it?'

He held her gaze. 'Yes. It's yours.'

She blushed. 'I've never owned anything so special in my whole life. The rest of my furniture is from IKEA.'

'Would it make you feel better if I gave it an unpronounce-able Scandinavian name?'

'Definitely.'

He paused in the middle of unwrapping the long side pieces. 'How about Sloplard? Or Murkburgerslappen?' Zoe giggled. 'Or Pantsplatnurfle? If they're no good then give Basil some random consonants and see what he comes up with.'

'Pantsplatnurfle is my favourite,' said Zoe. 'And if you ever decide you've had enough of wood then I'm sure the marketing department at IKEA would have you in a heartbeat.'

He grinned at her and snapped on his tool belt. 'Can you lift the footboard for me and I'll start putting it together?'

It was the first time he had ever assembled it. He had wanted it to be a surprise for Lucy on their wedding night. However, Lucy only liked surprises if she had planned them out in advance. She told him which ring she wanted him to propose with, and when, where and how the proposal should take place. When he'd let it slip he was making a bed for her, she didn't stop badgering him until she'd seen it. At which point her face said it all. It was never going to go with the modern aesthetic she was after.

He'd made it in the basement of the family townhouse in Edinburgh, which he'd turned into a workshop after his father had died. Looking back, he realised how pivotal that moment had been. Caught up in the chaos, disorder and earthiness of the room, Lucy must have known there was always going to be a limit to how much she could mould him into the man she wanted him to be.

As he fitted the pieces together, with Zoe helping, he noticed how perfectly he had made it. Every joint was exact. It was the opposite of his relationship with Lucy, where each crack and gaping hole had been covered with designer wallpaper. He was glad Zoe was having it. It was meant for the cabin and it was meant for her.

'This is going to be even stronger than the front door,' she marvelled.

Her voice snapped him out of his daydreams. 'I like to make things that can last generations.'

'I'll have to make sure I leave it to Basil in my will when I'm gone.'

'I forgot how much you know about the rat life cycle. At least you haven't got him a girlfriend.'

'Oh, I'm still considering it. I can't have him lonely when I'm out.'

He looked at her and she smiled back innocently.

She helped him heft the pieces of the bed together until all that was left was the headboard. He hesitated before unwrapping it, his fingers pausing on the buckle of the ratchet strap. *Just get on with it.* He tugged the straps apart and the blankets fell to the floor with a heavy thwump.

'Can you take the other end and we'll get it into place?'

There was no reply from Zoe. He held his breath.

She had seen it.

۞

'IS THAT ME?' SHE ASKED IN A HUSHED TONE, WALKING forward.

In the centre of the headboard, in the middle of the tree canopy, where before there had been a circle of unfinished wood, was now her face, her long curls waving out to join in with the leaves of the tree. The carving was of her head, neck and bare shoulders. She could have been wearing a low-cut dress, or she could have been a naked wood nymph. Sitting on her left shoulder, peeking out from behind a single curl of her glorious hair, was Basil.

A lump formed in her throat. It was like looking at her reflection staring out from a mirror of gold, a mirror that hid all your flaws and showed you the beauty often only others could see. She didn't want to believe it was her and yet knew to her soul that it was. Did he see her like that? She was beautiful, ethereal. And yet there was also a glint of humour in her expression, a Mona Lisa smile.

His face was blurry through her tears. 'Is that really me?' He nodded. 'It's incredible. Did you use a photo?' she asked, her voice a whisper.

He shook his head. 'I didn't need one. My head's so filled with you, there's no room for anything else. You're the only thing I see.'

His eyes were so bright, as if he was trying to offer up his soul to her. But there was something else too. Something desperate. She blinked, then the look had gone.

He lifted up the headboard. 'Can you hold this up for me?'

She complied, watching him absorbed in his work, his

strong hands gently tapping in wooden pins. In a painful moment of clarity she realised she had fallen into an endless abyss of love. A love she had never experienced before. No one else had ever touched her heart in this way. When they met in the courtyard, he had been a physical god. Now, that physical attraction had deepened into something else, something luminous and transcendent. She had seen his strength, his vulnerability, his humour, his creativity, his commitment to any task set before him. She knew the outer shell of his looks was just a fantastic illusion. The true treasure lay within.

When the slats were fitted, Rory pulled the cover off the mattress and they heaved it into place. The bed was vast; an entire city state. Zoe shivered in anticipation and went to the boxes containing her bedding.

She brought out a soft wool mattress protector and Rory went to the other side of the bed by the wall to help her put it on. She felt a thrill watching him. The task of making a bed so mundane, and yet with him, and this bed, in this place, it was so magical her heart almost stopped. His movements were so confident and strong, his gaze so intent.

She put the folded bottom sheet in the middle of the mattress and he took it and shook it out.

'Do you know how to make a bed properly?' he asked.

'What?'

'It was one of the first things I learned in the army. And now, you're going to learn the vital skill that has kept our country safe for so long.'

She giggled. 'Do I have to be able to bounce a bullet off it at the end?'

Rory raised an eyebrow and her heart rate spiked. 'I could bounce a grenade.'

Desire shot like lightning through her body. The skin of her breasts contracted, her nipples tingling. Nervous anticipation fluttered in her tummy, and a pulse throbbed deep inside her. She grabbed the sheet. 'Okay then, Rambo, show me how it's done.'

They both took the sheet and lifted it into the air. It billowed like a parachute above them, then settled slowly onto the bed. Rory lined it up so the crease line lay exactly down the middle, then smoothed the surface out with his big hands.

'Would you like me to get the tape measure?' she asked snarkily.

He stared at her. She looked quickly away, immolated by the fire in his eyes.

'Okay. We're going to do the corners first. Take the long bit out like this, then we're going to tuck this end underneath to make the corner neat and tight and tuck it under like so.' His demonstration was masterful.

'Oh! Hospital corners. I always do them.' She deftly tucked in the corners of the sheet on her side, as he had done. He deflated.

'Have I saved the free world yet?' she asked.

He straightened. 'Only if you can put a duvet cover on within thirty seconds.'

'You're on.' She took out the duvet, placing it the right way around on the bed, then unfolded the cover, laying it on top. She moved her head from side to side and jogged on the spot. 'Right. Count me down.' She flexed her knees, and spread her fingers, ready for action.

Rory looked at his watch. 'Five, four, three, two, one, go!'

Zoe's hands flew forward. She ran them into the duvet cover, finding the far corners and grabbing them. She then tugged them towards her down the bed and seized the corners of one end of the duvet, lifting it and flipping the cover inside out. She then bounded along the side of the bed, pulling the duvet cover down one long end, before throwing herself onto the bed and rolling over to the other side next to Rory to pull the other side of the cover down.

'Done!'

'Hang on, it was inside out to begin with. That's cheating! And you haven't done the buttons up.'

Zoe grabbed the end and fiddled with the buttons.

'Five, four, three, two, one. And we're done,' finished Rory.

Zoe threw the duvet down. 'Dammit! I would have done it in time if you hadn't distracted me.'

Rory laughed. 'I thought the roll across the bed was particularly good. It reminded me of basic training. And the forethought to already have the cover inside out was masterful.'

Zoe crawled back over the bed and threw three pillows at him followed by a pile of pillowcases. 'No creases now. I'm a princess, remember.'

She did up the buttons of the duvet, her fingers trembling. Her internal wiring was shorting out, sending surges of power through her, exploding in a fire of burning sparks. When the bed was made this was it. They were going to have sex. *Oh god. What if he doesn't like what he sees? Should I try and keep my clothes on?*

When the pillows were finished Rory smoothed out the duvet and she reached into the bottom of one of the boxes to pull out an enormous blanket. Working in the charity shop for so many years, her mother often came across cashmere jumpers that were donated but had too many holes or were too threadbare in the elbows to sell. She'd made a donation, then taken them home, cutting squares from what was still good quality, and stitching them together into a glorious soft patchwork. It had taken her years to finish and she had backed it with brushed cotton and given it to Zoe when she moved into her flat.

Zoe folded it in half and they placed it at the end of the bed.

Rory eyed it. 'Did you make it?'

'My mum did mainly and I helped. If you see some wonky blanket stitch then it's definitely mine.'

As he touched it, a thrill ran across her skin. 'It's so soft. It's beautiful.'

'Cashmere. It's the classiest thing about me.'

'Oh, I don't know about that,' he replied softly.

They were standing opposite each other, the bed between them, their eyes locked. The heat from Rory's gaze seared through her clothes, scorching her skin. The ache between her legs was now a throbbing pain. She wanted him so much it hurt.

He swallowed.

This was it.

19

Zoe pulled off her jumper and T-shirt in one swift movement, leaving her in a white bra, her nipples already hard and pushing through the lacy fabric.

A fire ran across Rory's cheeks, his lips parted and his pupils flooded black. Before her nerve gave out, she scooted across the bed and kneeled in front of him, pressing her breasts into his chest. She scored her nails through his hair, running the tip of her tongue up the length of his neck to the soft skin where it met his ear. She tugged on the lobe with her teeth.

He closed his eyes and raised his head to the ceiling, his jaw tight. 'Fuck!' he hissed, as if trying to keep his inner animal on a tight leash.

'Yes please,' she whispered into his ear.

He dropped his face into her hair, and brought his hands up around her. His touch was light as he skimmed the soft skin of her back. She spread her knees, and circled her hips into the bulge where his cock was straining against his trousers. He pushed her away, breathing rapidly. 'Zoe, you can't do that.'

She kissed her way to his mouth, pushing into him. 'Why not?' she murmured against his lips.

He held her hips firm, his jaw clenched. 'Because I want this to be good for you, and if you keep that up, you're going to break me.'

Zoe smiled against his lips. 'So how do you intend to stop me, Rory?' She ran the tip of her tongue between the seam of his lips, and rubbed her breasts into his chest.

He lifted and plopped her backwards on the bed. She shrieked with laughter as he covered her, pinning both of her legs with one of his, locking her arms by her sides. He kissed up her neck, darting his tongue out to taste her skin, sending her from squirming to soft. He nuzzled below her ear and tugged the lobe, vibrating his tongue over the soft edge. She moaned, and he hummed with satisfaction.

'This is how I'm going to stop you,' he purred.

'Well, if you insist.'

Rory chuckled. 'Oh, I do.'

He cradled her face, bringing his forehead to rest on hers. She could feel his restraint, the repressed power, and she thrilled inside. He held her reverently, kissing her, running his nose into her hairline, breathing her in. She closed her eyes and let herself sink into the sensations.

He kissed her freckles, running his fingers into her hair, cupping the back of her head as he gently brought his lips down to meet hers. He ran the tip of his tongue along her top lip, then gently sucked on the lower one. Zoe whimpered at his tenderness, the way he held her. His tongue slipped into her mouth, exploring it, tasting her, wringing out sweetness till she was dizzy.

He slowly ran a single finger down her side, skimming the curve of her breast, until he reached her bottom, squeezing it. He shifted, pulling her towards his thigh, and she wrapped her legs around it, pressing herself against the solid expanse of muscle.

She grabbed his hair, dragging him closer. His mouth was so hot. She wanted every part of him inside her. She fumbled to undo the buttons of his trousers, feeling his hard arousal. He took her hand away, up to his neck and ran his fingers down the side of her body again; long, tantalising strokes around the swell of her breast.

She whimpered, twisting towards him. He was maddeningly slow; teasing the edges of her breast, until finally he brushed across her nipple and she jerked, ripping her mouth from his and panting into his neck.

'Oh god, Rory.'

He responded to the sound of his name by locking their lips together, devouring her as he rubbed her hard nipple through the fabric. She cried out against him, alternately trying to get away and get closer, her body flooding with pleasure. He reached behind and unfastened her bra, then knelt on the bed, tearing it off and tossing it to the side. His eyes raked hungrily over her.

'You're so fucking beautiful,' he said huskily.

He trailed his fingers along her collarbone, then down her front, each hand mirroring the other, circling into the centre of her breasts, lightly pinching the nipples, then rubbing his calluses over the sensitive tips; sending intense and agonising pleasure spiralling out through her body.

She was lost to him, floating in a sea of sensory overload. Every part of her was fluid, ebbing and overflowing with sensation. He kept his hands on her breasts and dropped his head to her belly, licking her skin as her abdomen trembled under him, her breathing fitful. She felt his soft, golden curls, the hot wet heat of his tongue, the cooling air that followed it, and the sharp darts of pleasure shooting to her centre.

She grabbed handfuls of his hair, clinging to him, trying to anchor herself, to find a still point in the storm. He growled, sending vibrations through her abdomen. He licked his way to her breasts, taking a nipple into his mouth, rasping the roughness of his tongue over the tip.

Sensation was scorching through her, the insistent throbbing in her groin growing into a desperate, pounding need. She was so hot, so swollen. She bucked against his thigh, clenching it between hers, desperate for release. He pulled his leg away, unfastened her jeans, and pushed inside her underwear. He groaned as he stroked the wetness up and down the length of her opening.

Slowly and deliberately he ran his fingers to her clitoris, and she jerked, crying out. He rubbed her wetness over her nub, licking and sucking each breast in turn, as she shook beneath him.

He dipped back into her core, pushing two fingers inside her, growling as she tensed around him. Any illusion she had of control dissipated. He circled her clitoris with his thumb, inexorably increasing the speed and the pressure. She cried his name, giving her body over to pleasure, over to him.

He held behind her head and anchored his mouth to hers, swallowing the sounds of his name. Her climax began to ignite, building within her, a light getting brighter and brighter until it exploded in wave after wave of pleasure. She stiffened, her jaw locking, as the orgasm ripped through her. He kept the rhythm going with his hand, eking out every last ounce of feeling until she jerked and collapsed back onto the bed.

Her breathing was heavy, her limbs like lead. She stared at the cabin roof, the wool insulation like fluffy clouds above her. He tugged off her jeans and pants, then lay by her side, tracing her freckles.

'You're so beautiful. I don't think I could ever get enough of you,' he murmured.

Zoe flushed, seeing the intensity in his eyes, her nakedness in contrast to his clothed body. 'I haven't had any of you yet,' she replied softly. She reached down to unbutton his trousers and he stopped her, shifting till he was crouched above her, clasping her arms by her sides on the mattress. His hold around her wrists was soft, but when she tried to move, it became steel.

'Rory?'

'I can wait. I haven't finished with you yet.'

He touched his lips to the freckles at the base of her throat. Zoe felt his soft kisses, the caress of his tongue, the tickling of his hair as it brushed against her skin. He was frustratingly slow; teasing her, kissing down to her breasts and around them, but never quite reaching the centre. Her desire uncoiled itself within her again, searching for more. She moved, trying to angle herself into his mouth, a sound of frustration whimpering out, as she fought to free her arms. 'Rory, please.'

He kept her anchored to the bed and licked across the tip of one nipple. She jerked, a flash of sensation shooting down through her. He licked the other one and she cried out. Her legs were restless, her feet pointing and flexing, trying to relieve the tingles that fizzed through them. The soles of her feet were itchy, desperate to be scratched, needing a physical release of any kind. He spread one of his powerful legs across hers, keeping her still on the mattress as he took a nipple, greedily sucking on it, rubbing his tongue over it, as she panted and arched up against him.

He moved to the other breast, moving his stubble lightly across the end, taking it in his mouth as she sobbed with her need for release. Her desire was trapped within her, contained by his weight, agonising flashes of intensity rushing through her.

He released her wrists and she buried her hands in his hair, scratching her nails over his scalp and pulling at the roots. He kissed down to her belly button, swirling his tongue inside, then spread her legs.

Freed, she opened to him, panting, delirious with desire. He spread her soft lips and buried his tongue in her, humming his enjoyment. Another orgasm was building, a deep fire he was stoking with the hot and hard movement of his tongue. He held tightly behind her thighs, licking up her length, lapping at her clitoris, feasting on her. Her breath quickened and she tensed her inner muscles, chasing her pleasure. Her legs shuddered and he sped up the movement of his tongue, driving her over the edge. She screamed his name and clamped his head between her thighs, arching her back up, her body wracked with sensation. He held on, sweeping and sucking, as she convulsed, calling out his name, again and again.

Her legs fell back to the mattress, fingers fisting into the duvet beneath her. He brought his tongue to her opening and licked slowly up to her sensitive bud. She jerked beneath him, her breathing ragged, her legs twitching.

'God, Rory, I can't,' she protested feebly, her hands fluttering off the duvet then dropping back down again with a resigned thump.

He licked deliberately again, inching two fingers slowly into her. She clenched around him, spreading her legs wider, needing more. He increased the speed of his tongue, thrusting his fingers in and out. She arched back, stiffening, her arms and legs rigid as another orgasm tore through her.

She pulled at his hair, urging him upwards. He moved up beside her, stroking down her body. She stared drowsily at him, her heart overflowing, seeing her own feelings reflected back at her.

'What just happened?' she asked.

'You happened. You're incredible.'

Zoe blushed. 'And why do you still have your clothes on?' she asked, frowning.

He grinned and smoothed her hair off her forehead, damp with a thin sheen of sweat. 'I told you I wanted to make it good for you,' he whispered.

'Good? You've ruined me for bloody life. How could anyone else ever compare to that?'

Rory swallowed and blinked. 'I'd do anything for you. Anything.' There was a desperate edge to his voice, as if they were loving each other at the edge of oblivion. She stroked down his jaw, soothing him.

'Well, you can start by taking off your clothes and finishing what you've started,' she replied with a smile.

Rory knelt above her and unbuttoned his shirt. Zoe's mouth ran dry. He was the most gorgeous man she had ever known. She remembered the first time she saw him in the castle courtyard, the sight of his muscles moving as he buried the axe in the wood. And now it wouldn't just be his shirt that was off, it would be everything. Her breath caught in her throat as she watched him. He undid the last button and she gasped, her stomach fluttering. She clamped her hands over her mouth.

He stilled. 'Please tell me you aren't about to laugh? My ego was feeling quite good until about ten seconds ago.'

Zoe leapt up, sounds hiccupping in her throat. 'I'm so sorry. It's just you're so fucking gorgeous, I can't believe this is happening. And I'm nervous you won't enjoy it, and I haven't done this for such a long time, and, and—' She broke off, beginning to hyperventilate.

He took her in his arms, holding her into the warmth of his body. 'Shhh. Breathe. It's all okay. In through the nose and out through the mouth.'

Soothed by his voice and his touch, Zoe followed his directions, and her laughter slowly sputtered to a halt. She sagged and he shifted against her. She stared at him in surprise. 'You're still, erm...' she trailed off, looking downwards.

'Hard?' replied Rory. 'You're in my arms and you're naked. Of course I'm hard. You make me hard when you're fully clothed and five miles away.'

Zoe blushed. 'Maybe if I help take off your clothes, that might help my nerves?' she suggested shyly.

He nuzzled her cheek. 'I'm up for that.'

She turned her head to find his lips, their warm softness melting her to the bones. She kissed him with her soul, trying to tell him what she was too unsure to say with words. As she slipped the tip of her tongue into his mouth, she pushed the shirt off his shoulders, down and off to the bed behind him.

She ran her fingers up the expanse of his back; ripples of muscles defined by a life of work outdoors. She pressed her lips tightly against his, running a hand into his hair, pressing her breasts into the hot skin of his chest. Her heart thudded as he held her to him.

Her whole body was pulsating, pushing at the inside of her skin. She reached between them, pulling at his trousers. A tremor ran through him, but he didn't try to stop her. She undid the buttons, tugging them and his boxers away from his jutting arousal and down. She touched his cock, the skin as soft as silk, encasing a rod as hard as steel. He was huge. Her heart pounded as she stroked up the length, encircling him, rubbing the wetness at the tip over the swollen head. She didn't know how she would fit him in but she would sure as hell try.

She broke the kiss. 'Do you have a condom?'

Rory stared at her blankly, breathing heavily, his pupils big and dark. 'I didn't want to presume,' he replied. 'Do you?'

Zoe shook her head, then scooted out of his arms and off the bed. 'Luckily my friend Sam did the presuming for both of us.' She grabbed the package she'd picked up from the post office and brought it back to the bed. 'She sent us a present,' Zoe told him, opening it up.

She pulled out a box. 'You have got to be fucking kidding me.' She showed it to Rory, who laughed.

Sam had wrapped the box of condoms in white paper. On the outside, in thick black pen, she had written 'How desperate are you?' and encased the box in an entire roll of Sellotape. Zoe picked at it with her nails, wailing as she failed to find a way in. Rory took his Leatherman out of his trouser pocket. He flipped open the blade and deftly cut through the tape, passing it back to Zoe to open as he ripped his trousers and boxers off.

She excavated the box from its Sellotape tomb. They were XL sized. 'She obviously knows you well,' she said with a smirk.

Rory's cheeks burned. He took the box from her, pulled out a condom and ripped the packet open. He looked at Zoe and she nodded, watching him as he unfurled it down over his length. The sky was darkening outside and the light was getting lower, making his muscles more defined. She wanted his body on hers, to feel him inside her. She scooted back on the bed, reaching out to draw him to her. He exhaled a long tense breath.

'You're so beautiful, Zoe.'

Her heart skittered out of control. He exuded raw, unfettered masculinity. She pulled him to her, spreading her legs, angling her hips up to meet him. He settled between them, cradling her head, teasing open her mouth with his tongue. He gently nudged at her opening, pushing against her tightness.

He was so big, she involuntarily tensed, not knowing how she could take him in. He held her hips still with one hand, taking the other to stroke along the line of her jaw, soothing her, his tongue caressing her mouth. She sighed, and let him ease her into relaxation, the hot tip of his tongue trailing fire across her lips as he slowly inched his cock into her. With every lick, he pressed deeper, her muscles prickling with the sweet invasion.

He moved so slowly, so tenderly, as he filled her completely. She trailed her fingers down his back, feeling the movement of his hips, each thrust sending a tingling deep inside as she adjusted to his size. She let his kisses soften her, his breadth stretching her until she was completely wrapped around him. She clasped him to her and he stilled, his cock buried deep, his tongue in her mouth, his body on hers. She felt a fullness, a unity, an all-encompassing love.

She tensed her muscles around him and he tore his lips from hers, panting into her hair. 'Fuck! Zoe, Jesus!'

She could feel his body vibrating with the effort of holding back. He drew shallow breaths into her neck, fisting his hands into her curls, as he began a slow rhythm; withdrawing slowly, then plunging deep within her.

Zoe cried out, clawing at his back, wanting, needing more. Each thrust sent a shower of sparks through her, igniting a fire that throbbed and burned. She brought her legs over his, tucking her feet under his thighs, and raked her nails into his hair and down his spine, holding onto the rock-solid muscles of his bottom, pushing him deeper. He growled into her neck, nipping at it and thrusting harder as she brought her hips up to meet him.

She felt his restraint but wanted more, clenching as he

withdrew, dragging her pelvic floor against him. Each time he sank his cock deep, she gasped, light tearing up through her body. Another release unfurled within her, flames licking down her inner thighs and up into her abdomen. She reached between them to touch herself. She saw him watching, as her fingers circled her wet clitoris.

'Fuck, Zoe! I can't, I can't hold on,' he hissed through gritted teeth.

But she was gone, crying his name, bucking her hips up to him, her muscles spasming, her body imploding around him.

He let go, thrusting into her, roaring her name. She clutched at him, his orgasm pumping deep within her. He collapsed on top of her, fighting for breath, shaking in her arms.

He tried to move his weight from her but she clutched at him with a fierce strength, wanting to keep him inside for as long as possible. His face was buried in her neck, his hair lying like a blanket over her face. He flicked it off her and she kissed him. He stared at her as if she was the dawn of creation, the Holy Grail, nirvana. She smiled and he blinked, as if trying to reassure himself she was still there and not a figment of his imagination.

Zoe tried to speak but his weight was too much. He immediately shifted, withdrawing from her and lying on his side, head propped up on his hand. He traced from freckle to freckle down her body. She ran her fingers over the hard ridges of his abdomen, and her toes through the hairs on his legs.

She stared at him, the breath stopping in her throat. He was the most beautiful man she had ever seen, the most desirable human on the planet. Even dipping him in chocolate couldn't increase his appeal any further. That thought sent a reminder from her stomach to her brain she hadn't eaten for a while.

'Are you hungry?'

'Always,' he replied, taking her nipple in his mouth, licking it with languid strokes, his free hand rubbing the tip of the other. It hardened under his touch.

'No, I, I mean, I mean food. Do you want— Ah!' She broke off as he gently squeezed her nipple, rolling it as she writhed beneath him.

He blew a steady stream of cool air across the wet tip. 'Oh, I want to eat all right,' he promised, and reached for the box of condoms on the bed, taking out another. He took the used condom off his hard cock, tied a knot in the end and dropped it over the side of the bed onto the floor.

Zoe was confused. 'What? Again?'

Rory kissed down the centre line of her abdomen, swirling his tongue in her belly button, then kissing into her curls. He gave her a devilish smile. 'Oh yes. Only this time there'll be a bit more finesse.'

THE NEXT MORNING ZOE SAT AT HER CHAIR IN THE LIBRARY, a dopey smile on her face. It hadn't been a dream. They'd had sex. A lot of sex. Universe-shattering sex. They had continued to make love as the cabin darkened into night, all thought of food abandoned. Rory promised he would make it up to her with a meal the next night, and when he'd finally left to get back to Bandit, she had flopped back onto the bed and passed out in a blissful haze.

Now, back at the library, she mixed work and pleasure by editing the photos from the photoshoot. They went into three folders: one for the generic castle shots, one for the photos of Rory, and one for the pictures Fiona had taken of the two of them. She decided to come to the wedding album last.

The pictures of him in his kilt made her shift about on the

plastic chair, her heart beating faster. In the library, the least erotic space in Kinloch, she was feeling extremely hot and bothered. She tried to look objectively at the photos, imagining different people finding the website. What would they see?

She knew in her heart of hearts what they would see. They would see a male in his prime, a fantasy, no matter if you were young or old, gay or straight. For many, it would be a purely sexual one, as they took in his perfect form, his virility, his eyes staring out at you from the screen. For some it would be a fantasy about how they wished they looked, what would happen if they woke up one day in his body instead of their own. For others it would be a historical fantasy, a reimagining of the past, when the world was shaped by warriors, not politicians.

To her, he was everything. Strong, funny, caring, and hot as hell. She couldn't stop flicking through the photos. In the end, the homepage was entirely made up of the one of him on the battlements, sword in one hand, flag in the other. She used the one with his shirt on, but you could still see his muscular chest underneath. The main text read 'Discover the Power of Kinloch Castle'. She added more text in a block underneath, then went to the other pages she had written, adding more photos and playing about with the layout.

Finally, she came to the photos of her and Rory together. They seemed like a couple in love, a couple who saw only each other. She didn't know if she could ever use them on the castle's website. There was a rawness, an intimacy about them. Should she send Sam a photo of her and Rory in their wedding outfits? Title it 'Thanks for the condoms, look what we did today!'

She sniggered to herself. The thought of her reaction was almost enough for her to do it, but then Sam would ring her parents, they would raise their freak-out level to DEFCON two, drop whatever they were doing and drive up. So, she resisted the temptation and instead went back to the website. Rory had texted her his email address, the descriptive 'rory184@ymail.co.uk', and she emailed him a long list of questions about the history of the castle she hoped he would be able to answer. She then went online to do a more thorough search for information.

Ten minutes later she found a few references to the estate on the Highland council website. She opened the one with the most recent date on it and flicked over the text. It was a planning application for a spa and retreat centre. She scanned the details, seeing the name Stuart MacGinley, then the map of the site. It couldn't be right? The area was by the loch, and her land was right in the middle of it.

As her brain processed the information, she fell apart. Her heart stopped with a shooting pain, and her stomach rolled, trying to empty its contents. She gripped the edge of the desk, her head swimming, reading and re-reading. Trying to find a way to convince herself what she was looking at was incorrect, that she was wrong, that it was all wrong. She was falling out of a heavenly dream into a living hell, as she tried to control the mouse to print out the web page.

She stuffed her things into her bag, desperately trying not to cry, grabbed the sheet from the printer and dashed out the building. She had to get back to the cabin.

20

R ory knew his time was up when he heard the truck screech to a halt, the door slam and the sounds of her feet as she ran to the cabin, Bandit barking to greet her. He leaned forward against the kitchen units he was making, his head bowed, adrenaline surging through him.

She pushed open the door, kicked off her boots and ran to the back of the cabin to a stack of boxes. She pulled them down and rifled frantically through them. Bandit, seeing Zoe, an open door and smelling a rat, bounded in barking excitedly, running for Basil's cage. Rory bundled him out the door, and turned to Zoe. She was standing, papers strewn around her feet, her face white.

'You, you...' Her lower lip was trembling, her eyes flashing with hurt and rage, struggling to speak. 'You bastard. You lied to me. All this time.'

Rory swallowed. The speeches he had prepared for this moment vanished from his mind. All he could feel was her pain.

'You think I wouldn't find out? Put it all together? All of

this?' She threw her arms out indicating the cabin. 'I thought it was odd the rest of Willie's furniture wasn't here when I arrived, and how quickly you made everything.' She brought her fists to her forehead, then dropped them. 'You wanted to live here. Whilst Willie was down south dying, you were planning your move. I bet he wasn't even dead when you started making the front door. Then I showed up. First you won't sell me wood. Then I get your childish and pathetic attempts to hound me out, and when that doesn't work you seduce me? For what end? To move yourself in with benefits?'

He could see her fighting to hold back tears.

'This is my cabin and my land. But you just couldn't accept that, could you? You had your own plans for it. So, you stole from me. You stole my copy of the lease agreement so I had no way of proving this was mine.'

'What?'

Zoe indicated the papers on the floor. 'The lease agreement. The proof this belongs to me. It's gone. I had it with my passport, birth certificate, all my most important papers. I checked it was there after the first night when you said it wasn't my land. It was there then and it isn't there now. You're a fucking liar and a fucking thief and you need to leave.'

'Zoe—'

'Now!' she screamed.

Bandit was barking and whining outside.

'Zoe, please listen to me. Yes, I wanted to move in. I had no idea anyone would want to live here. But you did and it's yours, I accept that. I didn't take anything. I promise. I have no plans for the cabin. Please believe me.'

'Then what the fuck is this?' she yelled, tugging a sheet of paper out her bag and thrusting it at him like a knife.

He took it, scanning the page then shook his head. 'This is fucking bullshit,' he said quietly. 'And it's not going to happen.'

'Says who? You're not the boss! It's a planning application to turn my land into a bloody spa and retreat centre. How can I fight that without the lease agreement?'

He crumpled the piece of paper in his fist, walked to the Rayburn and threw it in the firebox. 'I'm going to go back to the estate office now to get the other copy. I know it's there. This application isn't going anywhere and neither are you.'

He held her gaze, seeing her uncertainty. The ground was slipping from under him. Sooner or later she was going to find out exactly who he was, but right now he couldn't leave her without a home.

'I'm so sorry, Zoe. I'm sorry for everything. There are some things I've done that I can't undo. But this is something I can fix. Can I come back when I've sorted it? Please?'

She gave him a terse nod. 'Just go now,' she said quietly.

BY THE TIME HE FINALLY FOUND HIS MOTHER ON THE MAIN staircase of the castle, he was filthy and fuming. He'd turned the estate office upside down until the room had gone from untidy to burgled and the air was thick with dust. But the papers he'd been given by the solicitor were nowhere to be found.

He stood at the bottom of the staircase, watching his mother as she glided down from the first floor. Barbara noticed him, paused to take in his expression, then continued on, unperturbed.

'Mother, when were you going to tell me about that ridiculous application? We can't apply for permission for land that isn't ours.'

She took his arm, and steered him down the long corridor. 'Darling. You said it yourself. She won't last the winter. And besides, who's to say there was even a legal agreement between

William and your grandfather? The proposals for the croft are only a small part of the plans Lucy and I have for the future of the castle.'

Rory stopped abruptly and pulled his arm away. 'Lucy?'

'Darling, that's no surprise. You know the part Lucy plays in her family's company. If you get into bed with Colquhoun Asset Management, then you, well, you know what I mean. Anyway, I know how stressful things have been for you recently, so I've been doing my bit to help behind the scenes.'

She went to take his arm again but he didn't budge.

'And by helping, you mean trespassing on Zoe's land, breaking into her home, stealing her property, removing the second copy of the agreement from the office, and going behind my back with an insane plan for a bloody spa by the loch?'

Rory was used to reading people during his army tours, but Barbara's face was impressively impassive.

'I don't know what you're talking about,' she replied smoothly. 'The estate is experiencing some difficulties, and Lucy and her family are trying to help. The land by the loch is a prime asset for development, and part of a much bigger plan we've been working on for you. Colquhoun Asset Management have had some very positive discussions with the planning board, and we believe the meeting next week is a mere formality. This is happening, darling, whether you like it or not, and I'm not going to sit back and allow it to be derailed by a cheap little tart who's turned your head.'

Rory lifted his hands as if to throttle her, hesitated, then dropped them to his sides. He was done. He'd never been able to please his father and he was giving up trying to please his mother, here and now.

'I want to make myself absolutely clear,' he said. 'I am going to get a new agreement drawn up for Zoe, and they aren't going to be leasehold, they're going to be freehold. The cabin and the land will belong to her forever and she can do what the hell she likes with it. Whatever deals with Colquhoun Asset Management you've agreed to are off, as of right now.'

'You can't do that! They've invested significant time and money into the estate. You can't cut them off,' Barbara protested.

'I can, and I will. I never wanted to go along with their ideas for the castle anyway, I did it for you and because I saw no other way. But now there *is* another way: Zoe's. I'm following her advice from now on. I don't want anything more to do with the Colquhouns or their money. I want them out of our lives for good. My future, our future, the castle's future is in my hands, and hers if she'll still have me.'

Barbara's mouth opened. Her pale skin went puce with rage. She grabbed his arm. 'You can't do this to me. I can't live here!'

Rory carefully pulled his mother's fingers away. 'We need to accept that Kinloch is our home now. This is happening whether you like it or not, and there is nothing you can do to stop me.' He strode down the corridor, her protestations echoing off the walls around him.

Rory showered off the dust from the office, redressed, and drove straight to Inverness. He went first to the Highland council offices and withdrew every application Colquhoun Asset Management had lodged on behalf of the estate, then strode along the high street for an impromptu meeting with Alastair McCarthy. He instructed him to draw up a new set of freehold lease agreements for the cabin with Zoe's name on them, and to have them ready as soon as possible. He also informed them in no uncertain terms that from now on, the only person able to speak for the estate was him.

He then went home, dropped Bandit off, picked up some supplies and drove out to the cabin. Heavy rain chilled the air and the sky was darkening with dusk when he rounded the final bend of the track and cut the engine. He could see Zoe inside the cabin, facing away from him. She was lit up by the lamps inside, her curly hair a glowing halo of light around her head.

He could think of nothing but her. She was like a virus, endlessly replicating herself inside him. Every thought he had, every movement he made, she was there. It was like staring into the sun, then away again, a spot of light still burned into his vision, overlaying itself on top of everything else he tried to look at.

And it wasn't just her beauty that captivated him, it was everything else that went with it. She was funny, sweet, resourceful, determined. Her reaction to the arrival of Basil had been totally unexpected, and she wasn't shy in telling him when he'd been a complete arse. She had left the safety of a secure job and the loving arms of family and friends to discover something about herself up here. She wasn't running away as he had always done, she was running to try and find something new, even if it meant living in a hovel in another country.

Time passed with Rory suspended in it, the rain drumming on the roof and blurring the windscreen, his mind detached from everything but her. The raindrops seemed to settle on him, drenching him in a deep realisation. He loved her. He loved every single crazy and magical part of her. A blinding pain lacerated his heart. She deserved the world. And what had he offered her? Lies.

He wanted to run. Fly to Tibet, join a monastery, hitch a

ride to Mars. Or just drive home, put his old army Bergen on his back and run north. Run till his body screamed for mercy, run until he collapsed. He started the engine. He needed to leave before she noticed the truck. Now he was a coward as well as a liar. He shook his head at himself, disgusted.

'Rory!'

He jerked up. She was standing on the porch waving at him. He cut the engine, got out and walked up the steps. Her beauty dumbstruck him.

'Well? Did you find the lease agreement?'

Rory nodded. 'It's with the lawyers. They're making another copy. It will be ready within a couple of days.'

Her shoulders sagged. 'Thank you.'

'I'm sorry. I don't know what happened to your agreement, but you've got a proper door now, so no one can get in.'

'I hope so.' She didn't sound convinced.

'You're the only one with keys. It shouldn't happen again.' Rory turned to go.

She grabbed his arm. 'Where are you going?'

'I thought, after earlier, it was best...'

'You promised me dinner. Surely that's the least you could do to make it up to me?' she replied. 'I was looking forward to something a little better than tinned soup or pasta.'

'Are you sure?'

She folded her arms but was smiling. 'Yes. I'm bloody starving.'

The light from her smile stabbed him in the chest and made a beeline for his groin. He had to tell her who he was tonight. He couldn't put it off any longer, no matter how happy she made him.

'Get yourself out of the rain. I'll get things going,' he told her, stepping off the porch and walking back to the truck.

Five minutes later she poked her head around the cabin

door. He was crouched down at the end of the porch. 'What are you doing?' she asked.

He stood, showing her the barbeque he had brought. Wisps of wood smoke curled up into the cold air.

'I thought you could do with a proper meal.'

Her eyebrows lifted. 'What's on the menu?'

'Dry-aged steaks from the estate's herd. Food miles about four, flavour out of this world.'

'Sounds amazing. When's it ready?'

'It depends how you like your steak. I have mine so blue they're practically still moo-ing. I've also brought steak knives and proper plates. There's no way I'm eating these off plastic ones. Despite what you think of me, I do have some standards.'

She grinned. 'I'll have mine rare then. I'm ready whenever you are, just give me the plates and I'll set the table.'

He passed her a box containing the crockery. 'How many do you want?'

'What do you mean?'

'How many steaks do you want?'

'Er, one? Isn't that the normal amount?' Rory raised an eyebrow. 'You may be a mountain, but I'm only a few inches taller than a normal, er, man, so one should do fine thank you very much.' She walked back to the door, and paused. 'Although, they are average-sized, aren't they? They aren't small?' she asked, sounding worried.

'I would confidently say they are *way* above average, and therefore perfectly sized,' he deadpanned back.

Zoe flushed to the roots of her hair and fled back into the cabin.

A few minutes later, Rory entered carrying a massive wooden board, piled high with steaming steaks. He kicked off his boots and put the board on the table where Zoe was sitting. He bowed deeply. 'Dinner is served.'

'Thank you, it smells incredible. Careful of the plates, I've been warming them in the Rayburn.'

Rory served her an enormous steak, then went to serve himself two even bigger ones. He looked between the board and the plate, trying to reconcile the amount of meat he intended to consume with the size of the plate that was meant to carry it. Maybe if he stared long enough, a solution would present itself.

'Oh, for goodness sake!' Zoe cried.

She pulled her sleeve over her hand to move his hot plate away and pushed the board in front of him. 'Eat.'

He gave her a relieved smile, then went to the door and put his boots back on.

'What now?'

'I forgot something. Eat, don't wait for me.'

21

Rory went back to the end of the porch. He had thought about what Zoe might have missed most about her previous life, apart from her friends, family and a hot bath, so had brought with him a bottle of Prosecco. He carefully poured her a glass, then went back to the door.

He opened it to see Zoe at the table, her head thrown back, groaning with ecstasy as she ate a piece of steak. It was the most erotic sight he had ever seen and he stood staring at her, his mouth open and his cock rigid, as the door slammed shut behind him.

Zoe's eyes snapped open in horror and she started to choke. He moved forward, one arm raised as if to thwack her on the back. She held up her hands in alarm to stop him and he stepped away.

'You okay?'

She nodded, still coughing, and gestured for a glass of water. Rory gave her the glass he was holding. She gulped at it, then coughed and spluttered even more, looking from the glass to him.

'It's Prosecco. I thought you might be missing one of your five a day.'

Zoe's coughs turned into giggles and hiccups, followed by the most enormous burp that burst out of her. She clamped her hands to her mouth as he started laughing.

'Shut up!' she finally managed.

He sat down, still smiling, and tucked in. Zoe looked at the glass in her hand. 'Don't you want some?' she asked.

Rory swallowed before replying. 'No thanks, I don't drink.'

'But what about the other week when you helped me rescue Basil from the tree?'

'Rescue *Basil*?'

'You said you were going to go home and drink a bottle of whisky.'

He grinned at her. 'That's the power you have. You could drive any man to drink.'

'As far as I know, I've only driven one man so nuts he's bought a rat to scare me away and chased a herd of yaks into my back garden.'

Heat ran across Rory's high cheekbones. 'You're right. You drive me absolutely crazy.'

There was silence, a tingling current of electricity fizzed in the air between them.

Rory swallowed. 'Is it okay? The steak.'

Zoe dropped her cutlery. 'Oh my god, yes! I'm having a foodgasm. It's the most incredible meal I've ever eaten in my entire life. If only I could eat like this every day.'

'You can. This is pretty much all I eat.'

'What? You just eat steak? For breakfast?'

'I eat other meat too, and fish and eggs and occasionally dairy, but mainly beef.'

Zoe's mouth dropped open. 'What? But you eat fruit and veg, right?'

'Nope. Plants are overrated.'

'But?' she sounded utterly bewildered. 'Bread? Cereal? Pasta? Nuts?'

'Nope, nope, nope, nope. Just meat.'

'But won't you get scurvy?'

Rory flashed her a killer smile, showing off his perfect white teeth. 'Not in the last four years.'

'FOUR YEARS? Doesn't your mother force-feed you spinach?'

'She gave up trying long ago,' he replied with a grin.

He could see her confusion and questions so decided to help her out. 'No, it's not expensive if you eat the whole animal. My food bill is less than it used to be. I'm far less worried now about cancer and heart disease than I was before, and I presume you want to know how my bowels function? They're now perfect.'

Zoe was beetroot red. 'But, doesn't it get boring?' she asked sceptically.

He looked intently at her. 'Are you bored right now?'

She swallowed, and shook her head.

They ate in a companionable silence for a few minutes. Rory mirrored Zoe's smiles, but his guts were churning. When should he tell her? And how? He kept stalling, hoping that Prosecco and the best steak in the world might soften the blow. She finished eating before him and sat back in her chair, studying him. When he finished eating she leaned forward, her elbows on the table, resting her chin on her hands.

'Okay, come on, out with it,' she said, her dark eyes pinning him to the chair. 'What's up? You look like a condemned man having his last meal before facing the firing squad.'

He swallowed and put down his knife and fork, tugging at

the top of his shirt. Anxious prickles of heat scuttering down his neck. 'I, I don't know how to explain, I've got no excuses. I should have told you weeks ago,' he began. He was desperate, haunted. He knew this was it. He was about to step off into the void.

'Who's Lucy?'

Rory's gaze flicked to the bed behind her, then back, his pulse racing.

Zoe cocked her head. 'Did you make the bed for her?'

Rory's cheeks burned. He nodded. 'But she's not, I mean that's not what I—'

'Who is she?' Zoe interrupted, taking her elbows off the table and sitting up straight.

Rory sighed, and ran his fingers into his hair. This was not going well. Zoe sat back in her chair and crossed her arms. He dropped his hands into his lap and stared at them.

'Lucy is the daughter of my mother's best friend. We grew up knowing each other but we never spent much time together as adults. When my father died and I came back to Edinburgh, Mum wanted me to settle down, marry Lucy. We got together two months after he passed away, I proposed six months after that, and she broke it off four months later. That was about a year ago. Four months ago we had to sell the family house in Edinburgh, and move to Kinloch. The bed was meant to be a wedding present, but it never got finished. She didn't want it. She didn't want me.'

'Did you love her?'

Rory nodded. 'I thought I did. But with all the upheaval in my life at the time, I think I clung to her as an idea rather than the reality. We had nothing in common. It was like we were from different planets. I think she saw me as a project. A scruffy oik who could be tidied up and tamed.'

'Being a scruffy oik is part of your charm.'

He raised his eyes to her, seeing a glimmer of humour in them. 'When she left, it was the last straw. It nearly broke me. So I made a decision to get rid of anything I didn't need, be on my own, cultivate my inner monk.'

'Did it work?'

'Until a few weeks ago. Then you showed up, and my inner monk buggered off.' They stared at each other. Rory's stomach twisted around his heart and squeezed. 'You deserve the moon on a stick,' he said, his voice cracking. 'You deserve everything. You deserve more than me.'

He stood abruptly, and began clearing the table. 'I'll wash up and get going.'

Zoe's forehead puckered with confusion. 'You're leaving?'

Rory nodded and carried what was on the table to the front door, returning to fill the kettle and put it on the Rayburn to boil.

'I'm sorry, Zoe. For everything.'

She got out of her chair. 'But what about pudding?'

His body was crisscrossed with darts of shame and desire. 'I'm sorry. I'm not the man you think I am, or the man you deserve.'

Zoe took the kettle off the Rayburn and turned him to face her. She held his hands and rubbed her thumbs across the back of his knuckles. 'I want you. Just the way you are. I'm not Lucy. I'm not asking you to change.'

'But, what if things were different, I was different?'

'You think I want a fancy-pants life? The bright lights of a city? If I'd wanted that I would have stayed in London. Sure, it would be great if the cabin had a bathroom and a kitchen, but just because I have an eye mask that says 'Princess' on it doesn't mean I want to live in a castle. I don't need that kind of bullshit in my life. Being with Prince Charming is the last thing I would ever want. I want a simple life. Here. With you.'

His insides stretched, as he was pulled apart. How could he have fucked this up so badly?

Zoe kissed him.

'I have to go,' he said, his voice taut.

She sighed, and put her arms around his broad shoulders, pressing tightly against him. 'There is one part of your body that always speaks the truth and it's telling me it wants you to stay,' she said, kissing him again. 'Why does it have to be so hard to seduce you?'

HE LOOKED INTO HER DEEP BROWN EYES. HE HAD NEVER been so bewitched by a woman. She was the perfect fit, her tall, willowy body moulding to his. Her eyes were pools of chocolate, her freckles a dusting of cocoa powder, her hair spirals of spun sugar. She was the most delicious creature he had ever known, and he couldn't get enough. Her lips were parted, and she ran her tongue across them, the movement sending a bolt of lightning straight to his straining cock. He pursed his lips and let out a long slow breath. She was impossible to resist.

He lowered his mouth to hers, the battle lost, and she sighed, her tongue darting out to meet his. He ran one hand up her back, under her clothes, and unfastened her bra. He groaned, grabbing her bottom as she ground herself against him.

All his dreams, all his fantasies, nothing ever compared to the reality of having her in his arms. The feelings blinded him. Every movement she made sent fire raging out of control through his body. No woman had ever had this effect on him. If he thought himself caught up in desire before then it was an illusion, a pale imitation, a candle next to an inferno.

As her tongue danced with his, he cupped her breasts,

rolling and pinching her nipples, feeling her tremble, pushing her body into him. Every circle she made, each time she ground her hips forward poured more fuel onto the fire. He gripped her bottom tighter, her muscles clenching as she pushed herself against him, her legs spreading to anchor the strained ridge of him between her thighs. Darts of pleasure were shooting up his legs and down his chest, coalescing in his groin, drawing his balls up tightly.

He tore her top up and off, throwing it with her bra to the floor. He raked his eyes over her, taking her in. She looked drowsy with desire, her lips pink and swollen, air rushing past them as she breathed. He was overwhelmed with her beauty.

'Jesus, Zoe.' He swallowed, his mouth dry.

He fell on her breasts, thirstily sucking and rubbing as she whimpered and clawed at him. The roughness of his tongue and his fingers rasped over the sensitive tips, and she cried out, grabbing handfuls of his hair, kneading like a cat. Blood pounded through him, he couldn't hold back much longer. He needed to taste her.

He unzipped her jeans and knelt on the floor, yanking them and her pants down her legs and off. He held her bottom, pulling her onto his tongue, pushing it between her folds, groaning as he dived into her wet heat. She bent forwards, holding onto his head for support.

'God, Rory, I, I can't—'

He spread her legs, scooped his arms under her thighs, and lifted her off the ground, his mouth still anchored over her swollen mound, his tongue inside her. He carried her to the table and lay her on it, her bottom by the edge. He reached one foot back behind him, catching the chair leg and dragging it towards him. He sat, his hands locked under her thighs, and licked up the length of her, drinking in her sweetness. His thirst for her was unquenchable. He'd found his heaven between her thighs and never wanted to leave. He lapped at her clitoris, holding her still as she shook under him.

'Rory, Rory, Rory,' she gasped.

The sound of his name sent blazing heat through him. He increased the pressure of his tongue and her cries became louder, repeating his name over and over again. He licked faster and faster, rushing her upwards, holding her as she shuddered beneath him, pulling at his hair.

Her body suddenly stiffened, her thighs clamping around his head as she screamed his name. He felt a rush of pleasure, a rush of power.

She quivered beneath him, her nails raking over his scalp. She propped herself up to look at him, her eyes dazed. 'That was the best pudding I've ever had,' she murmured. 'Now go and get the condoms.'

He got up and brought the box back to her. She was sitting on the table, her legs dangling over the edge, her wild curly hair cascading over her shoulders. She took the box from him.

'Now take your clothes off and sit down,' she instructed.

'Yes, Ma'am,' he replied with a grin.

In a few seconds he was sitting, and Zoe unfurled the condom down over his length. She stood with her legs either side of him and took his mouth in a deep kiss. He ran his hands up her back and into her hair, their tongues tangling, as she positioned herself at the head of his cock, and slowly began inching herself onto him.

He tore his head from hers, his jaw tensed, his eyes shut, and gripped the edges of the chair.

'Jesus, Zoe, you're so fucking tight,' he hissed.

She brought her mouth to his ear. 'And you're so fucking huge,' she whispered, gyrating herself deeper onto him.

He let out a tortured laugh, and cupped her breasts, pulling their weight together as he flicked his tongue back and forth over the tips of her nipples. She tensed around him, threw her head back and moaned. He hungrily sucked as she sank her weight down, taking the whole of him in. He was red hot. Blinding flashes pulsing through his body and into hers.

She tensed her inner muscles and lifted her hips, dragging them against him as she withdrew, then dropped her weight back into his lap, burying him in her. He was teetering at the edge of oblivion, his breathing ragged as he tugged on her nipple. Every movement she made was a torturous lesson in control, attempting to hold back the rushing tide, trying to give her more until the dam burst. And each time she clenched around him, another fuse was lit.

He rubbed her wetness over her clitoris, his mouth anchored to her nipple, his other hand gripping her bottom tightly. He was on the edge, his balls drawn up, his cock rigid. Every movement she made, every sound of her pleasure brought him closer to climax. She was his ecstasy, his divine bliss. He worshipped at the temple of her body, learning how to touch her, how to kiss her, responding to the subtle shifts as her orgasm built within her.

She moved faster, calling his name like an invocation. He couldn't hold back much longer. He let go of her breast, resting his forehead on her chest, his teeth gritted.

'Zoe, slow down, you have to—'

But she was gone, pounding harder onto his cock, pushing her pelvis forward, crying his name. He felt his body rushing upward, the earth disappearing beneath them. The two of them were in a rocket of sensation, flying higher and higher.

Her muscles spasmed around him and he lost control. Thrusting hard up into her, a deep and guttural sound forced itself out of his throat as the climax shattered through him. He could hear the blood roaring in his ears, feel his seed emptying into her, searing pleasure consuming him. Every part of him was light, every part of him was her.

❧ 22 ❧

Zoe woke the next morning in the middle of her huge bed, engulfed in the duvet, happiness bubbling inside her. She pushed up her eye mask and looked around. To her right the sturdy logs of the cabin wall, above her the underside of the roof, with its own duvet of sheep's wool, and to her left the rest of the cabin and the Rayburn she alternately loved and hated.

She pulled out her earplugs and listened to the sounds of the birds outside. No traffic noise, no distant aeroplanes, no sirens, no shouting, no barking, no screaming. Just the sounds and stillness of nature. This was what she had come here for. She had come for this moment. This perfect moment of peace and contentment. Warm and well fed, on the side of a Scottish hillside, in the cabin she had held in her heart for so long.

And yet her new life was so much more. Fiona, Morag, Jamie, a rat named Basil, her new job as a social media guru and marketer extraordinaire for the castle – and Rory. He had made love to her with a desperate intensity late into the night and she had fallen asleep in his arms, listening to his heartbeat

as he stroked her hair. She was drunk with remembered pleasure, luxuriating in the feelings of contentment humming
through every cell. He was now part of her very make up. He
had twisted himself around the double helix of her DNA,
creating a triple one. She could no more remove him than
breathe underwater or walk on the moon.

She sat up in bed, stretched, and swivelled her legs around
to begin the slow process of getting up. As she pottered about,
she saw the Rayburn was already filled with wood, the washing
up from last night was done. The floor had been swept and
everything was tidy. He was definitely a keeper. She made
herself some porridge and prepared to go to the library. The
website was nearly finished and she couldn't wait to make it
live. There was also a phone signal there and she wanted to see
if Rory had messaged her.

At the library she emptied her bag and switched her
phone on. It pinged happily at her with a message.

**Man-bear, yeti, mutant-redneck-hobbit, hobo:
Good morning, princess, hope you slept well? I'm
picking up some fittings for the kitchen this morning,
then I'll head to the cabin. See you later. Rory X**

Her tummy fluttered and her skin prickled with excitement. She didn't know how life could get any better than this.

**Zoe: Slept like the dead. I think you broke me. See
you later xxx**

She worked for a couple of hours on the website, until she
couldn't hold her yawns in. It was lunchtime, but rather than
visit Morag and Fiona, she wanted to get back to the cabin and
to Rory. She packed up and left the library to drive home.

Walking across the car park towards her was a striking
woman, her gaze fixed on her, and a brittle smile on her face.

Confused, Zoe glanced behind her, in case she was looking at someone else, but they were the only people there. It was starting to rain, so she quickly unlocked the truck door and threw in her bag. She was about to jump in when she heard her name.

'Zoe?'

She turned to see the woman standing in front of her. She was smaller than Zoe, older, and incredibly beautiful, with short blonde hair and piercing blue eyes. She was holding an umbrella over her head. Zoe stared blankly at her, wondering who she was, how she knew who she was, and whether she could get into her car to avoid the rain without seeming rude.

'So, you are the famous Zoe I've been hearing so much about,' she said, her face neutral. The woman's voice was soft and melodious, high cultured Scottish.

Unease crawled across her skin. The woman didn't sound particularly pleased to have finally met her. 'Er, hi?'

'I knew your mother when I was growing up. Such a high-spirited woman, just like you, and so popular with the men. I haven't seen her since she ran off with your father. How is she? Are they still together?'

A drop of icy rain slipped inside the collar of Zoe's coat and down her neck. Who was this woman, and what the hell did she want? She thought of her mother managing the local charity shop, her father working as a cashier at the bank in the next town, the love they had for each other and for her, and the sacrifices they had made.

'My parents are simply wonderful thank you,' she said artlessly, with the poshest voice she could muster. 'My father is in banking and my mother does a lot of work for charity.'

The woman looked a tiny bit put out but covered it well. 'How splendid. I'm so pleased to hear that,' she said, whilst appearing anything but. 'I've heard about your plans for the castle. The earl is very taken with the changes you've proposed,' she continued.

'Oh?' replied Zoe. How the hell did she know?

'I'm Countess Kinloch,' she explained.

Oh god. The countess? Why was she here and not in London?

'That's great,' said Zoe. 'I hope it will make a big difference.'

The woman ignored her. 'And now the estate is going to be all over social media. How very modern. Still, if Lord Kinloch agrees with such a course then there's no swaying him.'

Zoe's veneer of politeness was wearing thin. What was going on? She didn't know this woman. She wanted to get out of the rain and back to the cabin and Rory.

'Okay,' she said brightly. 'It's been lovely to meet you, but I need to be getting home now.'

She made a move to go but the woman laid a cool hand on her arm. 'A little word of advice, my dear, leave the earl alone.'

Zoe was confused. 'I've never met the man.'

The woman gave a tinkling laugh that sounded like a crystal bauble being dropped onto a stone floor. Her umbrella shook droplets of frigid water onto Zoe. 'How ridiculous. You haven't been able to keep your grubby mitts off him since you arrived.'

'The earl? Lord Kinloch? The one who lives in London?'

Her grip on Zoe's arm intensified, her fingers digging like sharp talons into her flesh. 'He doesn't live in London, he lives here. And he's my son, Stuart.'

Was the woman mad? 'I don't know anyone called Stuart.'

Her face stiffened. 'He likes to call himself Rory.'

'But, Rory's not the earl. He's just a scruffy bloke with a dog.'

The woman wrinkled her nose. 'Bandit?'

Zoe couldn't breathe. 'Rory can't be the earl, he just works for Lord Kinloch,' she stammered.

'My husband passed on two years ago and the title went to our son. He most certainly is the earl, and his future will never contain someone like you. You've outstayed your welcome and need to leave.' She dropped Zoe's arm and walked off, the rain parting before her.

Zoe bent forward, clutching at her belly, a low keening sound issuing from her lips. It couldn't be true, it couldn't. Rory worked for the estate, that was all. He wasn't an upper-class tosspot who did what they liked with no fear of repercussions. He wasn't the son of the man who had treated her great-uncle so badly. He hadn't stolen her lease and her heart. He hadn't lied to her, all the time laughing at her behind her back as if she was some sort of stupid peasant. He wasn't the earl. He couldn't be.

The icy rain battered her. It cut like knives through her body, the truth slicing with clinical clarity through the fog of her delusions. Everything had been a lie. Her dreams had been twisted into a sick nightmare by the man she had fallen in love with.

The fucking Earl of Kinloch.

She got into the truck and drove out of the car park, her breathing fractured, too shocked yet to cry. The drive to the cabin was taken care of by her unconscious mind. She was aware of none of the journey until the transition from smooth road to muddy track jolted her back into the present. She saw Rory's truck, parked by the cabin. Rage boiled up, so intense it was blinding. She saw the MacGinley family coat of arms emblazoned on the side of the driver's door, the truth hiding in plain sight, taunting her. She remembered the bull bars on the front of her truck, a ridiculous addition she thought she would never need. Then she put her right foot to the floor and drove her truck straight into Rory's.

The distance wasn't far but the impact was big. She reversed to see the entire driver's door bent in. Bandit leapt off the porch barking, and Rory came running out of the cabin. She wound down the window.

'What is your name?' she screamed at him.

His face was white. 'Rory.'

'Not Stuart?' she yelled.

Silence.

She put her foot down and floored her truck again into his. *SMASH*! The sound of crunching metal amplified the adrenaline rushing through her.

She reversed again, seeing the damage she had made. The driver's door was staved in, the bottom of the window bent, the window cracked. The coat of arms was scuffed and twisted. It was getting difficult to make it out. She wanted to obliterate it.

He ran off the porch to her truck, holding the edge of the window. 'Zoe, stop! Please, I'm sorry!'

'Say it. Tell me your name.'

'Stuart Somhairle Archibald William Rory MacGinley. I'm the Earl of Kinloch. Zoe, I'm so sorry. I was going to tell you, I just didn't know how—'

'Go! Get off my fucking land. Now!'

He paused, looking at her desperately. She revved the engine. He tried to open the driver's door but it was bent shut. He whistled to Bandit and walked around the other side, getting in and shuffling across. He reversed up the track, and was gone.

Zoe wound the window up, killed the engine and walked over the sodden ground to the cabin. Inside she sat on the sofa, staring out into space. The only time she had come close to this level of shock was when her mother was diagnosed with cancer. This hurt was different but it cut as deep. It was as if she had been ripped in two, the torn edges of her body flapping noisily in a bitter wind. She still couldn't process anything, so curled up on her side and closed her eyes, praying that when she woke up, this would all have been a terrible dream.

ZOE WAS WOKEN BY THE SOUND OF LOUD BANGING ON THE cabin door. Startled, she sat up. The cabin was almost in darkness and getting cold. How long had she been asleep? Had he come back?

'Hang on.'

Her arm was tingling with pins and needles from lying awkwardly, and she shook it to get the circulation back. She glanced at her watch. Half past three. She walked to the door and opened it.

Standing on the porch were two police officers: a bearded man who looked like he arm-wrestled bears for fun, and a woman taller than her, with her dark hair scraped back into a no-nonsense bun. Behind them was a police car and a police van.

This didn't look good.

The woman spoke. 'Good afternoon, I'm PC Ballantyne and this is PC Fraser. We're investigating several allegations. Can you confirm your name for me please?'

'Zoe Maxwell,' she stammered.

'Can we come in?'

Zoe nodded, and retreated into the cabin, her heart hammering. Was this because of Rory's truck? Had he called the police?

'Can we sit down?' asked PC Ballantyne.

Zoe nodded again, and sat at the table across from the two officers.

PC Ballantyne gave Zoe a perfunctory smile. 'We want to let you know someone has identified you as being responsible for criminal damage, trespass, theft and attempted murder. I'm arresting you for these offences. You are not obliged to say anything but anything you do say will be noted and may be used in evidence. Do you understand?'

'What? No, I don't understand. Attempted murder? You are shitting me! Theft of what? Trespass where?' Zoe replied, her voice getting higher.

'Here. You are being accused of squatting in this property.'

Her brain was pushing on the inside of her skull, lights flashing on and off behind her eyes. 'This, this is my home!' Her hiccupping breath turning into a panicked hysterical laugh. 'This is mine.'

'Do you have any documentation to prove that?'

Zoe stared at them wildly, her laughter now coming out in heaving gasps. The two PCs looked at each other. 'Are you okay, Zoe?'

Zoe shook her head violently and stood, the chair falling back behind her to the floor with a crash. The PCs came around the table towards her. She held up her hands, and staggered to the sofa, curling up in a ball, until her cries ended in tears. PC Ballantyne crouched down beside her.

'Zoe, we're going to search your property and vehicle now. Please could you give me your keys, phone, laptop and other electronic devices?'

'Why?'

'Because they may contain evidence to support the allegations. When we've done our search, and removed the property you're alleged to have stolen, you'll accompany me back to the station and we can discuss this further. Our Scene Examiners may attend the property later.'

AN HOUR LATER IT WAS DARK, AND ZOE LEFT THE CABIN with the officers. She had made sure Basil had enough food and water, and banked the Rayburn, but there was no way she could contact anyone, tell them what was going on. It was like inhabiting an alternate reality. She was starring in a TV show, which would all end happily in an hour and she could then go and make a cup of tea and move onto other entertainment.

The police officers had taken photos of the chairs Rory had given her from the castle, then put them in the back of the van. They had searched the cabin and her truck from top to bottom, and also photographed the bull bars and taken a sample of paint from the front which had scraped off the side of Rory's truck. They had then searched her, and by the time she got into the back of the police car to follow the van into Inverness, she didn't even have the keys to her own front door.

Would she ever get them back? Had he done this? Had his betrayal run this deep? The pain was overwhelming. Her love for him had expanded to fill all of her body, and now it had been ripped away, leaving a gaping hole. She desperately wanted her parents. Each time they came to her mind she flinched as if punched. She imagined what they would go through when they found out. The thought of their pain was worse than what she was going through. She had put them through enough by her sudden move up here. She knew how much they worried and how much they wanted her back home. Well, it looked like they were going to be getting their wish sooner than they had hoped. If she wasn't banged up for the foreseeable future.

She just couldn't reconcile what she knew of Rory with the

accusations against her. Squatting? He'd been furious when she'd shown him the planning application for the cabin. He had promised the other copy of the lease agreement was with the lawyer. He'd said she could have the chairs from the castle. Had he been so furious that she'd driven into his truck he'd called the police? Had she been that wrong about him? Attempted murder? Had he lost his mind? She hugged her arms across her heart, trying to find some comfort as she stared out into the darkness, the spots of rain on the window illuminated by passing cars.

When they arrived at the station, PC Ballantyne told her that due to the high volume of people they were currently processing she would have to wait in the back of the car until they were ready for her. Whilst the officer sat in the front of the car writing up her notes, Zoe took off her seat belt and lay on the back seat, running every conversation she had ever had, each encounter through her mind with a new lens. The lens that showed Rory was the Earl of Kinloch, Lord MacGinley.

Why had he lied? What was the point? *His future will never contain someone like you.* His mother's words echoed around her head. Was that it? He was using her brains without having to publicly admit he knew her? But nobody seemed to know who he was. None of it made any sense.

She forced herself to go through every moment she'd spent with him, seeing his reticence to be with her, how he had tried to talk to her, how increasingly agonised he had been. *I'm not the man you think I am. I'm sorry. You deserve more than me.* She couldn't believe he would then go back on everything he'd said, call the police? Accuse her of trying to kill him? But if it wasn't him that had done this, then who? She thought back to the library car park, his mother's grip on her arm, the look of hatred in her eyes. She remembered sitting outside the bothy with Rory, watching the sun rise, hearing the pain in his voice describing a mother who put his bullying father first. This was his mum. The woman who waved her son off to boarding school in England aged seven. The woman who wanted her son to marry someone better.

Zoe wrapped her arms tighter around her body. It must have been her who told the businesses in Kinloch not to use her as an accountant. You didn't say no to the Countess of Kinloch when she was such an ice queen. She had to get the police officers to call Rory. He would explain everything. Or would he? Would he betray his own mother to save her?

Two hours later Zoe was brought into the overly bright police station, breathalysed, searched again, and taken to the custody suite. The custody officer, a woman half Zoe's height, with short black hair, sat her down and detailed the charges against her.

According to the accuser, Zoe had broken into the castle, stolen three priceless antique chairs, was squatting in the cabin that belonged to the estate, and had tried to murder the Earl of Kinloch by driving into his truck when he was sitting in it. Zoe shook her head in disbelief. This was insane.

'Ms Maxwell, I'm reminding you you're still under caution. Do you understand why you are being detained?'

Zoe nodded.

'Do you have anything you want to say?'

Zoe roused herself. 'Yes, yes I do. This is nuts. The cabin is mine, I swear, and the chairs were lent to me. The only thing I did was drive my truck twice into the side of Rory's, but he wasn't sitting in it. You need to ring him. He'll tell you this is all a mistake.'

'Rory? Rory who?'

'Stuart something something something Rory MacGinley.

The Earl of Kinloch,' Zoe replied, the words tasting like sawdust in her mouth. 'His number's in my phone.'

She paused, remembering what she called him. 'He's not in my contacts as that,' she said, sinking her head.

'What name will we find him under?'

'Man-bear, yeti, mutant-redneck-hobbit, hobo,' said Zoe with a whisper.

The officer made a note. 'Okay, we'll do that shortly. Now, before we take you to your cell, you are allowed to contact a solicitor.'

'I don't know any solicitors.'

'Do you want to use the duty solicitor? It's a busy night so you'll have to wait a while but he will be available.'

Zoe nodded.

'Okay, Ms Maxwell, I'll let him know. Now, if you could remove your shoes, we'll take you to the cells.'

'My shoes? Why?'

'The laces. We remove anything from your person that could be used to self-harm.'

ZOE LAY ON THE BENCH ALONG THE BACK WALL OF THE CELL, looking at the ceiling, trying to make out the scratched names and obscenities. She could hear drunks singing in other cells, repeatedly kicking the doors, and smell the acrid tang of vomit and bleach. She knew Scottish winter nights were long, but this was an eternity. Stress hormones flooded through her, her heart thudding quicker and louder than normal in her ears. As the hours went by, she kept repeating to herself *'this too shall pass'* over and over again like a mantra.

Eventually the custody officer opened the hatch in the door. 'Miss Maxwell, another solicitor has arrived offering to represent you.'

Zoe jumped up. 'What? Who?'

'Mr Alastair McCarthy. From MacLennan and McCarthy? He wants you to know he's here at the request of the Earl of Kinloch. Would you like him to represent you instead of the duty solicitor?'

Zoe wavered. She was so tired and strung out she didn't want to make the wrong decision. Rory had sent help. He couldn't have been the one who called the police on her.

'Yes, yes, I'll have him instead,' she replied.

Half an hour later, a very thin old man entered the cell carrying a large leather bag. He stood in front of Zoe and cleared his throat noisily. 'Miss Maxwell, I am Alastair McCarthy. May I sit?'

Zoe nodded and scooted to the end of the bench. He slowly levered himself down, his craggy features softening. 'Ahem, I must first offer an apology on behalf of the earl. He is, ahem, extremely, ahem, agitated by what has occurred today. He is currently giving a statement at the front desk refuting all the charges made against you.'

Zoe slumped back, tears rolling unchecked down her cheeks. A clean hanky was passed to her. 'I'm so sorry,' she said.

'No, no, it is not you, ahem, who should be apologising. There will be an interview at some point in the next couple of hours which I will attend with you. It is a mere formality. After that you will be free to go.'

TWO HOURS LATER, ZOE COLLECTED HER BELONGINGS AND walked out into the reception of the police station with Alastair. Sitting waiting for her was Jamie.

He stood up awkwardly. 'Hey, Zo. You okay?'

'How did you know I was here?' she asked in a daze.

'That Rory bloke came to find Mum.'

Alastair turned to her. 'Miss Maxwell, I trust I will see you again. Under, ahem, better circumstances.'

'Thank you for all your help,' she replied.

He gave her a short nod and left.

Jamie turned to her. 'Mum's made Fi's old bed for you tonight if you want to come back to ours? Fi popped to yours earlier to fill the Rayburn and get you some clothes. She even brought your pet back with her and Mum didn't say a word, which shows how much she loves you.'

Zoe clenched her jaw shut against the tide of emotion that was pushing to get out.

Jamie's eyes crinkled with concern. 'Zoe, what's going on?'

She tried to speak but a sob burst out.

Jamie held out his arms and she stumbled into them. 'Come on, Zo, let's get you to Mum's.'

23

Zoe woke to the smell of bacon the following lunchtime. She lay in the warmth and comfort of Fiona's childhood bedroom, pulling her consciousness back into her body as she stared at the ceiling, so different from the one in the prison cell. Without allowing herself any thoughts or tears, she got up, showered, put on the clean clothes Fiona had brought her and went to find Morag in her pinny by the stove.

'Ah, there you are, my darling!' exclaimed Morag. 'Sit down and I'll get you a cup of tea. I'm making you brunch.' She put her arms around Zoe, enveloping her in a hug. 'Oh, you make me feel so small! How did you sleep? Sorry I missed you last night, I just couldn't keep my eyes open, and Jamie had to go to work so he's missed you too, and Fi's at a class with Liam, so she sends her apologies and wants you to ring her as soon as you can.'

'I'm so much better now, thank you.' She blinked away tears.

Morag sat her down in a chair. 'My poor wee lass, what a

to-do, eh? Let's get some food in you, then we can have a chat.'

Morag put the kettle on and finished making Zoe an enormous pile of bacon, eggs, mushrooms, black pudding and toast, while chatting merrily away. When Zoe was eating, she kept up the verbal barrage, ensuring all Zoe had to do was chew, swallow and nod. When the plate was clear, Zoe sat back, puffing out her cheeks.

'Thank you, Morag, thank you for everything. I feel slightly more human now.'

Morag stroked down Zoe's arm.

'I'm so sorry, love. I just can't believe Rory is Stuart MacGinley. The earl? We're all in shock. He stormed into the post office yesterday looking like the world was about to end and when he told me you'd been arrested, I couldn't take any more in.' Morag picked up Zoe's plate, put it on the side, then sat down again, fiddling with her cuticles. 'Why the secrecy? What else is he hiding? And what does this mean for the village?' She looked up. 'You know, love, it must have been him that spoke to Chantelle and Sally, told them not to use you. But I don't understand why he would do that?'

'He didn't. It was his mum.'

'Barbara? Is she in Kinloch as well?'

Zoe nodded. 'Yeah, and she doesn't much like me.'

Morag scoffed. 'She doesn't much like anyone who's not got a direct line to the queen. Honestly, her grandfather was a sheep farmer, lived in a croft smaller than yours, could hardly write his own name, and yet she acts like she's to the manor born just because she managed to snag that miserable so-and-so Stuart MacGinley. Just you wait till I tell everyone what she's done. You'll have so much work, you'll be richer than her.'

Zoe gave her a wan smile. 'Thanks, Morag, but I'm not sure I'm going to stay.'

The colour fell out of Morag's cheeks. 'No! Why not? You can't let them win!'

Zoe shrugged.

'All my life I did what I knew I should do. I never did anything crazy, never went travelling, never took drugs, never got a tattoo. I got a useful qualification, got a sensible job, never went into debt. But when Willie died, all the crazy that had been bottled up just exploded, and I ditched everything to come and live here. It's the first time I've ever done anything like this, and it's been a mistake. I should have listened to Mum and Dad.'

Morag took her hand, shaking her head vehemently. 'No, Zoe, a life half lived is a life not lived at all. And your ma's one to talk! She gave a good show of being well-behaved, especially to avoid trouble from your dragon of a granny, but *she* was the one dragging me over walls to scrump for apples, and making cider in the shed. And look what happened when your father showed up. Within a week she was off. Best decision she ever made.'

AFTER BRUNCH, ZOE WAS ITCHING TO GET BACK TO THE cabin. She needed time alone, time to think. Fiona had given Jamie a lift up that morning to collect her truck, so after assuring Morag she was okay and she'd ring Fiona, she drove home with her bags and Basil's cage on the back seat.

The cabin was quiet, left in stasis from the previous day. Rory's work looked abandoned in a hurry, the tools still lying about, sawdust on the floor. The bed was still unmade. The last time she'd slept in it, she'd also slept with Rory. She stared at the carving he'd made of her in the centre of the headboard, then took her patchwork blanket and draped it over, hiding it from view.

The police told her she could collect her chairs later, so she filled the Rayburn with wood to get it back to temperature, tidied away Rory's tools and swept the floor. She had been back less than fifteen minutes when she heard a vehicle driving up the track. She went to the window to see a tiny car driving up. An enormous man unfolded himself out of it.

Rory.

Her heart jumped, and she put her palm on her chest, as if pushing it back inside, moving away from the window. There was a knock at the door. She ignored it, rooted to the spot.

'Zoe, it's me,' he called out. 'I have the lease for the cabin.'

'Leave it outside the door,' she called back.

'I can't. I need a signature from you on both copies, one for you and one for the estate. I'll go and wait in the car and you can sign them, then I'll take a copy away.'

She heard him stepping off the porch. She opened the door, pulled the folder inside, and took it to the sofa.

She flipped through the two copies. They were different from what she remembered. These were brand new. She read the document, making sense of the legal jargon. The penny finally dropped that these were for a freehold lease. She would own the cabin outright. She could live here forever, or she could sell it and start again, put a deposit on a flat back home. Why had he done this? To finally get her and the cabin out of his hair? To say sorry? To get back at his mum? She signed both copies, put one with her important documents, the other outside the front door, then waited for him to return.

When she heard his footsteps on the porch, she opened the door a crack and looked at him.

Emotions scudded across his face. 'Zoe, I'm so sorry.' His voice was a whisper, he looked exhausted.

'Why did you lie to me?'

He paused, his jaw working but no words coming out.

Finally, he spoke. 'Do you want the long answer or the short answer?'

'Short.'

He dropped his head, sighed, then pinned her with his wolf eyes. Inside she lit up, but kept her expression neutral.

'I don't want to be Stuart MacGinley. I don't want to be the earl. I don't want to be saving an estate from the mess my father made. I don't want any of it. When I came back to Kinloch, I didn't tell anyone because I didn't want it to be real. I wanted to fix the castle and leave. But I didn't know what I was doing. Then I met you. You didn't know who I was but you still liked me. I didn't have to be the earl, just myself. Being with you was like a perfect dream, and I didn't want it to end.'

Zoe remembered laying her body and soul open to him, the intimacies they had shared. Hurt spiralled up again into anger. 'Anything else you haven't told me? Any wives in the attic, children in the cupboard, or bodies under the patio?'

Rory shook his head and swallowed. 'You know about Lucy, and that I made the bed for her. I was addicted to opiates for a year after an injury in the army. That's why I don't drink. I've killed men in combat. Lots. And... And it was my mother who told the local businesses not to employ you, who stole your lease, and had you arrested.'

'I know all this. But why? What the actual fuck have I ever done to her?'

'Nothing. You've done nothing. She's, she... It's complicated.'

'Complicated?' Zoe shouted. 'It's fucked up, that's what it is. It's toxic and I don't want anything to do with it, her or you.'

She could feel her lower jaw trembling. He was everything to her. And now?

'Zoe, I—'

'Do you have any idea what yesterday was like for me? What you and your family have done?' she asked, emotion spilling out.

Rory ran his hands into his hair. 'Zoe, I'm so sorry. Lying to you was the worst thing I've ever done. I'll never forgive myself.' His eyes mirrored her pain.

'Do I embarrass you? Am I not good enough? Are you ashamed to be seen with me?'

'No! God no. Zoe, I, I—'

'You know, just leave,' she interrupted. 'We're done.'

She closed the door, walked over to Basil's cage, gently lifted him out and took him back to the sofa. She stroked his soft warm body as her tears fell, listening to the sound of Rory driving away.

THE NEXT MORNING ZOE DROVE TO FIONA'S HOUSE AND knocked on the door. Fiona opened it, hugged her even harder than Morag had done and whisked her into the kitchen where she was feeding Liam his breakfast in a highchair.

'Zo, I am so sorry, are you okay? Sit down, this won't take a min then I'll get the kettle on. God, I swear, all men are bastards. Apart from Dad, and Dunc and Liam of course.'

Zoe couldn't help but giggle. 'What about Jamie?'

Fiona held up her hand, rocking it from side to side as if evaluating her brother. 'On balance he's a good one, but give me five minutes in his company he'll have annoyed me so much I'll be kicking his shins and flicking his ear.'

'Oh, Fi, I've never been so pleased to see him as I was the other night.'

Fiona sat, her face crumpling with a frown. 'What. A. Bitch. I can't believe anyone would behave like that! Jamie said you were arrested for attempted murder! For fuck's sake. The only people about to commit murder are me and Mum, but we don't know who to start with, Rory or his bloody mother.' She finished feeding Liam and began to clean him up. 'I just can't believe it. Everyone's in shock.'

'Fi,' Zoe began, embarrassment and hurt fighting inside her. 'I slept with him.'

Fiona lifted Liam out of his highchair, bouncing him up and down. 'I did wonder. At that photoshoot you looked so perfect together. I'm so sorry, Zo. What an arsehole.'

Zoe took a key out of her pocket and put it on the table. 'Would you be able to get this to Rory so he can pick up his tools from the cabin? I'm leaving this morning to go back to Mum and Dad's.'

Fiona stopped bouncing Liam. 'But you'll be back after Christmas, right?'

'I don't think so. I think I'm done.'

❧

RORY SAT ON THE FLOOR OF HIS WORKSHOP BY BANDIT'S bed, Bandit's head resting on his thighs. In his palm was a block of wood he was shaping with one of his small carving gouges. He hadn't spoken to his mother since returning from the police station in Inverness, and was now living in the workshop. Before he left for the station, he'd confronted her. She was unrepentant, thrusting an email at him she'd printed out from Colquhoun Asset Management, informing them they were suing the estate for breach of contract. It was only after he told her he would tell the police she'd lied to them she backed off. Every part of him was full of pain, so he channelled his thoughts into making delicate cuts in the piece of wood he was holding.

There was a knock at the door, and Bandit lifted his head. Rory pocketed the carving. 'It's open.' His voice sounded as rough as he felt.

Fiona poked her head around the door and walked in. She stood above him, holding out a key. 'Zoe wanted you to have this so you could collect your tools. When you've got them you can drop the key back at the post office with Mum.'

'Why do I need a key? Won't she be there?'

Fiona huffed. 'No. She's leaving.'

Rory jumped up. 'What do you mean leaving? For Christmas?'

Fiona thrust the key towards him like a knife. He took it. 'No, Rory. She's leaving for good.' She looked furious.

'What? When?' Icy fear was petrifying his bones.

She folded her arms across her body. 'Now.'

RORY BUNDLED BANDIT IN THE BACK OF THE COURTESY CAR he'd got from the insurance company and drove out of Kinloch. The rain lashed down, swelling the streams and sending sheets of water across the road. He tried to formulate the words he could say to her, the words that would convince her to stay but came up short with each thought.

He rounded the bend and saw with sickening dread that her truck was gone. He ran to the door, unlocked it and rushed in. His tools were by the door, the patchwork blanket had gone from the bed, Basil's cage was missing, and the Rayburn was cool to the touch.

That was it. She'd gone. He sat at the table and sank his head into his hands as Bandit whined. Could he catch her up? Not in that car. He had to ring her.

He drove up the road until he had signal and called her. It

cut to voicemail and he hung up, his palms sweating. How could he find the right words?

24

As soon as Zoe had left Fiona's house, she switched her phone off and headed south. She'd already packed up the truck the night before, and called her delighted parents to tell them she was coming home. Now she needed to get some distance between her and Rory, and if her phone was on she would be checking it obsessively to see if he'd messaged her. She drove all day, breaking only to refuel her truck, her tummy, and empty her bladder. It was seven o'clock when she finally arrived at her parents' bungalow. She stepped stiffly out onto the pavement and up to the low iron gate, pushing it open and walking along the small concrete path to the front door.

It was flung open before she could even get her key out, and she was enveloped in the arms of her parents.

'Our darling girl! You're home!' cried Mary.

'Come in, love, I'll get your bags and your pet,' said Arnold, patting her shoulder and kissing the top of her head. 'I've never met a Dumbo rat before.'

Zoe followed her parents into the house, familiarity

settling over her. She knew her surroundings and she knew her parents. There were no secrets, nothing unexpected under the stairs waiting to come out and bite her. Only unconditional love, warmth and the smell of home cooking.

'I'm so glad I'm here. What a drive,' Zoe groaned, as she took off her shoes and hung up her coat in the tiny hall. 'Can I smell lasagne?'

'Yes, darling, I made it just for you,' said her mother. 'Use the bathroom if you need it, then come on through and I'll dish up.'

Zoe went to the toilet and washed her hands, then walked through into the kitchen and sat at the small round table as Mary filled her plate and Arnold brought her bags in. He put Basil's cage on the floor by the back door and took a bottle of Prosecco out of the fridge, presenting it to Zoe as if he were a wine waiter.

'Would madame like a glass of fizz?'

'Yes please. That's exactly what I need right now,' replied Zoe with a sigh.

He uncorked the bottle and poured her a glass as her mother set a steaming plate of food in front of her. 'Here we go, darling,' she said. 'We're so glad you're home. Now things can go back to normal.'

WAKING THE NEXT MORNING IN HER OLD ROOM, SHE WAS drowsy with nostalgia. Memories of the latter part of her childhood, post her mother's diagnosis, after her time in Scotland with Willie floated around her, faded, and tinged with a sense of separation. They belonged to an old life, a distant one, one that didn't fit any more. It was like finding your favourite blanket from childhood and discovering it was smaller than you remembered and didn't smell right.

Last night she'd been glad to be back with her parents. She was safe within the walls of their home and their love. But now, did she want her life to go back to how it was? Was normal what she really wanted? Scotland seemed so far away, as if in another universe. But it was a universe of adventure, wide-open spaces, old friends and a man who had thrown her life upside down.

She took out her phone and switched it on. Beeps and pings filled the room as her home screen lit up like a firework show. Her heart rocketed into her throat as she opened a text message from Rory.

Man-bear, yeti, mutant-redneck-hobbit, hobo: I came to find you but you'd gone. I'm sorry for everything. You deserve more than I gave you, and I've got what I deserve. There's only one other secret I kept from you, because I didn't want to scare you off. I know it's too late now, but I need you to know. I love you, Zoe. My heart is yours and will be forever. Safe journey, Rory X

She stared at the screen, reading it over and over again, memories fluttering across her skin like butterfly kisses. He loved her. And she knew she loved him, at least the version of him she had known until a couple of days ago. But did she want him after everything that had happened? Did she want a life that involved the castle and his mother? She couldn't reply until she'd got her head straight, and that process would involve her best friend, Sam. She sent her a message, got out of bed and wandered into the living room to find her parents reading the papers.

It was such a familiar scene and tears welled up. Her dad got up and sat her on the sofa next to her mum. 'I'll put the kettle on,' he said, walking out.

Mary put her paper down and pulled Zoe in for a hug. 'You've had quite the adventure up there, my darling.'

Zoe nodded into her mum's shoulder. 'It was certainly that. I ended up being arrested for attempted murder.'

Mary sat up, staring at her with shock and disbelief. A loud crash came from the kitchen.

'Only a mug. Hang on, don't start without me,' Arnold called through.

Zoe disengaged from her mum's arms. 'It's okay now. I'm sure I'll find it funny in about ten years.'

Arnold came back into the room. 'I'm afraid tea will have to wait. If I don't find out what's going on, I might drop the kettle, and I'm allergic to boiling water. What's gone on, love?'

Zoe told them about meeting Rory, about their agreement for him to do up the cabin in return for her doing the website and marketing, about how she didn't know who he was, and what happened when she found out. She didn't tell them everything, but there was enough for them to read between the lines. When she finished speaking, they both sat back as if they'd survived a tsunami and needed to catch their breath.

'Well,' began Arnold, 'I didn't expect that.'

Mary shook her head. 'This is to do with me and Barbara, love, not you.'

Zoe sat up. 'What?'

'You know I always said the earl was a bully? When I was growing up, Stuart MacGinley was a force of nature. He was about ten years older than I was, and acted like the entire world was his for the taking, whether it wanted to be taken or not. Everything he wanted, he got. It didn't help that he was good looking and could be very charming—'

'Not as good looking or charming as me, mind,' Arnold butted in.

Mary looked at her husband. 'My darling, it's not possible for anyone to be as wonderful as you.'

Her parents smiled at each other and Zoe rolled her eyes.

'Anyway,' her mother continued, 'if he didn't get his own way then he could turn nasty. In my twenties, he took an interest in me. I avoided him like the plague, but Kinloch is a small place, and I couldn't avoid him forever. Barbara was much younger, about nineteen at the time I think, and she'd set her sights on him. She wanted to be the one who finally got him up the aisle. She saw me as a threat, and became obsessed with finding ways to get me out of a picture I didn't even want to be in. She made me into her nemesis, which was ridiculous as I didn't even want Stuart. It got totally out of hand. Rumours started, things went missing, and fingers of blame were pointed at me. I could never prove Barbara was behind any of it, but the more I protested my innocence, the worse it got. It got so bad I prayed for some kind of deliverance.'

'And that was when your knight in shining armour strode down from the glen. A man with rugged good looks, the brain of Einstein and the body of a god,' Arnold proclaimed before turning to Zoe. 'That was me, love.'

Zoe giggled. 'Did you challenge him to a duel?'

'I did not have to resort to violence,' her father replied. 'It wouldn't have been a fair fight anyway. He may have been the size of Goliath, but I was David.' Arnold thumped the middle of his chest, causing him to cough. 'No, your mother and I ran off into the sunset on the number 42 to Inverness, and took the train south. Happy ever after. The end,' he finished with a flourish.

'Well, that helps explain why his mum went to such lengths to try and get rid of me. I hope I never see her again,' said Zoe.

'You don't have to see any of them ever again if you don't

want to, darling,' assured Mary. 'And if Rory's anything like his parents I don't want you anywhere near him.'

ZOE SPENT THE NEXT COUPLE OF DAYS RESTING, THINKING about Rory and re-reading his text message. Was he like his parents? From what he'd told her, he'd spent most of his life trying to run away from his family, not emulate them. Fiona had messaged her every day, trying to encourage her back to Scotland. Fiona didn't do subtle, but her messages made Zoe feel loved, and she missed her friend.

Wanting a change of scenery, she left the house one morning to walk to the high street to do some Christmas shopping. Everything about the urban environment was so planned, so ordered, so manmade. The pollarded trees, the identical houses spaced evenly out. The concrete, tarmac, metal and paint. And the noise. It was so bloody noisy. She flinched at the squeal of brakes from the buses, the roar of cars so close to the pavement, the sounds of voices in all directions. She'd looked around a couple of shops before the music and crowds had got too much, then ran back to her parents' house. She craved the quiet and the openness of the Scottish country-side. Could she go back to a life in London she never really wanted in the first place?

THREE DAYS AFTER ZOE RETURNED FROM SCOTLAND, SAM finished her block of filming on the soap and was free for the Christmas break. Zoe put on make-up, skinny jeans and a black lace top and took the bus into central London to meet her in one of their old haunts. Sam was late as always, and Zoe sat at the bar, glugging her glass of Prosecco and fidgeting with her bag. The place was packed. Groups of people were out for Christmas drinks and had cranked their partying level up to the max. It was as if she was in the middle of a well-groomed mosh pit, assaulted by glossy hair, cloying perfume and stumbling strangers. She used to love the buzz of nights out, but now it all jarred. She felt awkward, out of place, hemmed in. Someone bumped into her, spilling her drink. She put the glass on the bar and wiped her hand on her jeans. She couldn't do this any more, she needed to get out and ring Sam.

'Babe!'

Sam was pushing through the crowds towards her, arms thrown wide. Thank god she was finally here.

They hugged each other, jumping up and down and laughing with joy. Sam held Zoe at arm's length and looked her over. 'I'm just inspecting for vermin. Do I need to check for lice as well?' Zoe shook her hair at her and Sam leapt back in mock horror. 'Get away! Don't infect me with the countryside.'

They sat at the bar to catch up, but hadn't been chatting long when they were approached by two men: city boy clones with slicked-back hair, sharp suits, big watches, and even bigger egos. They had tinsel draped around their necks. The leader zeroed in on Sam. 'Hey, are you Bethany? From *Elm Tree Lane?*'

Sam tossed her blonde hair back. 'I'm incognito. Here you can call me Sam,' she replied, preening at the recognition.

'Fuck, man, I knew it was you. Didn't I say it was her, Brett? Can I get a selfie?'

Zoe stepped down from her stool as Sam's number one fan muscled in to take her place. Brett, the wingman, held out his hand to Zoe. 'Hi, I'm Brett.'

'Zoe.'

She took it and he pulled her in for a kiss on the cheek, then broke away with a chuckle. 'Sorry about that, you're just well fit. We've just had our Christmas bonuses. Mine's fucking huge.'

Zoe stood with the bar digging into her back, forcing a smile as she was assailed by Brett's aftershave, the stench of Jägerbombs, and the details of just how enormous his bonus was. Every part of her was screaming to get away. But wasn't this the definition of a good night out? Drinks, loud music and the promise of sex with strangers?

Sam clutched her arm and leaned in to whisper in her ear. 'Are we having fun yet?' she asked sarcastically. She tugged Zoe away from the men. 'Excuse me, gentlemen, such a pleasure, but we need to powder our noses,' she said, winking at them and dragging Zoe towards the toilets.

The door shut behind them with a bang, muffling the sounds from the bar. Sam went to the mirror, pouting at her reflection. 'Well, I've never had that before. When I turned down the offer to autograph his dick, he offered me his right hand to sign so he'd think of me later when he jacked off. Charming.'

Zoe gave a shriek of horrified laughter. 'Oh my god, is this what being famous is like?'

Sam grinned. 'Nah, they're just pissed. Most of the time it's fine. I tie my hair back and put sunglasses on and no one bothers me. Anyway, pleased to be back?' she asked mischievously.

Zoe nodded vigorously. 'Yes, it's so great,' she said, her forced smile starting to hurt.

Sam narrowed her eyes. 'I can tell... Did you get my package?'

Zoe blushed. Sam folded her arms in front of her chest. 'Aha. So, tell me. What on earth are you doing in the trenches of sexual desperation, suffering the likes of those two idiots when you could be banging Thor in your shed?'

Zoe's blush spread down her chest. She stared at the floor. 'He lied to me about who he was, so I left. It's complicated.'

'Who is he then? Some local crim? The village idiot?'

Zoe shook her head. 'No, he's the Earl of Kinloch,' she mumbled.

Sam stood in stunned silence as the music from the bar pulsed through the door to fill the void. 'What? The actual Earl of Kinloch. The one with the castle?' she finally managed.

Zoe nodded.

'And he's single?'

Zoe nodded again.

'And he likes you?'

Zoe nodded.

'Has he told you he loves you?'

Zoe nodded imperceptibly.

'What? Fuck's sake, Zoe! Then why are you here?'

'I told you, it's complicated,' she said, her face twisting with pain.

'Try me.'

ZOE WOKE THE NEXT MORNING AS HER MUM BROUGHT IN A cup of tea and a package that had arrived in the post from Morag. She placed them on the bedside table and kissed her forehead.

'You get up in your own time, love, I'm glad you've finally seen Sam,' said Mary, leaving the room and gently closing the door behind her.

Zoe sat up in bed. Last night she had felt so out of place, like she was in an alien world. It had been amazing to see Sam, but as for everything else, it wasn't what she enjoyed or wanted any more. And despite the messages Sam had sent her in Scotland, begging her to return to 'civilisation', last night she had insisted Zoe go straight back up. Her parting words ran around Zoe's head on a circular loop.

You've always wanted this. Scotland is where you belong. Go back and be happy.

Zoe slurped some hot tea, and picked up the small parcel. It was from the post office, and the handwriting was Morag's. There was an object inside, about the size of a clementine, wrapped in tissue paper with the words 'for Zoe' written in pencil on the outside. Her pulse raced as she pulled off a strip of Sellotape and opened it up.

It was a small carving, slightly larger than a walnut, of a heart surrounded by oak leaves. The detail was exquisite. It was so fine and so carefully made it looked as if it had been crafted by woodland fairies. On the back were inscribed the words: 'Zoe, my heart is yours'.

She held it in her hand, rubbing her thumb gently over the words, her eyes pricking with tears. He had made this for her. Could she forgive him? Could she live with the thousand tonnes of baggage he came with? She sighed. Did her heart belong to him as his did to her? She picked up her phone. She needed to speak to Fiona.

25

Rory stood at the end of the great hall. Before him swirled a sea of people dressed up to the nines in their best kilts, tuxes, dresses and jewellery. Their eyes were bright, their cheeks reddened by alcohol and excitement. For the first time in decades, the castle felt alive. Putting on a Christmas ceilidh was his coming out party. A way of introducing himself to everyone and showing to them, and himself, that he was here to stay. He'd arranged with the landlord of the only pub in Kinloch to put on a bar at one end of the hall, and had paid for a ceilidh band at the other with yet another credit card.

His mother had refused to attend.

He had spent the first part of the evening meeting and greeting everyone. Trying to memorise their names, and what they wanted from him. He thought back to Lucy and how she would have loved this. She would have been in her element. On the arm of an earl, and finally seeing him inhabit the role he was born for. When she left him, it had broken his heart. He didn't resent her decision. He was grateful she'd recognised they weren't right for each other. The acute pain of her loss was infinitely preferable to the chronic pain he would have lived with if he'd married her.

He put the brakes on his memory trip and realised that thinking of her and that time had absolutely no effect on him any more. He tried another memory on for size and found it equally unmoving. He thought back to the depths of his despair and just felt sadness for the man he was then and the way he had suffered. He realised that Lucy had gone from his heart, burned to ash by the fire that was Zoe.

She had crashed into the waters of his life like a meteorite. Scorching through the sky and vaporising his sea of tranquillity. His feelings for her blinded him. She consumed every part of his body, mind and soul, drawing him into her endless light. But he knew with a dull certainty that if she had stayed, sooner or later the lure of city life would have come calling, like a tune you can't get out of your head, an itch that can't be scratched away.

What could Kinloch offer someone as mind-blowing as her? A crumbling castle serving dwindling numbers of tourists, an economy built mostly on jobs done far away, and a small-town mentality where everyone knew your business. She deserved more than he or Kinloch could ever offer, and he would rather live with his soul ripped out than have hers one day yearn to leave. Her happiness meant infinitely more to him than his own.

The band was warming up for the ceilidh, and people drifted to the sides of the room or paired up. As he turned away a flash of red snagged the edge of his vision and his head jerked instinctively towards it.

Standing at the far end of the hall – Zoe.

As their eyes locked, lightning arced through him and

blood roared in his ears. He blinked rapidly, trying to convince himself the goddess gliding towards him was real.

It looked like she had floated down from heaven, then been poured into a dress designed to send men to hell. It was black as sin, hugging her perfect curves and ending just above her knees. As she walked, the skirt split up the side, revealing a glimpse of her long, creamy thighs, kissed with freckles. Lust punched him in the groin.

Her hair was braided and pinned up, but with enough escaping curls for people to know she was a firework. He tried to move but his feet were rooted to the spot, his breathing ragged, a fire of love and want and need raging through his body. She smiled at him, and ran her tongue out to lick her bottom lip nervously.

She reached him and he drowned in the liquid warmth of her eyes. 'You scrub up well,' she said with a smile. 'I was looking for my scruffy boyfriend but he appears to have been replaced by James Bond.'

His throat constricted with emotion.

'Aren't you going to say something?'

'You're here. You came back,' he said hoarsely.

She took one of his hands in hers. 'And I'm staying. If you'll have me?'

He nodded and swallowed. 'I'll take whatever you want to give,' he whispered.

'You can have my heart,' she said softly.

The dam broke and he wrapped his arms around her, burying his head into the side of her neck, kissing up her jawline until he found her mouth, losing himself inside her with a groan. 'I love you, I love you, I love you,' he murmured between kisses. 'Oh god, Zoe, I love you.'

She stroked his hair, as if soothing a wild animal. 'Rory, maybe this can wait?'

He looked up. They were standing in the middle of the hall on their own, everyone watching with smiles on their faces. The silence was broken by the sound of the band's bass player playing '*Bow Chicka Wow Wow*' for their benefit. The room erupted with laughter, cheers and wolf whistles.

Rory's face flushed almost as much as Zoe's and he whispered in her ear. 'You make me forget which planet I'm on.'

He ran his fingers up and down her spine, revelling in the discovery that her dress was completely backless. 'Or maybe they've just noticed half your dress is missing.'

Zoe giggled. 'It's Fiona's. She bought it to wear for her husband.'

'And then, nine months later, their baby arrived,' he replied drolly. He kissed her earlobe, in no hurry to leave the dance floor, impervious to the uproar they were creating. 'What you're wearing isn't a dress,' he murmured, grazing his hand down to cup her bottom. 'It's just a scrap of material in my way. And in about five minutes, I'm going to remove it with my teeth.'

Zoe shivered. 'Can we dance first please?'

'One dance. Then we're leaving.'

'But isn't this your party?'

'They'll be fine without me.'

'Come on, at least two dances? This is my first ever ceilidh.'

'One. And that's my final offer,' he replied, reluctantly releasing her.

The fiddler played a chord.

Rory bowed deeply. 'Would you give me the honour of the first dance?'

Zoe nodded shyly, and he led her into position. 'I don't know what to do,' she whispered.

He squeezed her hand. 'Don't worry. They have a caller and they'll talk us through the steps.'

The caller had a microphone, a twinkle in his eyes, and the vigour of a man at least half his age. He made a beeline for Zoe, using her for the demonstration, complete with eyebrow wiggles and ostentatious fanning of his brow for comic effect that had everyone howling. At the end of his performance, he led her away, walking on tiptoe, his finger held up to his mouth telling his audience to shush until Rory tapped him on the shoulder and reclaimed her.

By now Zoe was puce with embarrassment. Rory bent down to her ear. 'You're even more gorgeous when you're ruffled,' he whispered, nuzzling her neck.

The music started and the dancing began.

Despite his assurances they would leave after one dance, as he whirled her around the floor, his heart overflowed with her happiness. One dance turned into two, two into three. He wanted everyone to know that the most intoxicating woman in the world belonged here, by his side. Finally, there were no secrets between them. She knew every part of who he was and she still wanted to be with him. Eventually she begged to sit down and rest.

He led her to a chair in the corner of the room and pulled it out for her, facing her away from the hall. He then grabbed one for himself and sat opposite, lifting her feet into his lap and slipping off her pumps. He kneaded the soles of her feet and she groaned.

'Thank you. I feel like Cinderella after her first ball.'

'Did you have fun?'

She smiled at him. 'I had the best time ever.'

He massaged her ankles, kneading up her legs. 'The night's not over yet,' he said softly.

Her eyelids fluttered as if she wanted to close them. She swallowed. 'Do you want to leave?'

He nodded, suddenly uncertain. Would she still want him at the cabin? 'Where do you want to go?' he asked quietly.

'Home. Our home.'

Emotion rushed through him again, obliterating his ability to speak.

'Although, I got a lift here from Fi and I've had a few, so I wondered if you knew of a handsome man who doesn't drink who might be able to put me to bed?'

He couldn't reply, but he could act. He grabbed her shoes, then scooped her out of the chair and into his arms.

'Rory! What are you doing!' she said, starting to giggle. 'I'm too heavy! Put me down!'

'Excuse me, coming through,' he boomed as he ploughed his way through the crowds.

'Rory!'

He stopped and raised an eyebrow at her. 'Would you prefer I put you over my shoulder? I've done it before and I'd quite like to do it again. Only this time I'm going to take a bite out of your peach of a bottom.'

She attempted to look sternly at him but her eyes were sparkling. 'You wouldn't dare.'

He hoiked her over his shoulder as if she weighed nothing and continued walking, nipping at her bottom as she shrieked. Everyone around them burst into whistles and applause.

❧

THE CABIN WAS WAITING FOR THEM, LIT BY TWINKLING fairy lights. Earlier, as Zoe was driving up from London, Fiona had lit the Rayburn and Jamie had collected her chairs from Inverness police station. By the time she arrived in the late afternoon, the cabin was warm, and all she needed to do was settle Basil and unpack her bags before getting a lift with

Fiona back to Morag's for her fairy-tale transformation. Cinderella had gone to the ball, found her Prince Charming and spent the evening dancing in his arms. Now they were alone, and the magic had gone from enchanting to alchemic.

It took them five minutes just to get in the door. Eventually Zoe tore her mouth from his and turned her back to him, shaking as she fumbled to get her key in the lock. He covered her from behind, kissing her neck, as he ran his hands inside her jacket, sending trails of fire across her bare skin. He found the button of the halterneck and undid it, pushing the front of her dress down, growling as he cupped her breasts.

She let her forehead rest on the door, gulping in air as he grazed the tips of her nipples with the calluses on his palms. Flashes of intense pleasure shot through her, and she pushed back into him, anchoring his hard length in the crease of her bottom and squeezing against it. He pushed the hem of her dress up, stroking over her sodden underwear.

'God, Zoe. You're so fucking wet,' he growled.

He slipped his finger under the elastic and slowly pushed it inside her, up to the hilt as she trembled in his arms. He added another, and slowly and deliberately drove them in and out.

'Zoe. Open. The. Door,' he hissed between thrusts, as she moaned, her muscles squeezing around him. She managed to turn the key and they tumbled into the cabin. He shut the door behind them, pushed Zoe up against it, pulled her jacket off her shoulders to the floor, then stood back, staring at her.

She felt faint from the intensity of his gaze. His eyes were burning, fire running across his high cheekbones, his full lips parted. He lifted the fingers that had been in her up to his mouth, and sucked hungrily at them. A spasm of need ripped through her, and she reached for him. He interlocked his free hand with hers, gripping her tightly, holding her up, as he angled his body away. Then he traced a wet path over her breasts, circling them, grazing her hard nipples, pinching them as her head dropped forward.

'Rory, god, Rory, please,' she begged, not even knowing what she was asking for any more, except release from his exquisite torture.

He nuzzled her face, coaxing it up, his hot breath on her forehead, her nose, her cheek. His lips finally found hers, binding her to him as he plundered her mouth with searching sweeps of his tongue, his other hand rolling her pebbled nipples. Licks of fire shot out across her skin. She was rushing towards a climax, her body fizzing and expanding, like a shaken bottle of champagne.

He let go of her breast and pulled her dress to her waist, hooking his thumb under the side of her pants and dragging them down her thighs. He drew away and rested his forehead on hers.

'You taste so sweet. God, I love you.'

Before she could reply, he dropped to his knees, tore her pants off, and spread her legs. She held onto him to keep herself upright as he licked his way up her inner thighs and flicked his tongue once over her clitoris. She jerked as the pleasure ricocheted through her body. He did it again and she cried out. There was no way she could remain standing. As if he could sense her onrushing climax, he brought his arms up underneath her thighs, holding her, as he clamped his mouth to her and began a relentless assault with his tongue.

She fell back against the door, letting her weight rest between the hard wood behind her and his strong arms beneath her. She pulled at his hair as the waves came faster and faster, closer and closer together. She could hear her voice crying out his name, see lights colliding and splitting behind her eyes. He hummed into her and the vibrations tipped her over the edge. She ground herself into him, as the orgasm obliterated her, slamming her body with wave upon wave of overwhelming pleasure, rolling on and on, battering her until she fell forward, delirious. He let her fall over him, then stood, carrying her over his shoulder to the bed and gently laying her down.

She stared up at him in wonder. He was a completely different species from any other man on the planet, like a pirate king who'd sailed in from faraway lands. He pulled her dress from where it had bunched up around her waist, up and off, then lay beside her, tracing and kissing her freckles.

'How come I'm naked and you're fully clothed? Again,' she asked groggily.

He raised his head. 'Well, on balance, most of the time I take my clothes off in front of you, you laugh,' he said with a grin. 'So, it's safer for my ego to remain dressed.' He went back to kissing her, roaming his hands over her with long, languorous strokes. 'Anyway,' he continued. 'Your body is beautiful, a miracle of nature. Mine's just a bloke's.'

Zoe sat up, pushed him onto his back and loosened his tie. 'I disagree. I think you're incredible. In every way. I've never met anyone like you before. I—' she broke off blushing.

'You what?' he asked, tilting her chin up.

She ignored his question and continued with his clothes, undoing his shirt and pulling it off him. She wanted to tell him that she loved him, but the words seemed too inadequate, too small to express the enormity of her feelings.

'You can say whatever you like to me, Zoe, you can tell me anything.'

She shook her head and undid the buckles of his kilt, opening the fabric and tugging it away. 'So, it's true that real Scotsmen are naked under their kilts?' she said, taking his hard length and stroking up and down.

He hissed a long, slow breath out. 'Do you think you can distract me like that?' he asked, squeezing his eyes shut.

'Yes. Is it working?'

Before he could answer, she leaned forward and sank her mouth down onto his cock, sucking him in deeply. He reacted as if he'd been shot, crying out and pulling away. 'Jesus Christ. Holy shit, Zoe, I was not expecting that.' He knelt on the bed, his hands fisting into his muscled thighs.

She crawled towards him. 'Would you like me to do it again?'

He looked desperately at her. 'Yes. No. Er. Not now. You're not going to distract me,' he said, sounding utterly flustered.

She licked her lips. 'I think I'm going to easily distract you.' She grinned and moved forwards.

In a flash she was on her back and he was on top of her. 'Really now?' he said, arching an eyebrow. 'I think we know how threats like that end.'

She giggled helplessly as he locked her arms by her sides, kissing and nipping down her neck until he reached her breasts. He licked from one nipple to the other, sucking on them and tugging them into his mouth. He pushed her legs apart and settled between her thighs, grinding his hips into her with slow, insistent circles.

Her giggles turned into gasps as she writhed beneath him, throbbing heat pooling between her legs, desire uncoiling itself again within her. He lifted his head. 'So, what did you want to tell me?' he asked, huskily. He flicked his tongue over her nipple and she moaned.

'I might be persuaded to talk if you were inside me,' she murmured.

'That can be arranged,' he replied, reaching for the box of condoms by the side of the bed. He knelt between her legs, ripped open a packet and rolled one down over his cock. She opened her legs wider, tilting her hips up to him. He propped himself on his elbows, his chest hovering just above her. He kissed her lightly.

'As you were saying?' he whispered.

'You're not inside me.' She frowned with frustration, and reached between their bodies.

Quick as a flash he moved, fixing her arms to the mattress. He rolled back on top, and the tip of his cock nudged at her opening. She bucked up to meet him and he moved away.

'Are you trying to drive me crazy?' she hissed at him.

He kissed her till she whimpered and nudged inside a little deeper. 'I'm just returning the favour,' he groaned.

She could hear his breathing changing, as he strained against the desire to bury himself inside her. He kept pushing in an inch, then retreating, as her muscles tightened around him. He brought his fingers down to her clitoris, rubbing her juices over the swollen nub, kissing her deeply. Sparks were shivering down her legs to the soles of her feet and up her chest to her throat. She was drowning in the middle of an ink-black ocean at night, fighting for air as shooting stars filled the sky, raining light down onto her.

He stared at her with passionate intensity. She felt the unbreakable connection between them. His cock nudged, rubbed and tormented her, as his fingers brought her towards another climax. His hand moved faster. Thunderclouds built, the wind picked up, and electricity rushed through her body. Rory was the storm, his eyes the lightning, his breath the wind. She was battered by desire, completely at his mercy.

Her legs widened, preparing to take in all he could give, pulses of energy building for a cataclysmic release. Her love for him, the words she wanted to say, bubbled up, pushing before them an unstoppable force of emotion. She couldn't contain it any longer.

'I love you,' she cried. 'I love you, Rory.'

His eyes widened and he plunged into her, stretching her, filling her, completing her. She stiffened and shattered into a million pieces of light, as her orgasm ripped through her body. She clenched her inner muscles tighter around him, the pleasure rolling through, wave after wave, exploding out through her skin, through the top of her head, obliterating her. He cried out above her, his own release pumping into her, as he gasped her name over and over again.

She had never experienced anything this intense before. The loss of all perspective, all rational thought, all sense of self. It was as if she had experienced the birth and death of the universe, the whole of time and space experienced in one perfect moment.

The sensations subsided and she drifted back into her body. The love she had for him overwhelmed her, pushing itself out in tears.

'God, Zoe, what's wrong? Did I hurt you?'

She shook her head. 'No, no you didn't,' she sobbed. 'It's just I love you so much.'

He rolled onto his back, pulling her with him and held her tightly. 'Not as much as I love you,' he replied.

He lent down and kissed her gently. 'I'm sorry for everything, Zoe. For what I did, for how my parents treated your mum and Willie, for what my mother did to you. I've spent my whole life chasing love and acceptance in all the wrong places. I should never have expected my parents to behave differently, to give more than they did.'

She pulled back from him, frowning. 'Stop that right this second. Now you listen to me, Rory lots-of-unpronounceable-Scottish-middle-names MacGinley, every child deserves unconditional love from their parents. It wasn't your failing, it was theirs.'

. . .

SHE WOKE THE NEXT MORNING TO A MUG OF TEA BY THE side of the bed and Rory behind her, kissing her neck and stroking down her body. She had never felt so present before, so complete.

'I love you,' she said happily.

He lifted his head to nuzzle her ear. 'Are you talking to me or the tea?' he asked, suspiciously.

She giggled and turned to face him. 'It's a close-run thing, but you can bring me a mug of tea, and a mug of tea can't bring me you. So, you're always going to come out on top.'

He kissed her. 'You're all my Christmases and birthdays rolled into one.' He swallowed, and a cloud of worry drifted across his face. 'Are you sure you still want me if I lose the castle and don't have a penny to my name?'

Zoe cupped the side of his face. 'I fell in love with a man who didn't have a castle and looked like he lived in a hedge. Nothing's changed. And we'll find a way to make it work, whatever happens.'

She grinned mischievously. 'Although if Brad Bauer shows up, he might give you a run for your money. Do you think we should put some posters of him around the cabin? I know how much you want to be like him.'

Rory raised an eyebrow and she let out a shriek of laughter, disappearing to hide under the covers. He burrowed in after her and trapped her under him, their faces almost touching in the half light of their duvet cave. He brushed her lips with a tender kiss. 'I love you, Zoe,' he whispered. 'I want to make you so happy Brad Bauer wouldn't stand a chance.'

She wrapped her arms around him. 'That sounds like a good plan to me.' She sighed happily, pulling his mouth to hers.

❦ 26 ❦

After a leisurely morning in bed, Rory reluctantly allowed Zoe to drag him out so they could go to Morag's for a late lunch. Before they'd left the castle the night before, he had brought a small bag with clean clothes with him from the workshop, so after washing on the porch he dressed in a slightly rumpled shirt and a pair of smart trousers. Zoe looked him up and down and raised her eyebrows as he brought out a comb and attempted to drag it through his damp hair.

'Are you trying to impress someone?'

He felt the heat in his cheeks. 'I want to make an effort. It could take years to get in Morag and Fiona's good books.'

Zoe wrapped her arms around him and hugged him tightly. 'It's going to be fine. If I'm happy, they're happy.'

He stared into her chocolate brown eyes as his heart burst its banks. She had brought him to a river, the border between two countries, the boundary between two lives, taken his hand and walked him over a bridge he never even knew was there.

His life was the same but different. Forever changed, forever better. The castle, his mother, Lucy, memories of his father, the wars he'd fought, everything that had weighed down on him for years was now gone. He was lighter, calmer, free.

He stroked his thumb over her adorable freckles, as if reassuring himself she was actually in his arms. She was everything he never even knew he wanted or needed, and so much more.

'I should be scared by how much I love you,' he said. 'But I'm so happy right now, there's no room for anything else.'

She smiled and reached up to kiss him. 'I'm sure there's room for a couple of steaks.'

∞

ZOE EXPERIENCED A MIX OF HEART-POPPING PRIDE AND overwhelming shyness arriving at Morag's back door, her hand encased in Rory's. The door was flung open by Morag, dressed to the nines. She craned her neck as she looked up at them. 'Ah, there you are. I don't know whether to bow or curtsey.'

Rory blushed. 'Please don't do either, Morag.' He bowed low and presented her with a dusty bottle of wine he'd taken from the castle cellars.

Morag whistled. 'Well, this didn't come from Lidl.' She looked up at him. 'Thank you, love. Very lah-di-dah. I fear it's wasted on the likes of us.'

Rory smiled. 'Not at all, and I'd reserve judgement until you've tried it.'

'Well, I'll take one for the team and make sure I get the first glass, eh?' Morag joked, giving him a nudge. She dragged them into the small kitchen which was filled with the mouth-watering scent of roast beef. 'I hope you're both hungry, I've got half a cow in there, and even our Jamie looks daunted.'

Fiona came into the kitchen and gave Zoe a hug. 'How you doing? Recovered from last night yet? You danced so much you couldn't walk by the end,' she finished innocently, before collapsing into fits of laughter.

Morag batted her daughter's arm. 'Oh, leave them alone or I'll tell them about your courtship of Duncan.'

Fiona's eyes were dancing. 'Fair point, we are in polite company after all. Come on, let's get you out of Mum's hair,' she replied, leading them through to the sitting room where Jamie and Duncan sat, Liam on the floor between them playing with his toys.

Duncan and Jamie stood up as Zoe introduced Rory to them. Fiona, caught in the middle of a sea of tall people, pushed them back into chairs. 'Sit down, you're making me feel like a bloody munchkin,' she complained.

Jamie sat back. 'Height of a child, maturity of a child, mouth of a sailor.' He sighed, shaking his head sadly.

Fiona threw a sofa cushion at him and he laughed.

'Shut it, you big lump, you're always going to be younger than me,' she replied good-naturedly. 'Now, Zoe, Rory, what can I get you to drink?'

ZOE SAT BACK ON THE SOFA NEXT TO RORY, HIS THUMB moving in small circles over the back of her hand, as the conversation flowed around her. Fiona and Jamie were the siblings she never had, and Morag was her second mum. This wonderful family, that had been so important to her at the most critical part of her childhood, were once again surrounding her with love. The sense of belonging, of finding her true home were back and amplified. This was where she belonged.

And the love Morag and her family had for her was willingly shared with Rory. She sneaked glances across at him; his powerful thighs pressing against hers, their hands intertwined, his brilliant smile. To begin with, he'd been shy and slightly awkward. But now his face was dazzling. So open, so bright, so at ease. Morag and her family had welcomed him as if he had always been there, the past completely forgotten, his mother never mentioned.

When Morag called them through to the dining room, they sat down with a collective and reverential silence as they beheld the beef joint sitting in the middle of the table.

'Bloody hell. I'm glad I've got my fat pants on.' Jamie whistled.

They held hands and closed their eyes. 'Dear you upstairs,' Morag began. 'Bless this family and bless this meal. Thank you for Zoe, and for bringing Rory into our family. Thank you for Duncan, who takes Fiona off my hands every two weeks, and for whoever you're lining up to take our Jamie out from under my feet. Thank you for Liam, and if it isn't too much trouble, I'd be much obliged if you could make his first word Nana. Keep safe in your love the ones who are no longer with us. Amen.'

A squeeze rippled through everyone's hands, Zoe squeezing Rory's extra tightly, then they opened their eyes.

'So, Mr Earl, Rory love, would you do the honours?' asked Morag, handing him the carving knife.

He stood up, towering over the table. He swallowed and smiled hesitantly. Zoe's heart burst with happiness.

'Thank you, Morag. How hungry is everyone?'

'Fat pants!' cried Jamie.

'Me too!' said Duncan and Fiona at the same time, and the table dissolved into laughter.

The afternoon passed in a warm haze of good food and good company. Rory got into a long and technical discussion about electrics, as Duncan and Jamie argued between themselves about the best approach to wiring the cabin, and Fiona and Morag wanted to hear all about Zoe's plans for the castle and how the website was coming on.

Talking about it, she realised how excited she was about making it work, how passionate she was about taking on such a big project and making it her own. There was no guarantee of success; in fact, she knew all too well how precarious the situation was, but the uncertainty and the challenge were part of the adventure. For the first time in her life, she was following her own path, charting her own future, supported by the man she loved. She was truly living, and she had never been happier.

THE END.

❀

THANK YOU SO MUCH FOR READING HIGHLAND GAMES! Rory and Zoe return in Hollywood Games. Fancy a sneak peek? Here's the prologue and first chapter!

HOLLYWOOD GAMES

PROLOGUE

THE SCOTTISH HIGHLAND INSTITUTE OF TARTAN Excellence in Los Angeles, known to locals as 'LA Shite', had never before hosted a celebrity of this calibre. Situated in a small strip mall in the Valley, its only claim to fame came three years ago when a minor TV starlet, high on meth, stopped to ask for directions. Now, Hollywood's biggest and brightest star was naked on the floor of its conference room.

The chairman and sole staff member, Hamish, had been approached a few weeks before by a tall thin man with a straggly beard that reached the middle of his chest. He was dressed in a long dark robe that marked him out as a priest of some kind, but there was no aura of the divine about him. He smelled of decay and debauchery, and his eyes had the bleak, inescapable finality of a black hole. He may have appeared to Hamish like an emissary from hell, yet he'd promised him heaven in the form of a movie megastar and a quarter of a million dollar hire fee. All Hamish had to do in return was create a family tree linking the man back to Robert the Bruce, sign a non-disclosure agreement, and disable the smoke alarms. That, and split the fee with the so-called priest, and throw in a case of whisky.

Hamish had promised not to enter the room, but as the pungent smoke seeped under the door like marsh mist, he crept to the back of the building. He stood on top of a dumpster, and peered through the gap in the small window he had insisted stay propped open for safety/snooping purposes. Inside, the most famous man in Hollywood was sitting on the floor, naked except for a length of tartan fabric draped over his equally famous manhood. The priest was waving a bundle of smoking leaves above him, chanting indecipherably, with the cadence of a song by the Wu-Tang Clan. He stopped the incantation with a jolt and raised both hands.

'It is as I have foreseen.'

The seated man swayed, as if he'd just stepped off a sailboat and was trying to remember the floor was no longer moving. 'Tell me what you see.' His voice was excited, but distant, as if he were in a trance.

'I see trees of green,' the priest continued. 'Red ro—'

'Red hair! I knew it! Tell me more.'

The priest cleared his throat. 'She is a wild woman of Scotland. Her hair is red and curly. And she is brave.'

The man on the floor nodded as he swayed, making 'hmmhmm' sounds of satisfaction.

'You have been married across multiple lives.'

'Knew it,' the man whispered.

'I see a bear. You will fight it.'

Hollywood's most famous head jerked up. 'Are there bears in Scotland?'

'A man-bear,' the priest replied smoothly. 'A man with the heart of a bear. You will defeat him and claim the ultimate prize.'

The nodding recommenced. 'Yeahhhh.'

'Her spirit is waiting for you. She approves your vision.'

The nod turned into a shake. 'No. She's real.' The man thumped himself hard in the chest. 'I feel it here.'

'Her *spirit* is real—'

'No. *She's* real. And when I'm in Scotland, I'm going to find her.'

CHAPTER ONE

THIS WAS IT. SHE WAS GOING TO DIE.

Zoe gripped the steering wheel of the hire car, her knuckles white. She'd made a rash decision and it looked likely to be her last. Fat flakes of snow slapped angrily against the windscreen. The storm screamed around her. Death would come from slipping into oncoming traffic, or by flying off the road down the side of the mountain. She stared ahead, following the tracks of the cars in front. She'd never driven in

snow before and wasn't sure of the rules. Was the logic backwards, like for skidding? Did you have to speed up in snow
rather than slow down? Her jaw set with determination. A
snowstorm was nothing. She'd drive into an active volcano if it
meant today she'd get to be with with the hottest man she had
ever known.

Two months earlier she'd left her job, her friends, her
family to build a new life in the Highlands of Scotland. She
moved into a dilapidated cabin left to her by her great-uncle,
chasing a childhood memory of open spaces and freedom. It
was the craziest decision she'd ever made, and seemed doomed
to fail. Then she met Rory. Six foot five, shaggy blond hair,
arctic blue eyes, and the body of a god. The Earl of Kinloch
was scruffy, sexy, and all hers. A week ago she'd gone back to to
England to spend a quiet few days over Christmas with her
parents. Now she was rushing back to be with Rory for
Hogmanay. But when her flight from London that morning
had been cancelled, she hired a car. Her love for him had made
her defy her family, common sense, the weather forecast and
an airline. She was now willingly driving into a Scottish blizzard with no phone signal, no emergency supplies, and no plan
B. Used to a four-wheel drive truck, her five-foot-ten frame
was now squeezed into a tiny car. A car that was white. *White –
in a fucking blizzard!* She was a snowball with headlights, sand-
wiched between lorries, counting down the seconds on her
life.

As daylight faded, she drove into the Highlands. The roads
became smaller, steeper, snowier. Soon there were no tyre
tracks left to follow. She had to rely on guesswork, hope and
prayers. Her forehead prickled with sweat. Chasing the man of
her dreams had led into a living nightmare. She shivered with
fear, struggling to see past the swirling snow as it thumped on
the windscreen. There was no space left in her brain to lust

after Rory or curse her own stupidity. Every synapse was focused on keeping her alive.

Soon it was dark, and she was the only vehicle left on a road that had disappeared. She slowed to a crawl, heart pounding as she drove up the last mountain before Kinloch, the wind buffeting the sides of the car. At the top of the glen, she skidded. Her foot slammed onto the accelerator with fright, taking her out of the skid into a half slide down the winding road. Her cabin was a few miles out of the village, hidden down a dirt track, and she nearly missed the turning. She yanked the steering wheel to the left as she saw it, hit the brakes and came to a grateful stop, buried in a snowdrift. Switching the engine off, she shook with adrenaline, gulping in air as she oscillated between laughter and tears. She was alive. She'd made it. Now she just needed to get her bags, make it down the track, and into the arms of the love of her life.

She pushed open the door into the howling storm. The wind whipped stinging snow into her face. She walked carefully, head bent, the darkness lit by the torch on her phone. The potholes were hidden, and she stumbled, pushing on until she rounded the last bend. Through the flurries she could see her little cabin gently illuminated by the battery-powered lights inside. There wasn't any electricity, running water, bathroom or phone signal, but the roof, windows and door were secure and it had a wood-fired Rayburn stove. It also had a huge bed, which hopefully contained Thor's better-looking brother. He was the entire reason she'd just driven into the next ice age.

Zoe reached the front of the cabin, and saw with lurching horror her truck wasn't there, which meant neither was Rory. She faced the full brunt of the storm as it shrieked from the loch towards her. Where was he? Could he not make it up the hill from Kinloch? Had he come off the road? *Shit, shit, shit!* She hurried up the steps to the porch that ran along the front edge of the cabin. She needed to get inside, change into wellies and waterproofs, then head back out to try and discover what had happened.

She fumbled to unlock the door, threw her bags and herself in, shut it behind her and rested back against it, eyes closed in relief. The solid wood muffled the noise outside. Everything was warm and still. She drew in a breath, smelling the familiar scent of woodsmoke. She was home. She opened her eyes then blinked rapidly. Home wasn't quite as she remembered.

The sparsely furnished cabin had been transformed. In the far right-hand corner was now a boxed-in bathroom; above it, a large hot water tank. Pipes ran down the side wall to the Rayburn stove, now surrounded by kitchen cupboards, from the bathroom at one end to the front wall of the cabin at the other. There was a sink and draining board built into the worktop, with a wooden draining rack mounted above on the wall, and a large freestanding fridge freezer. Had he got her water *and* electricity?

She saw a switch on the wall, just inside the front door. She pushed it up. Lights went on around the cabin. She flicked it off and on, as if daring the miracle to repeat itself, then went to the kitchen and opened the fridge. It was full of food, milk and a bottle of Prosecco. Zoe's heart squeezed. He had done all of this for her. At the sink she turned on the taps, noticing a smaller one to the side, with a note by it. *This is for drinking. More info on the table.* She poured herself a glass of water, then went to read what Rory had written.

WELCOME BACK, PRINCESS.

If you're reading this then you arrived safely. I've filled the firebox of the Rayburn, but fill it again as soon as you get in. You have limited

289

electricity coming off two solar panels by the outhouse. There is a battery, but don't go power crazy. I've dug out under the porch and filled it with wood so we won't run out. There's still plenty on the deck and I've covered it with a tarp to protect it from the snow. Drinking water is the small tap on the side of the sink. Basil is fine and has missed you, but not as much as I have. There is a surprise for you in the bathroom. It's not the most romantic present, but I think you'll like it. I wanted to be there when you arrived, but have to go back to get a bag of grit. I'll be there as soon as I can.

Rory XXX

ZOE PUT DOWN THE NOTE AND WENT TO CHECK ON THE cage in the corner of the cabin, where Basil, her big-eared, fluffy little Dumbo rat, was sleeping. She then went to see her new bathroom. An enormous two-person shower ran down the left-hand side; a long shelf at hip height along the back wall; a built-in sink, with a huge mirror on the wall above; a heated towel rail on the side wall, and under the window, a toilet. However, this was not a compost toilet as they had planned. This toilet was flushable. Rory had stuck a note on the seat. *Who said romance was dead? Your surprise is a septic tank. Only put down loo roll and what comes out of you. Rory XXX.* She blinked back tears. He was the most incredible man she had ever known.

But he wasn't here. He was stuck on the road or back in Kinloch. And her parents... *Oh god*, what had she done? She leaned on the edge of the sink, her head light. What the fucking fuck had she done? She looked up, the mirror reflecting her horror back at her. By the time she'd felt brave enough to ring her parents about driving up after her flight was cancelled, there was no phone signal. They would now know the plane hadn't taken off and would be panicking. And

Rory? She'd rung him north of Manchester and promised she'd stop if the roads got bad. But she hadn't. She'd pushed on. And for what? The people she loved most in the world didn't know if she was alive or dead. She hung her head. She needed to go back out into the storm, make it up the mountain until she found a signal, and let them know she was okay.

She wrapped up, grabbed a powerful torch, and opened the door into the storm. It assaulted her as she stepped out of the cabin and she staggered. The snow had piled in drifts onto the porch, covering the tarpaulin protecting her wood supply. She stepped gingerly down the steps, reached the ground and sank into snow that fell into the top of her boots.

She forged ahead, hunched over. The biting wind slapped her with ice each time she tried to look up. When she finally got to the main road, she only knew it was there by the absence of trees, and the giant snowball that was her car. She shone the torch left and right, peering into the darkness. No vehicles had passed since she'd stopped. The snow was too deep for anything other than a tractor or a snowplough and was showing no signs of abating. It was suicide to try and walk the distance needed to get a signal, and she'd already used all nine of her lives on the drive up. Her mother would be having a fit. And Rory? *Fuck!* It might be days before she could get out, or anyone could get to her. Her throat tightened. How could she have been so selfish and stupid?

By the time she got back to the cabin her tears were frozen, her fingers numb. She hung her clothes to dry in front of the Rayburn, put on her pyjamas, and made herself dinner on the stove top. She was meant to have arrived that morning, spent the day in bed with Rory, then driven into Kinloch to celebrate Hogmanay with Morag – her mum's old school friend and Zoe's second mum – along with Fiona and Jamie, Morag's children and Zoe's closest friends in Scotland. That was never going to happen now.

Exhausted, she lay on the bed, listening to the screaming wind. Hopefully the storm would have passed by morning and she could get out to find a signal.

On the edge of sleep, she heard a thumping sound outside on the porch. She sat up, alert. There it was again. She shrieked with joy and shock, switched on the lights, ran across the cabin, and threw open the door to let in an extremely cold Rory and a mountain of snow. He was dressed in ski boots, ski pants and a long jacket with an enormous rucksack on his back. Ice was encrusted in his hair and his lips were blue. Her very own yeti had found his way through the snow to her.

She threw her arms around him and kissed his frozen lips. 'Oh my god! How did you get here? Did you drive?' she asked.

Rory rested his forehead against hers and let out a sigh. 'I skied. It took bloody hours getting here from Kinloch.'

He shuffled off his backpack and it hit the floor with a thud. 'What were you thinking? You could've died!'

Zoe swallowed. He was right. Hot shame burned through her.

Rory turned away and tugged off his jacket, ski pants and socks. A T-shirt and long johns clung to the muscled outline of his body. He shook his head. 'I'm just glad you're alive.'

'I'm sorry,' she began, trying to keep her voice steady. 'You're right. I didn't think, and I had no idea what I was driving into. You know more than anyone how impetuous I can be.' He gave a huff but his features were softening.

She picked up his jacket, ski pants and socks. They were soaked through. She hung them over chairs in front of the Rayburn.

'I've never seen a storm like this before,' said Rory quietly. 'Slates were flying off the castle roof when I left.' He sighed.

'I'm going to take a shower.' He stopped by the bathroom door. 'Er, would you...'

She looked up, a spark of hope in her chest.

He stared intently at her. 'Would you like to join me?'

HOLLYWOOD GAMES RELEASES APRIL 4TH. PRE-ORDER YOUR copy now at mybook.to/HollywoodGames

REVIEW HIGHLAND GAMES
WRITE A REVIEW & MAKE MY DAY!

Writing a review is absolute gold for an author. It helps people find our books, and lets us know which bits you particularly enjoyed and connected with.

Knowing what you love helps me plan future stories, as ultimately, I'm writing for you! No matter how long or short your review, it is so appreciated. You can review Highland Games on Amazon, Goodreads, BookBub and anywhere else you like!

Thank you so much,

PRE-ORDER HOLLYWOOD GAMES

Liked Highland Games? The sequel, Hollywood Games, is available for pre-order now. Want more of Zoe and Rory? Want to meet Zoe's best friend Sam? Rory's best mate Charlie? And want to see what happens when Barbara's credit card is declined in Lidl? Order Hollywood Games today!

mybook.to/HollywoodGames

⚜

HOLLYWOOD GAMES
Brace yourself, Scotland. Hollywood's coming...

Rory's found the love of his life but can he be sure Zoe feels the same? What can he offer her when his job's on the line, and his mother's out to destroy her? When Hollywood superstar, Brad Bauer, shows up wanting to film Braveheart 2 at Kinloch castle, it seems like the answer to all his prayers. However, there's a catch.

Zoe's had a crush on Brad since she was a teen. Now he's here, hotter than ever, and convinced he was married to her in a past life. As Hollywood descends on the tiny village of Kinloch, it's not just the castle that's under siege.

A mystical holy man, a sexy starlet, an intense megastar and a couple pushed to the edge. Can Rory navigate the glitter storm and keep his eye on the prize, or by saving the estate, is he about to lose the best thing that's ever happened to him?

☙❧

Pre-order   Hollywood   Games   now   at mybook.to/HollywoodGames

Can't wait to read Hollywood Games? The prologue and first two chapters are available exclusively for newsletter subscribers. Sign up now to read the hot and heavy start to Hollywood Games, plus a whole lot more...

www.eviealexanderauthor.com/subscribe/

NEWSLETTER SIGN-UP

Newsletter goodies are waiting just for you...

In my newsletter you get Evie news before anyone else, as well as exclusive content. Newsletter subscribers are my extra special friends, and get everything from 19,000 words of steamy deleted scenes, the start of books not yet published, extracts from my current works-in-progress, and bonus epilogues.

Hop aboard the Evie Express and sign up for my newsletter today!

www.eviealexanderauthor.com/subscribe/

SEX INDEX

(AKA THE GOOD BITS)

If you fancy re-reading the steamier moments from Highland Games, then here we have my amazing new idea – a sex index! Enjoy...

Page 179 – Four-poster Foreplay
Page 201 – What time is it? It's sexy time...
Page 229 – Pleasure for pudding
Page 273 – Coming home

And if that wasn't enough, don't forget I've got nineteen thousand words of super-hot deleted sex scenes available exclusively for newsletter subscribers... If you want some extra Zoe and Rory action, then get yourself signed up today!

www.eviealexanderauthor.com/subscribe/

ACKNOWLEDGMENTS

Even though Highland Games is dedicated to Pash Baker, I'd also like to thank her here. This book, and in fact the entire Kinloch series wouldn't exist without my amazing friend. In the summer of 2019 she helped me extricate myself from a situation that was crushing my soul. Once out, she told me I had to write for half an hour a day and send her what I'd written. I started in June, and by the end of October, I had two hundred thousand words that became Highland and Hollywood Games. Pash is my alpha reader, my sounding board and my ultimate cheerleader. I could not have done it without her.

When I wrote the words 'The end' in the autumn of 2019, I should have ended with a question mark, not a full stop. The Highland Games you've just read is verrrrrrrrry different from my first draft. Helping me batter it into submission in the nicest possible way, has been an army of truly wonderful readers and writers. I am indebted to my first beta readers. They taught me so much about writing and how to hone my craft. Thank you especially to Julia, Kelly, and Margaret, who have been with me from the start, and become such incredible friends. Margaret deserves a medal for reading this book at least fifty times over the last two years, and spending far too much of her precious time making me laugh and helping me fix the seemingly unfixable.

Thank you to my outstandingly supportive friends, in particular Ali, Dilara, Jacqui, Linden, Sarah and Satz. Thank you for reading my early drafts and always believing in me, even when I don't believe in myself.

A huge thanks goes to my editor, Aimee Walker. I am truly blessed to have her. She is an incredible editor and a phenomenal human being. She has my back and keeps me steady, steering the good ship Evie in the right direction, no matter which storm I have accidentally blundered into.

I'd also like to thank two Mikes. If you ever want an absolutely brutal assessment of a romance novel, then you need to send it to 'Indent' Mike or 'Storage Yard' Mike. One is a six-foot-six, skinhead, ex-copper crime novelist, and the other is a six-foot-two, professional copywriter who writes novels about the horrors of World War One in his spare time. Neither of them had read a romance novel until Highland Games... Their comments and suggestions were not always easy to hear, but they made this book infinitely better and I am incredibly grateful to both of them for their insights.

My team at Emlin Press: Victoria, Mandy and Taryn. Thank you for doing everything I can't, won't, or don't have time for. Thank you for tolerating my foul mouth, and laughing at my unfunny jokes.

To my cover designer Bailey McGinn, thank you for designing the perfect cover for Highland Games. I love it!

My family of course gets a special mention, in particular the two people who suffer the Evie Experience on a daily basis. Husband, you are the best decision I have ever made. Elway, you are the best luck I have ever had. I love you to the end of the universe and back.

And finally, before I dissolve into an emotional puddle, I want to thank YOU! Yes, you the reader. Because, really, at the end of the day, every word I write is for you. So thank you for letting me introduce you to Zoe and Rory, and I can't wait to bring you more adventures with them and their friends in 2022!

Evie ♡

Ps - I love love LOVE hearing from my readers so please get in touch via email or social media to ask me anything or just tell me about your day!

ABOUT THE AUTHOR

Evie Alexander is the author of sexy romantic comedies with a very British sense of humour.

She takes a method approach to her work, believing her capacity to repeatedly fail at life and love is what has given her such a rich supply of material for her writing.

Her interests include reading, eating, saving the world, and fantasising about people who only exist between the pages of her books. She lives in the West Country with her family.

RESOURCES

My editor is Aimee Walker. Find her at www.aimeewalkerproofreader.com

My cover designer is Bailey McGinn. Find her at www.baileydesignsbooks.com

My author photos were taken by Mark Karasick. Find him at www.markkarasick.com

Find me at www.eviealexanderauthor.com and on social media!

THE KINLOCH SERIES

Highland Games

Zoe's given up everything for a ramshackle cabin in Scotland. She wants a new life, but her scorching hot neighbour wants her out. As their worlds collide, will Rory succeed in destroying her dream? Or has he finally met his match? Let the games begin...

Hollywood Games

The only way for Rory to save Kinloch castle is to throw open the doors to a Hollywood megastar. However, Brad's plans for Braveheart 2 involve Rory's girlfriend as well as his home. By saving his estate, is Rory about to lose the love of his life?

Kissing Games

September 2022

Valentina's worked without a break to craft her acting career. But she's never truly lived, and everything's built on a lie. Bodyguard Charlie's done too much living, and is on the run from his demons. Can they let go of the past, or will their love remain a Highland fling?

Musical Games

Early 2023

After lying to a Hollywood megastar, Sam needs Jamie to write an album with her in one week. He's got the voice of an angel and the body of a god, but fame is the last thing on his mind. Will he help make her dreams come true?

By Evie Alexander and Kelly Kay

EVIE & KELLY'S HOLIDAY DISASTERS SERIES

Evie and Kelly's Holiday Disasters are a series of hot and hilarious romantic comedies with interconnected characters, focusing on one holiday and one trope at a time.

Cupid Calamity

Featuring Animal Attraction & Stupid Cupid

Patrick and Sabina have ditched their blind dates for each other. Ben's fighting a crazed chimp for Laurie's love. Insta-love meets insta-disaster in these laugh-out-loud Valentine's day novellas.

Cookout Carnage - June 2022

Featuring Off With a Bang & Up in Smoke

Cute farm boy Jonathan clings to a love ideal, blissfully ignoring what the universe has planned, while keeping track of his pet pig. Posh Brit follows his heart into the American Midwest in search of Sherilyn, his digital dream love.

Christmas Chaos - November 2022

Featuring No way in a Manger, & No Crib and No Bed

In Scotland, Zoe and Rory attempt to have a civilised and respectable rite of passage, but straightforward is not their style. In Sonoma, Bax and Tabi attempt to throw a meaningful Christmas celebration. But there are too many people involved and it's nothing like they expect.

Made in the USA
Las Vegas, NV
30 April 2022